TEFFI

SUBTLY WORDED

AND OTHER STORIES

Translated from the Russian by Anne Marie Jackson
with Robert and Elizabeth Chandler, Clare Kitson,
Irina Steinberg and Natalia Wase

PUSHKIN PRESS
LONDON

Pushkin Press
71–75 Shelton Street, London WC2H 9JQ

The stories in this volume are selected from
Teffi's entire body of work, 1910–1952

This translation first published by Pushkin Press in 2014

ISBN 978 1 782270 37 9

ИНСТИТУТ ПЕРЕВОДА

AD VERBUM

Published with the support of the Institute for Literary Translation, Russia.

Frontispiece: Teffi in her apartment, 1910–12

Set in 10 on 13 Monotype Baskerville by Tetragon, London

Proudly printed and bound in Great Britain by TJ International,
Padstow, Cornwall on Munken Premium White 80gsm

www.pushkinpress.com

CONTENTS

Introduction   7

Part I · Before the Revolution

A Radiant Easter   21

The Corsican   28

Will-Power   32

The Hat   35

The Lifeless Beast   40

Jealousy   50

The Quiet Backwater   57

Duty and Honour   66

Part II · 1916–19: Rasputin, Revolution and Civil War

Petrograd Monologue   75

One Day in the Future   79

One of Us   84

Rasputin   91

Part III · 1920s and 1930s in Paris

Que Faire?	139
Subtly Worded	144
Marquita	149
My First Tolstoy	159
Heart of a Valkyrie	165
Ernest with the Languages	173

Part IV · 1930s: Magic Tales

"The Kind that Walk"	187
The Dog (A Story from a Stranger)	196

Part V · Last Stories

The Blind One	235
Thy Will	245
And Time Was No More	269

Acknowledgements	291
Notes	293

INTRODUCTION

IN THE YEARS before the Revolution, Teffi was a literary star. People quoted lines from her work in conversation. Strangers recognized her on the streets of St Petersburg. So broad was her appeal that her fans included such disparate figures as Vladimir Lenin and Tsar Nicholas II.[1] As well as being popular with the reading public, Teffi was greatly admired by fellow writers such as Ivan Bunin, Fyodor Sologub and Mikhail Zoshchenko, to name but a few.

Although she is still often seen primarily as a humorist, the scope of her work was, almost from the beginning, broader and deeper. As often as not, her stories are small tragedies. The greatest of Soviet humorists, Mikhail Zoshchenko, once wrote: "Just try retelling one of her stories, even the funniest, and it will no longer be funny. It will come out absurd, maybe even tragic."[2] Or, in the words of the Russian critic Lidiya Spiridonova, Teffi's stories are "funny on the outside, tragic on the inside".[3]

Teffi, or Nadezhda Alexandrovna Lokhvitskaya, was born in 1872 into a prominent St Petersburg family. Her father was an eminent criminologist and a gifted raconteur, her mother a cultured woman who loved literature and passed this love on to her children. Along with her sisters and brother, Teffi was immersed in books and writing from an early age. Teffi's older sister was the well-known poet Mirra Lokhvitskaya, dubbed the "Russian Sappho" by Ivan Bunin. Her other sisters were also published writers. Around 1890 Teffi married and went to live with her husband in the provinces, where they had three children. A decade later, however, she left her family and returned to St Petersburg. As Teffi wrote to her elder daughter in 1946, if she had remained in the marriage it would have been the end of her.

Later, as an émigrée in Paris, Teffi explained the origin of her pseudonym. She had written a play, but people kept telling her that no one would even read it unless she had theatre contacts or a big name. She felt she needed to come up with an attention-grabbing pen name, a name that might belong to either a man or a woman. When she cast about for the name of a fool—because fools were believed to be lucky—a certain Stefan came to mind, called "Steffi" by his friends. Out of delicacy, she got rid of the initial S and arrived at "Teffi". When the press first encountered this pen name, someone assumed it was an allusion to Rudyard Kipling's character "Taffy". The explanation stuck and Teffi did little to discourage it.

Teffi's first publication—a poem—appeared in 1901, but it was not until 1904 that her work began appearing with any regularity. Her satirical articles were published in a broad range of periodicals, and in 1905 she even contributed briefly to a Bolshevik newspaper. Teffi was closely associated with the journal *Satyricon* (*New Satyricon* after 1913) and the daily newspaper *The Russian Word*.[4] *The Russian Word* usually published literature only in its holiday editions, but Teffi recalls in her memoirs that the editor Vlas Doroshevich interceded on her behalf, saying, "Let her write what she wants to write. You don't use a pure-bred Arab to haul water." Gradually articles gave way to fiction and, by 1911, Teffi was publishing mostly short stories.

The political reforms of 1905 had been followed by a conservative backlash; even schoolchildren were often arrested. Such absurdities furnished material for Teffi's prose collection *Humorous Stories*, one volume of which was published in 1910, followed by another in 1911. *Humorous Stories* was so successful that it was reissued three times in quick succession. Similar success would accompany Teffi throughout her literary career.

In this, as in later collections, Teffi usually writes about ordinary people, whose folly she ridicules but for whom she retains a certain tenderness. 'The Corsican' is about a police agent trying to learn revolutionary songs so that he can become an agent provocateur and thus improve his career prospects. In 'A Radiant Easter', a parody of a recognized genre of sentimental and moralistic Easter stories, a petty official attempts to make a good impression on his boss, but the plan backfires. Teffi regarded marriage with a certain scepticism, and 'Duty and Honour', first published in the collection *Carousel* in 1913, pokes fun at the banality of a woman attempting to enforce a friend's adherence to convention.

One day Teffi received a three-layered box of candies from an anonymous admirer. They were in colourful wrappers, each emblazoned with her pen name and portrait. Overjoyed, she telephoned her friends, inviting them round to sample the "Teffi" candies. She began sampling them herself and, before she realized it, had devoured nearly all three layers. "I had gorged on fame until I'd made myself ill. That's when I understood its flip side. [...] Instead of happily celebrating with my friends, I had to invite a doctor round."[5] From then on, she appears to have remained indifferent to the trappings of her celebrity.

The Lifeless Beast (1916) is generally seen as the most accomplished collection that Teffi published before emigrating. In the preface she warned readers expecting light-hearted humour that "this book contains a great deal that isn't cheerful". 'The Quiet Backwater' rivals Chekhov at his best in its evocation of the language and mindset of an elderly peasant couple. Many years before, while her husband was away fighting, the wife had borne an illegitimate child. Teffi's evocation of the silences and evasions that enable them to cope with this threat to their marriage is extraordinarily subtle. The title story, 'The Lifeless Beast', is told from the perspective of a young child all but forgotten amid the collapse of her parents' marriage. The child's world is inhabited almost entirely by beasts of one kind or another—animate and inanimate, animal and human. In 'Jealousy' a little girl, distressed by the attention her nanny is paying to another little girl, first wishes this girl to die and then determines to die herself. Robert Chandler writes, "Like Andrei Platonov, Teffi has a remarkable ability to evoke the inner world of a child. And like Platonov, she knows how fluid the boundary between life and death can seem to a child":

> Liza went round the lime tree, scrambling over its stout roots. In among these roots was plenty to catch the eye. In one little corner lived a dead beetle. Its wings were like the dried husks inside a cedar nut. Liza flipped the beetle onto its back with a little stick, and then onto its front, but it wasn't afraid and didn't run away. It was completely dead and living a peaceful life.

In 1916 Teffi was invited to two dinners attended by Rasputin. Later, in Paris, she wrote a vivid account of these meetings, all the more remarkable for the way she manages—in spite of the horror Rasputin evoked in her—to release him from cliché.

Many of Teffi's stories and articles from the period of the Revolution and the Civil War have only recently been published in book form. Several of these pieces are included here. In 'Petrograd Monologue', Teffi manages to write with humour about the terrible food shortage of these years. "Funny on the outside, tragic on the inside" indeed! Social class is central to 'One of Us', in which a promising acquaintance between two balletomanes is nipped in the bud; even in 1918 there was evidently no escape from snobbery. And in 'One Day in the Future' (written and published in the St Petersburg journal *New Satyricon* not long before it was closed down) class snobbery is turned on its head; the story portrays a world in which knowledge and ability are spurned in favour of membership in the ranks of the proletariat.

In 1919, following the closure of *The Russian Word*, Teffi left St Petersburg to go on tour in Ukraine. She never saw Russia again. As the Bolsheviks continued to advance, Teffi was evacuated first from Kiev, then from Odessa, then from Novorossiysk. After passing, like so many other émigrés, through Constantinople, she ended up in Paris, settling there in 1920.

Teffi quickly became a major figure in the émigré world. '*Que Faire?*'—her first feuilleton published in Paris—was a huge hit and still remains one of her best-known works. Teffi's title alludes to Chernyshevsky's novel *What Is to Be Done*, a phrase later put to use by Lenin as a revolutionary slogan. Teffi reverses the implication by putting the words into the mouth of a White general. They quickly became a catchphrase among émigrés. Full of clever interlingual word play, '*Que Faire?*' brilliantly portrays the squabbling

Russian émigré community, unable to find any kind of internal solidarity:

> We—*les russes*, as they call us—live the strangest of lives here, nothing like other people's. We stick together, for example, not like planets, by mutual attraction, but by a force quite contrary to the laws of physics—mutual repulsion. Every *lesrusse* hates all the others—hates them just as fervently as the others hate him.

The blackly humorous 'Subtly Worded', from Teffi's 1923 collection *Lynx*, captures the anxiety people were experiencing with regard to what was happening back in Russia. A comparison of 'Subtly Worded' with Teffi's earlier letter-writing story, 'Duty and Honour', reveals a great deal about just how much both Teffi and Russia had changed over the intervening decade.

The collection *Gorodok* was published in 1927. A *gorodok*—or "little town"—is essentially what the émigré community had become: a little town within the confines of Paris that refused to integrate into its host society. Rather, it sought to "preserve the values and traditions of Russian culture"[6] in anticipation of going home, and carried on doing so even after any such hopes had faded. In this little town we find Sashenka, a young mother who nightly appears as "Marquita", performing Spanish songs in a café where all the waitresses are "daughters of provincial governors". She ruins her chances of a good marriage when she mistakenly accepts a friend's advice to pretend to be a femme fatale. As Robert Chandler remarks:

> Many writers have written about people pretending to be better than they really are; Teffi, with characteristic originality, shows us a woman who inadvertently ruins her chance of a better life by consciously pretending to be worse than she really is.

Like the majority of the Russian émigrés in Paris, Teffi did not expect to remain in exile from her homeland. As hope gave way to resignation, a new theme entered Teffi's work: nostalgia. She contemplated not only a world left behind, but a way of life that no longer existed. 'Ernest with the Languages' comes from a trio of stories about private tutors on Russian country estates. Other stories from these years are autobiographical: in 'My First Tolstoy' the young Teffi pays a visit to Leo Tolstoy to plead her case for saving the life of Prince Andrei Bolkonsky.

When asked in 1943 which of her works she most valued, Teffi named her collection *Witch*. "This book," she writes, "contains our ancient Slavic gods, the way they exist even now in the people's psyche—in legends, superstitions, customs. It's all as I found it, in the Russian provinces, as a child."[7] In 'The Kind that Walk' a Jewish carpenter who returns to a village after an absence of thirty years is viewed by the peasants as one of the living dead. 'The Dog' is set against the background of the First World War and, in the words of Robert Chandler:

> it provides a fine example of a writer drawing on folk-lore not for ornament but as a source of psychological truth. Just as D.H. Lawrence sometimes draws on the paranormal, so Teffi draws on folklore to convey how, at moments of crisis, we can be overwhelmed by the most primitive aspects of the psyche.[8]

Teffi remained in occupied Paris throughout the war. When the émigré newspapers and journals were shut down she lost her only source of income; her difficulties were compounded by the tendency of Western critics—many of whom were at least to some degree pro-Soviet—to dismiss Russian émigré literature.[9] While she was not exactly left to starve, the gifts that Teffi received from fans and supporters were often somewhat impractical. She once wrote to her daughter about a lady who wanted to send her a velvet dressing gown for her name day, and another who sent her 3,000 francs for a new umbrella, although she already had one that was perfectly serviceable.

Deteriorating health notwithstanding, Teffi continued to give occasional readings during these years. Ever-dwindling audiences, however, attested to the attrition of the Russian community in Paris. In 1945 Teffi's own death was rumoured; one New York journal even published her obituary. Teffi laid these rumours to rest in a letter-feuilleton which eloquently summed up the state of émigré Paris at the time. After expressing her regret that there was not yet a recognized etiquette for such letters, she suggested that such an etiquette was sure to be established soon: one was, after all, only too often bumping into people whose departure from life had already been noted in prayers and obituaries. She went on to say that this was actually a most rational phenomenon, as:

> it is now more normal to die than to live. Can someone who is weak, elderly and ailing really be expected to survive the winter—in an unheated building, on a hungry stomach, with the wail of sirens and the roar of bombs, and in a state of grief and despair? […] Of course not! Obviously he has died![10]

Earthly Rainbow, Teffi's final collection, was published in 1952, the year Teffi really did die. Shortly before her death she wrote, "An anecdote is funny when it's being told, but when someone lives it, it's a tragedy. And my life has been sheer anecdote, that is—a tragedy."[11] Parallels can be drawn between Teffi's own suffering and that of her character Anna Brown, the pianist in 'Thy Will'. Both Teffi and Anna seem to come to a recognition that there is no controlling the pain in the world. Only days, perhaps hours, before Teffi died, in great pain and no longer able to speak, she scrawled onto a sheet of paper: "There is no love greater than that of someone giving his own morphine to his brother."[12] Like a true friend, Teffi shares her morphine with Anna Brown. 'The Blind One', one of Teffi's favourites in this collection,[13] juxtaposes the self-inflicted misery of a well-to-do woman with the joy and buoyancy of a poor blind girl from the neighbouring orphanage. The blind girl's ability to "see" the beauty around her—on a "wan [...] tear-stained" day, beside a sea that is "utterly stagnant and dead"—seems to mirror Teffi's own ability to see what is wonderful in the most unlikely of places. The present collection closes with the extraordinary 'And Time Was No More', narrated by a fictive Teffi. Following an injection of morphine, this Teffi opens her eyes to find herself in a little house that she used to draw as a child. This begins a sequence of memories, dreams and illuminations into the nature of death, the soul and eternity. It is a kind of summing up of Teffi's spiritual life as she prepares to depart her earthly existence.

Teffi died on 6 October 1952. She was buried in the Russian cemetery at Sainte-Geneviève-des-Bois.

The poet and critic Georgy Ivanov described Teffi as "an inimitable presence in Russian literature, a genuine wonder" and predicted that she would still be "amazing readers a hundred years from now".[14] Unfortunately, following Teffi's death, she fell off the literary map. There are several possible explanations: she was a woman; she had been typecast as a lightweight humorist; she was an émigrée. But beginning in the 1990s, nearly half a century after Teffi's death, a new generation of Russian readers began to discover and appreciate Teffi's special genius. Georgy Ivanov—now himself becoming recognized as one of the greatest Russian poets of the last century—was right. Teffi's time has come—or rather, her time has come again.

ANNE MARIE JACKSON

PART I

Before the Revolution

A RADIANT EASTER

Like a torch, they passed the good news one to another,
and, as if from a torch, each lit from it his own flame.

— From *Legends about the Lives of the First Christians*

S AMOSOV STOOD there gloomily, watching the deacon with the incense and thinking, "Go on, swing that incense, swing that incense! Think you can swing yourself into a bishopric? Some hope!"

Wanting to move closer to his boss, who was also praying in the church, he slowly but surely elbowed away a small boy. He wanted his boss to know he was there—this was why he had come.

"He's brought his wife along," muttered Samosov, crossing himself. "A right bitch she is! Forty lovers—and off she goes to church with her pencilled eyebrows! Here at least, in the presence of God, you might think she'd show a little shame. The man's a fool, too—he imagined she had a dowry. And she, of course, didn't want to starve to death—she was only too ready to marry him."

"Christ is risen!" proclaimed the priest.

"He is risen indeed!" Samosov responded with feeling. And then, in an undertone: "And he's brought his mother-in-law along too! Of course! If he left her at home, she'd be either smashing the china or forcing the safe. All she cares about is getting those daughters of hers married off. They're a gaggle of monsters—she's trying to get them off her hands as cheap as she can. And *they* can't even buy the old woman a decent hat! *Their* idea of fun is to stick an old galosh on her head. To make everyone laugh. A fine show of respect for an old woman... But like it or not, she did bring you monsters into the world! There's no getting away from that... Go on, swing that incense! They'll make you an archimandrite! A metropolitan!"

The service came to an end. With dignified deference Samosov approached his boss.

"Yes, risen indeed!"

They exchanged kisses.

He kissed the hand of the boss's wife. He kissed the hand of the boss's mother-in-law.

"Yes, yes! It brings me such joy to see this crowd of simple people professing their faith in the timelessness of ordinances... which... My wife? No, she's stayed behind, you see, managing the household... A regular Martha from the New Testament."

He left the church, continuing for a while to sense both an inner glow from this meeting with a superior and the scent of floral eau de Cologne on his moustache. But little by little he returned to his senses.

"He might have invited me back to his home—so we could all break our fast together! The women were *glad to see me*! They stuck their hands out for a kiss. I suppose there aren't many people eager to kiss their manky paws."

He went home.

His wife and daughter were already at table, about to eat their ham and *paskha*.[1]

His wife had the hurt and confused look of someone who is constantly being scolded.

His daughter's large nose slanted slightly to the right, dragging along with it a squinting left eye that peered out at the world with suspicion.

Samosov thought for a moment: "Oh, I like that! They think I've got presents for them!"

He banged his fist on the table.

"Who the devil gave you permission to break fast without me?"

"What do you mean?" asked his wife in amazement. "We thought you were at your boss's. You said yourself—"

"A man can't even get any peace in his own home!" said Samosov, almost in tears. He very much wanted some ham, but it didn't seem right to start eating in the middle of a family row. "Have some tea brought to my room!"

He slammed the door after him.

"Anyone else would have come back from church and said, 'The Lord has blessed us'," said the daughter, looking at her mother with one eye and at her plate with the other. "But we never do anything like normal people!"

"Who is it you're referring to?" asked the mother. "Your father? How dare you speak like that! Day in, day out, without a moment's rest, your father ploughs away with his pen like a real workhorse. Then he comes home to break his fast and his daughter won't even exchange Easter greetings with him. Still thinking about Andrei Petrovich, are you? I'm sure you're ever so important to him! And how is it you try to charm him? By being rude to your parents? A girl with any self-respect does what she can to make life easier for her parents. She tries to earn a little money herself. Yulia... What's her name? You know the name, that bearded lady... Yulia Pastrana's been supporting her parents since the age of two. She's been helping her other relatives as well."

"So am I to blame that I wasn't given a brilliant education? It's easy enough to find secretarial work if you've been brilliantly educated."

The mother stood up in a dignified manner.

"I'll have tea sent up to my room! Thank you! You've ruined the entire holiday."

She walked out.

Looking around brightly, her face flushed and joyful, the cook came into the dining room with a red-painted egg in her hands.

"Christhasrisenmiss! The Lord grantyouonlythebest! And a good husband! A capital young husband!"

"The Devil take you! Cheeky creature! Slobbering all over my face like that!"

"The Lord have mercy!" said the cook, taking a step back.

"Why on earth… How can you refuse a fellow Christian an Easter kiss? So what if my visage is somewhat flushed? I'm speechless for words… All day long I've done nothing but bake and boil—the mere exhaustion of it all's enough to make a woman red in the visage. The stove's been alight all day—there's such an inflammation in there you can hardly breathe. And it's hot outside, too, though it did mizzle a bit in the morning! Last year was a thousand times cooler! It snowed on our way to Mass."

"Oh, leave me in peace!" squealed the young lady. "Or I'll tell mother to give you the sack."

She spun on her heels and left the room, strutting off in the manner of all mistresses who have just quarrelled with one of their servants.

"Oo-ooh, I'm terrible scared!" the cook sang out after her. "Oo-ooh, you've put the fear of God in me… Huh! Pay me my wages and you can do as you please! I don't think I've sniffed five kopeks from you since Christmas. I'll clear the table, but then I'm lying down and I'm not making no one no tea. If it's slave labour you want, you can find yourselves a convict. He can make tea for you even in the middle of the night."

She took a dirty plate from the table and then, keeping to the system followed by every maid-of-all-work, placed a spoon on the plate, another plate on top of the spoon, a glass on this second plate, and a dish of ham on the glass. She was about to place a tray of cups on top of the ham when everything crashed to the floor.

"Oh, to hell with it all!"

All she had left in her hand was the original plate.

The cook thought for a while, then tossed the plate into the pile too.

After scratching behind one ear, underneath her head-scarf, she suddenly, as if remembering something, went back into the kitchen.

On a stool, lapping up milk and water from a little dish, was a scrawny cat. A little girl—*an orphan, just to wash the dishes*—was squatting down in front of this cat, looking at her and repeating, "Drink it up, my little darling, drink it up! Yes, you've fasted enough. Let's hope some good food will plump you up quickly."

The cook seized the girl by one ear.

"Who's been smashing china in the dining room? Huh? Is that what they keep you here for? To smash up the china? Measly-faced little tyke! Huh? Who told you to go and clear up in the dining room? You little blockhead—tomorrow they'll give you what for!"

The little girl gave a frightened whimper and blew her nose in her apron. She rubbed her ear, blew her nose in the hem of her skirt, let out a sob, blew her nose in the corner of her headscarf, then suddenly rushed at the cat, pushed her onto the floor and gave her a good kick.

"To hell with you, you scrounging beast! You don't give us a moment's peace, you heathen creature. Milk, milk, milk—that's all *you* ever want! Well, I hope you snuff it before you die!"

Encouraged by the girl's foot, the cat leapt out onto the staircase, barely managing to get away with her tail, which was almost chopped off by the door.

She took refuge behind the dustbin and sat there for a long time without stirring, afraid that a mighty enemy might be searching for her.

Then she began to pour out her grief and bewilderment to the dustbin. But what did the dustbin care? It said nothing.

"Oo-au!"

That was all the cat knew.

"Oo-au!"

But who could make any sense of that?

1910

THE CORSICAN

T HE INTERROGATION had been dragging on, and the police officer felt exhausted; he declared a break and went off to his office for a rest.

With a sweet smile of satisfaction he was approaching the couch; suddenly he stopped, his face taking on a twisted look, as if he had seen something foul.

The other side of the wall, a loud bass voice was singing, clearly enunciating each word: "Forward, forward, O working class!"[1]

Not quite able to keep up with this, out of time and out of tune, a timid and hoarse little voice was singing: "Fowad, fowad!"

"What on earth's going on?" the officer exclaimed, pointing to the wall.

The clerk straightened up a little in his chair.

"I have already had occasion to report to you on the matter of this agent."

"What *are* you on about? Keep it simple."

"Agent Fialkin has expressed a pressing and imperative wish to enter the ranks of our provocateurs. This is the second winter running that he has been on duty by the Mikhailov tramway. He's a quiet chap. Only he's ambitious beyond his station in life. Here I am, he says, wasting my youth and expending the best of my strength on the trams. He is concerned about the slow progress of his career on the trams and the impossibility of applying his exceptional abilities—that is, supposing he possesses such abilities."

"For juthtith thake we thpill our blood," went the thin voice behind the wall.

"Out of tune!" said the bass.

"And is he talented?" asked the officer.

"He's ambitious—even excessively ambitious. He wants to become a provocateur, but he doesn't know a single revolutionary song. He's been moaning on and on about this. And so police constable No. 4711 has come to his rescue. No. 4711 knows every song perfectly—you'd think he had the music right there in front of him. Now, of course, most constables know the words well enough. You can hardly block your ears when you're out on the streets. But this one has a fine feel for music as well. So he's teaching Fialkin."

"Well, well! And so now they're belting out the 'Warszawianka'," the officer murmured dreamily. "Ambition's no bad thing. It can help a man get on in the world. Take Napoleon. A simple Corsican, but he achieved... quite something..."

"The people's flag is burning red. It's sheltered oft our martyred dead," growled constable No. 4711.

"They seem to be on another tune already," said the officer, suddenly suspicious. "Is he teaching him all the revolutionary songs in one go?"

"Every last one of them. Fialkin's in a hurry. He thinks there's an important conspiracy being hatched."

"Well, there's certainly no lack of ambition round here!"

"The see-eed of the future," Fialkin bleated from behind the wall.

"The energy of the Devil," sighed the officer. "They say that when Napoleon was just a simple Corsican…"

From the staircase below came muffled thumps and a kind of roar.

"And what's that?" asked the officer, raising his eyebrows.

"That's our lot, on the ground floor. They eat there. They're getting agitated."

"What about?"

"Seems they can hear the singing. They don't like it."

"Damn it! This really is a bit awkward. People out on the street might hear, too. They'll think there's a protest meeting here in this building."

"Damn you!" said the bass the other side of the wall. "Howling like a dog! Is that the way a revolutionary sings? A revolutionary sings with an open heart. He makes a clear sound. Every word can be heard. But you just whimper into your cheeks, and your eyes keep darting about. Keep your eyes still! I'm saying this for the last time. Or I'll up and leave. If you're really so keen to have lessons, you can go and find yourself a Maximalist!"[2]

"Now he's losing his temper," grinned the clerk. "A real Vera Figner."[3]

"Ambition! Ambition!" the officer repeated. "And he's

taken it into his head to be a provocateur… No, brother, there's no rose without thorns. Court martials don't have time for long deliberations. Get yourself arrested, brother, and no one will bother to check whether you're a revolutionary or whether you're the purest of provocateurs. You'll swing for it anyway."

"Gluttons grow fat on workers' sweat," roared the bass, letting himself go.

"Ow! It's even making my teeth ache! Can't anyone find a way to talk him out of all this?"

"But how can they?" sighed the clerk. "He's a man possessed. People are all such careerists nowadays."

"There must be some way to convince him. Tell him the fatherland needs competent sleuths every bit as much as it needs provocateurs. My tooth's really hurting…"

"You gave your life in sacrifice," roared constable No. 4711.

"You gave your life in sacrifice," the agent bleated pathetically.

"To hell with it all!" yelled the officer, and ran out of the room. "Get out of here!" he shouted down the corridor, his staccato voice hoarse with rage. "Scoundrels! Wanting to be provocateurs when they can't even sing the 'Marseillaise'! They'll put our whole institution to shame! Corsicans! I'll show you what happens to Corsicans!"

A door slammed. Everything went quiet. On the other side of the wall, someone let out a sob.

1910

WILL-POWER

Lips parted forlornly, Ivan Matveyich watched with glum resignation as the doctor's little hammer bounced up and down his stout sides.

"I thought as much," said the doctor, taking a step back. "You'll have to give up the booze, that's what. Drink much, do you?"

"A glass before breakfast and two before lunch. Cognac," replied the patient, with a mixture of sorrow and sincerity.

"Aha. That will have to stop then. Think of your liver—look at the size of it now! How can you keep treating it like this?"

Ivan Matveyich looked where the doctor was pointing. He saw his bulging side, naked and defenceless. He sighed.

"Of course, you have nothing to worry about really," continued the doctor. "With will-power like yours, you won't have any trouble kicking the habit."

"Yes, quite! Will-power I have in spades! That certainly isn't something I need to work on!"

"Jolly good then. I'll prescribe you some powders. Take them for a couple of weeks or so, then pop by and see me again. Thank you very much—you really don't have anything to worry about."

Ivan Matveyich mulled things over as he made his way down the street. "My liver's not in the right place. That's to say, it's not where it should be. Things don't look good... But as I have will-power, I can overcome anything, liver or no liver! And, it just so happens that I got to the end of a bottle today anyway, so fate is clearly on my side..."

On the corner right by his house, Ivan came to a halt, bewitched by the grocer's window display.

"Well, well, what have we here then? Liqueurs? Who, I ask you, needs liqueur on an empty stomach? Yet they've stuck them in the window. Fools! And what's that? Cognac? Well, *I'm* not going to be tempted! Those with will-power, my friend, have nothing to fear. I'll even go one better! I'll go in, buy a bottle and take it home with me. Yes I will! Just like that! Those who have will-power..."

On arriving home, he immediately locked the cognac away in the sideboard and sat down to lunch. He dished up his soup and fell into thought.

"I've put it away in the sideboard... But no, I can go one better than that, I'll put it on the table. Yes, that's what I'll do: I'll put it on the table... and even uncork it! Those who have will-power will never crack, my friend. No, not even if you pour out cognac right onto their noses!"

So he uncorked the bottle. He sat down, looked at it and began to think, moving his spoon around the bowl. Suddenly, he decided: "I can do better than that! I'll take the bottle and pour out a glass. And why stop there? I'll even drink one glassful. Yes! That's what I'll do. Why shouldn't

I? After all, those with will-power can stop whenever they want… and doing a little experiment on oneself can be fun!"

He drained the glass and, eyes bulging, looked around with surprise. He swallowed a couple of spoonfuls of soup and said with conviction: "No, I can do better still—I'll drink a second glass!"

He drank the second glass, grinned and winked.

"No, even better—let me do something I have never done before: let me drink a third glass. Really, it would be silly not to! Firstly, it will be enjoyable, and secondly, if I have will-power and can always stop in time, what do I have to fear? Why, for example, shouldn't I drink a fourth? Or better than that, a fourth and a fifth immediately after it! Yes, that's what I'll do. And then I'll send someone to get some more cognac. So there. Those with will-power…"

That evening, a friend saw a light at the window and decided to drop in. He was dumbfounded by the scene before him: Ivan Matveyich sitting on the dining-room floor, wagging his finger knowingly and resolutely at the table leg, saying with great feeling, "Perhaps *you* can't, my friend, but I can! I'm drunk. There, I admit it. And I'm going to go one better. I'm going to get drunk every day from now on. And *why*, you may ask? Well, because those with will-power… will-pow-er… can drink without anything to fear. And I have will-power aplenty, my friend, oh yes, I do. And because I have will-power, it means…"

1915

34

THE HAT

Varenka zvezdochetova, a member of the chorus of the Private Opera,[1] could have done with a bit more sleep, but she awoke in high spirits all the same.

She was short on sleep because she had stayed up half the night trying on a new hat—a deep-blue hat with a deep-blue bow and a deep-blue bird, a true bluebird of happiness.

And she was in high spirits because the poet Sineus Truvorov had promised to take her out for a drive.

The poet was someone very interesting.

He had not yet written any poems—he was still trying to come up with a pen name—but in spite of this he was very poetic and mysterious, perhaps even more so than many a real poet with real, ready-made poems.

Varenka quickly got dressed, grabbed her new hat and once again began trying it on.

"Absolutely stunning! Especially like this, from the side…"

Oh! What a woman can get away with when she's wearing a hat like this! Things that a woman wearing any old hat wouldn't even dare to dream of.

35

She can be arch, she can be tempestuous, or dreamy, or haughty. She can be anything—and whatever she does she can carry it off with style.

For the sake of comparison, Varenka took out her shabby old black hat and started putting on first it, then the dark-blue dream. She pinned on each hat, fastened her veil and tried out identical expressions with both. How tasteless, how pathetic they looked under the black hat, how irresistible under the wings of the bluebird of happiness.

At the sound of the bell and a familiar voice she dashed headlong into the front hall.

The poet with no poems was already standing there, smiling and gazing at her adoringly.

"Let's get going, the driver's waiting…"

She wanted to run back to her room and look at herself in the mirror one more time, but he wouldn't let her. He just bundled her into her coat and pulled her to the door.

"There's something about you today," he whispered, pressing her elbow to his side. "I don't understand what it is, but I just can't take my eyes off you."

"I know what it is," thought Varenka. "It's my new hat."

But she did not say this to the poet. Let him think she's always this pretty. After all, where would a true confession get her?

In response she just smiled and gave him a playful sideways look, and he pressed her arm still closer.

How lovely it was out of doors! It was a city spring, smelling of mould and cats, but the sun was the real thing, the same sun that shone on fields and meadows all over the world, the entire silly round world, and whirling about the sun were high-spirited little clouds—the lamb's-fleece clouds of spring.

On the bridge a little boy was selling lilies of the valley. He was running after the carriages, calling out in a heart-rending voice that he was selling the flowers at a loss.

The driver flicked the reins and the boy dropped behind. Mud splashed out from under the wheels—the high-spirited mud of spring. It splashed right onto the boy and a lady who was passing by. Varenka felt rich and important, and modestly pursed her lips so that the passers-by she had splashed with mud would not be too jealous.

"You are particularly lovely today," said the poet joyfully. "You are utterly, utterly remarkable…"

Indeed she was remarkable on this day. Her awareness of her own elegance lent her a certain boldness and gaiety of spirit.

Ah, if only she were rich, and every day, every single day, she could put on a new hat, and every day she would be beautiful in some new way!

"How do you like my hat?" she couldn't help but ask.

He glanced at it distractedly and said, "Oh yes, very much."

"Don't you love this deep blue?"

"Blue? Well, yes… but it's a very dark blue, almost black."

Varenka smirked. How poorly men understood colours! Even poets. Yes! Even when they are poets!

On the stairs they said goodbye. He had to hurry off somewhere. But, after he'd gone down a few steps, he suddenly ran back up and kissed Varenka right on the lips.

And then, leaning over the banister, she watched him go. She watched him adoringly, and brightly, and exultantly—in the way you can watch only when you are wearing a new hat, a hat with a bluebird of happiness on the brim.

Humming to herself, she went to her room.

Ah, if only she were rich, and every day she could wear a new...

She stopped in her tracks and her jaw fell open in surprise, practically in fright: there, on the table, next to its box, lay her deep-blue hat, her new deep-blue hat, with the deep-blue ribbon and the bluebird.

"Good heavens! I don't believe it!"

She ran to the mirror.

Yes, she was wearing her old black hat!

It must have been when she was trying on and comparing the two hats. She'd put on the old one, and when the poet appeared she had got confused and forgotten which hat she was wearing...

"That means he liked me for myself, and not because of the hat. How very strange! But what made me so very pretty today?"

She sat down on her bed and fell into thought.

Her brilliant philosophy about the happiness of those who were richly endowed with hats began to totter. It began to totter and then it collapsed—and there was nothing to plug the gap it left behind.

Varenka sighed, sat down in front of the mirror and began trying on first one hat, and then the other...

1918

THE LIFELESS BEAST

THE CHRISTMAS PARTY was fun. There were crowds of guests, big and small. There was even one boy who had been flogged that day—so Katya's nanny told her in a whisper. This was so intriguing that Katya barely left the boy's side all evening; she kept thinking he would say something special, and she watched him with respect and even fear. But the flogged boy behaved in the most ordinary manner; he kept begging for gingerbread, blowing a toy trumpet and pulling crackers. In the end, bitter though this was for her, Katya had to admit defeat and move away from the boy.

The evening was already drawing to a close, and the very smallest, loudly howling children were being got ready to go home, when Katya was given her main present—a large woolly ram. He was all soft, with a long, meek face and eyes that were quite human. He smelt of sour wool and, if you pulled his head down, he bleated affectionately and persistently: "Ba-a-a!"

Katya was so struck by the ram, by the way he looked, smelt and talked, that she even, to ease her conscience, asked, "Mama, are you sure he's not alive?"

Her mother turned her little bird-like face away and said nothing. She had long ago stopped answering Katya's questions—she never had time. Katya sighed and went to the dining room to give the ram some milk. She stuck the ram's face right into the milk jug, wetting it right up to the eyes. Then a young lady she didn't know came up to her, shaking her head: "Oh, dearie me, what *are* you doing? Really, giving living milk to a creature that isn't alive! It'll be the end of him. You need to give him pretend milk. Like this."

She scooped up some air in an empty cup, held it to the ram's mouth and smacked her lips.

"See?"

"Yes. But why does a cat get real milk?"

"That's just the way it is. Each according to its own. Live milk for the living. Pretend milk for the unliving."

The woollen ram at once made his home in the nursery, in the corner, behind Nanny's trunk. Katya loved him, and because of her love he got grubbier by the day. His fur got all clumpy and knotted and his affectionate "Ba-a-a" became quieter and quieter. And because he was so very grubby, Mama would no longer allow him to sit with Katya at lunch.

Lunchtimes became very gloomy. Papa didn't say anything; Mama didn't say anything. Nobody even looked round when, after eating her pastry, Katya curtsied and said, in the thin little voice of a clever little girl, "*Merci, Papa! Merci, Mama!*"

Once they began lunch without Mama being there at all; by the time she got back, they had already finished their

41

soup. Mama shouted out from the hall that there had been an awful lot of people at the skating rink. But when she came to the table, Papa took one look at her, then hurled a decanter down onto the floor.

"Why did you do that?" shouted Mama.

"Why's your blouse undone at the back?" shouted Papa.

He shouted something else, too, but Nanny snatched Katya from her chair and dragged her off to the nursery.

After that there were many days when Katya didn't so much as glimpse Papa or Mama; nothing in her life seemed real any longer. She was having the same lunch as the servants—it was brought up from the kitchen. The cook would come in and start whispering to Nanny, "And he said… and then she said… And as for you!… You've got to go! And *he* said… And then *she* said…"

There was no end to this whispering.

Old women with foxy faces began coming in from the kitchen, winking at Katya, asking Nanny questions, whispering, murmuring, hissing: "And then he said… You've got to go! And she said…"

Nanny often disappeared completely. Then the foxy women would make their way into the nursery, poking around in corners and wagging their knobbly fingers at Katya.

But when they weren't there it was even worse. It was terrifying.

Going into the big rooms was out of the question: they were empty and echoing. The door curtains billowed; the clock over the fireplace ticked on severely. And there was no getting away from the endless "And *he* said… And then *she* said…"

The corners of the nursery started to get dark before lunch. They seemed to be moving. And the little stove—the big stove's daughter—crackled away in the corner. She kept clicking her damper, baring her red teeth and gobbling up firewood. You couldn't go near her. She was vicious. Once she bit Katya's finger. No, you wouldn't catch Katya going near that little stove again.

Everything was restless; everything was different.

The only safe place was behind the trunk—the home of the woollen ram, the lifeless beast. The ram lived on pencils, old ribbons, Nanny's glasses—whatever the good Lord sent his way. He always looked at Katya with gentle affection. He never made any complaints or reproaches and he understood everything.

Once Katya was very naughty—and the ram joined in too. He was looking the other way, but she could see he was laughing. Another time, when he was ill and Katya bandaged his neck with an old rag, he looked so pitiful that Katya quietly began to cry.

It was worst of all at night. There was scampering and squealing everywhere, all kinds of commotion. Katya kept waking up and calling out.

"Shh!" said Nanny, when she came in. "Go back to sleep! It's only rats. But you watch out—or they'll bite your nose off!"

43

Katya would draw the blanket over her head. She would think about the woollen ram, and when she sensed him there, dear and lifeless, she would fall peacefully asleep.

One morning she and the ram were looking out of the window when they suddenly saw someone brown and hairless trotting across the yard. He looked like a cat, only he had a very long tail.

"Nanny, Nanny! Look! What a nasty cat!"

Nanny came to the window too.

"That's not a cat—it's a rat! And it isn't half big! A rat like that could make mincemeat of any cat. Yes, some rat!"

She spat out the last word so horribly, grimacing and baring her teeth as if she herself were an old cat, that Katya felt frightened and disgusted. She felt sick to the pit of her stomach.

Meanwhile, the rat, belly swaying, trotted up, in a business-like, proprietorial way, to a nearby shed and, crouching down, crawled under a slat and into the cellar.

The cook came in and said there were so many rats now that soon they'd be eating your head off. "Down in the storeroom they've gnawed away all the corners of the master's suitcase. The cheek of them! When I come in they just sit there. They don't stir an inch."

In the evening the fox-women came, bringing a bottle of something and some stinking fish. Along with Nanny, they took swigs from the bottle, swallowed down mouthfuls of fish and then started laughing at something or other.

"You still with that ram of yours?" a rather stout woman asked Katya. "He's only fit for the knacker's yard. He's going bald—and look at that leg of his! It's hanging on by a thread. I'd say he's had it."

"Stop teasing her," said Nanny. "Don't pick on a poor orphan!"

"I'm not teasing her. Just telling it how it is. The stuffing will all fall out and that'll be the end of him. A live body eats and drinks—and that's how it stays alive. You can molly-coddle a rag all you like but it'll always fall apart in the end. Anyway, the girl's not an orphan. For all we know, her mother drives past the house laughing into her sleeve: *Tee-hee-hee*!"

The women had worked up quite a sweat with laughing so much. Nanny dipped a lump of sugar in her glass and gave it to Katya to suck. The sugar lump clawed at Katya's throat and there was a ringing in her ears. She tugged at the ram's head.

"He's special. I tell you—he really bleats!"

"Tee-hee! You *are* a silly girl," said the stout woman, with more sniggering. "Even a door squeaks if you push it. A real ram squeals all by itself. You don't need to pull its head."

The women drank some more and went back to whispering the same old words: "And *he* said… You've got to go!… And then *she* said…"

Along with the ram, Katya went behind the trunk in the nursery, to be well and truly miserable.

The ram wasn't very alive. He was going to die soon. His stuffing would all fall out—and that would be the end of

45

him. If only she could get him to eat—if only she could find a way to get him to eat even the very littlest of little nibbles.

She took a baked rusk from the window sill, held it to the ram's mouth and looked the other way, in case he felt shy. Maybe he would bite a little bit off... She waited, then turned round again: no, the rusk was untouched.

"I'll nibble a little bit off myself. Maybe that'll encourage him."

She bit off a tiny corner, held the rusk out to the ram again, turned away and waited. And once again the ram did not touch the rusk.

"No? You can't? You can't 'cos you're not alive?"

And the woollen ram, the lifeless beast, answered with the whole of his meek, sad face, "I can't! I'm not a living beast. I can't!"

"Call out to me then! By yourself! Say 'Ba-a-a!' Go on: 'Ba-a-a!' You can't? You can't?"

And Katya's soul overflowed with pity and love for the poor lifeless one. She went straight to sleep, face pressed to her tear-soaked pillow—and found she was walking down a green path, and the ram was running along beside her, nibbling the grass, calling to her, shouting "Ba-a-a!" all by himself and laughing out loud. How strong and healthy he was. Yes, he would outlive the lot of them!

Morning came—dismal, dark and anxious—and suddenly there was Papa. He was looking grey and angry, his beard all shaggy, and he was scowling like a goat. He poked his hand out so Katya could kiss it, and he told Nanny to tidy everything up because a lady teacher would be coming soon. And off he went.

The next day there was a ring at the front door.

Nanny rushed out. She came back and started bustling around.

"Your teacher's arrived. To look at the face on her, you'd think she was some great dog. Just you wait!"

The teacher clicked her heels together and held out her hand to Katya. She really did look like an intelligent old watchdog; she even had some kind of yellow blotches around her eyes. And she had a way of turning her head very quickly and snapping her teeth, like a dog catching a fly.

She looked round the nursery and said to Nanny, "You're the nanny, are you? I want you to take all these toys, please. Put them somewhere well out of the way, so the child can't see them. All these donkeys and rams have to go. It's important to be truly rational and scientifical about toys. Otherwise we end up with morbidity of imagination and all the damage that ensues from that. Katya, come here!"

She took from her pocket a ball attached to a long rubber string. Snapping her teeth and rotating the ball on the string, she began singing out, "Hop, jump, up and down, bound and bounce! Repeat after me: hop, jump... Oh, what a backward child!"

Katya said nothing and smiled forlornly, to keep from crying. Nanny was carrying away the toys, and the ram let out a "Ba-a-a!" in the doorway.

"Pay attention to the surface of this ball! What do you see? You see that it is two-coloured. One side is light blue, the other white. Point to the light-blue side. Try to concentrate."

And off she went, holding out her hand to Katya and saying, "Tomorrow we're going to weave baskets!"

Katya was shaking all evening long. She couldn't eat anything. She was thinking about the ram, but she didn't dare say a word.

"It's hard being lifeless. What can he do? He can't say anything and he can't call out to me. And she said, 'He's got to go!'"

The words "got to go" made her whole soul turn cold.

The foxy women came, eating and drinking, whispering, "And *he* said... And *she* said..."

And again: "Go! Just got to go!"

Katya woke at dawn, feeling a fear and anguish the likes of which she had never known before. It was as if someone had called out to her. She sat up in bed, listening.

"Ba-a-a! Ba-a-a!"

The ram's call was pitiful and insistent. The lifeless beast was shouting.

All cold now, she leapt out of bed, clenching her hands and pressing them to her chest, listening. There it was again:

"Ba-a-a! Ba-a-a!"

From somewhere out in the corridor. He must be out there.

She opened the door.

"Ba-a-a!"

He was in the storeroom.

She pushed the door open. It wasn't locked. It was a dim, murky dawn, but there was enough light to see. The room was full of boxes and bundles.

"Ba-a-a! Ba-a-a!"

Just by the window was a flurry of dark shapes. The ram was over there too. Something dark jumped out, seized him by the head and began dragging him along.

"Ba-a-a! Ba-a-a!"

And then—two more of the dark shapes, tearing at his flanks, splitting open his skin.

"Rats!" thought Katya. "Rats!" She remembered how Nanny had bared her teeth. She trembled all over, clenching her fists still tighter. But the ram was no longer shouting. He was no more. A big fat rat was silently dragging some grey scraps of cloth, pulling at some soft bits and pieces, tossing the ram's stuffing about.

Katya hid away in her bed, pulling the blankets up over her head. She didn't say anything and she didn't cry. She was afraid Nanny would wake up, bare her teeth like a cat and laugh with the foxy women over the woollen death of the lifeless beast.

She went quite silent; she curled up into a little ball. From now on she was going to be a quiet little girl, oh so quiet, so that no one would ever find out.

1916

49

JEALOUSY

T HAT MORNING she had a sense of foreboding from the very first.

It began when instead of her usual white stockings she was given a pair of murky blue stockings, and Nanny grumbled that the laundress had put too much blue in the wash.

"I ask you, how can she give us the laundry in such a state? And all these airs and graces. If you're going to call yourself 'Matryona Karpovna', you had better ought to know your business and do things proper!"

Liza sat on the bed and examined the long, skinny legs on which she had walked about the great world for seven years. She looked at the murky blue stockings and thought, "This is bad. They look like death. Something's going to happen to me!"

Then, instead of Nanny, the chambermaid Kornelka came into the room—Kornelka with the oily head, oily hands and cunning oily eyes—and began brushing her hair.

Kornelka yanked so hard with the comb that it stung, but Lisa considered it beneath her dignity to whine in the maid's presence and so she just grunted instead.

"What makes your hands so oily?" she asked the maid.

Kornelka turned her short red hand this way and that, as though admiring it.

"It's work makes me hands shine. I work hard, that's why me hands shine so."

Out on the terrace, under the old lime tree, Nanny was cooking jam on a small clay stove.

The cook's little girl, Styoshka, was helping out, feeding wood chips into the little stove, fetching a spoon, fetching a plate, fanning flies away from the pan.

Nanny was encouraging the little girl. She was saying, "Very good, Styoshka! Oh, what a smart girl Styoshka is. Now she's going to go bring me some cold water. Run along, Styoshka, go fetch me some water. Little Styoshka is more precious than gold buttons!"

Liza went round the lime tree, scrambling over its stout roots. In among these roots was plenty to catch the eye. In one little corner lived a dead beetle. Its wings were like the dried husks inside a cedar nut. Liza flipped the beetle onto its back with a twig, and then onto its front, but it wasn't afraid and didn't run away. It was completely dead and living a peaceful life.

In another corner stretched a little web, and in the web reclined a tiny fly. The web was obviously a hammock for flies.

In a third corner sat a ladybird, minding her own business.

Liza lifted her up on the twig. She wanted to take her over and introduce her to the fly. But along the way the ladybird suddenly split down the middle, spread her wings and took flight.

Nanny was rapping a spoon against a plate and skimming the foam off the jam.

"Nanna! Let me have the foam!" begged Liza.

Nanny was all red and cross. She was trying to blow a fly off her upper lip, but the fly seemed to be stuck to the damp skin of her face and it kept trying to creep across either her nose or her cheek.

"Go away! Go away now! There's nothing for you here! How can you have the foam when it hasn't even boiled yet? Another child would have stayed in the nursery and looked at picture books. Can't you see Nanny's busy? What a fidget! Styoshka, my little love, feed it some more wood chips. Oh, what a good girl you are!"

Liza watched Styoshka mincing along on her bare feet, fetching the wood chips and diligently feeding them into the stove.

Styoshka had a scrawny pigtail tied with a dirty pale-blue ribbon, and under the pigtail her neck was dark and as thin as a stick.

"She's trying very hard indeed," thought Liza. "And she does it on purpose. The girl really *does* think she's clever. But Nanny's just trying to be kind."

Styoshka got up and Nanny stroked her head, saying, "Thank you, little Styoshka. Soon there'll be some foam for you."

Liza's temples began to pound, very loudly. She lay face down on the bench, kicking her legs about—in their "deathly" stockings. With a furious smile and trembling lips, she said, "I won't! I won't go! I don't want to and I won't!"

Nanny turned and flung her arms up in the air. "Lord have mercy! What have I done to deserve this? I put a fresh dress on her this morning, and look at her now, rolling around on that dirty bench—she's absolutely filthy! Well, are you going or not?"

"I don't want to and I won't!" Nanny was about to say something else, but just then a thick white foam appeared on top of the jam.

"Good heavens! The jam's boiling over."

Nanny rushed over to the pan, and Liza got up and began singing defiantly. And off she hopped.

Hopping out from under the lime tree, she came upon Styoshka carrying a dish of berries.

Styoshka was stepping along very carefully. And she was doing it on purpose. To show Liza what a clever girl she was.

Liza went up to her and whispered in a strangled voice, "Go! Go away from here, stupid!"

Styoshka put on a frightened face, on purpose, so Nanny would see. Now walking a bit faster, she went over to the lime tree.

Liza ran off into a thicket of gooseberry bushes, collapsed onto the grass and burst out into loud sobs.

Now her entire life was in ruins.

She lay there with her eyes closed, picturing Styoshka's scrawny pigtail, her soiled pale-blue rag of a ribbon and thin neck, dark as a stick. But Nanny would be petting her and saying, "What a clever girl you are, Styoshka! Soon there'll be some foam for you!"

"Fo-oam! Fo-oam! Fo-oam!" Liza moaned, and each time the very sound of the word "foam" was so painful, so bitter, that tears trickled from her eyes straight down into her ears.

"Fooooaam!"

"But maybe something will happen, maybe Styoshka will suddenly drop dead as she's fetching the wood chips! Then everything will be all right again!"

But it wouldn't be all right again. Nanny would be sad. She'd say, "Once there was this clever little girl, but she went and died. If only Liza had died instead." And once again the tears trickled down into Liza's ears.

"So she's got herself a bright little girl. But this little girl doesn't go to school. While I'm learning French. I know how to say *zhai*, *tu ah*, *eel ah*, *voozahvay*, *noozah*... I'll grow up and marry a general. Then I'll come back here and say, 'Who's this girl? Send her packing! She stole my blue rag for her pigtail.'"

Liza began to feel a little better, but then she remembered the foam.

"No!" she said to herself. "Nothing like that will ever happen."

Her life was over now. She wouldn't go back inside ever again. Why should she?

Just like Marya the old laundress had done, she would lie on her back to die. She would close her eyes and lie perfectly still.

God would see her and send His angels to fetch her sweet young soul.

The angels would come, their wings rustling—flutter, flutter, flutter—and carry her soul way up on high.

And at home everyone would sit down to dinner and wonder: "What's wrong with Liza?" "Why isn't Liza eating?" "Why has our Liza grown so pale?" But she would go all quiet and wouldn't say a word.

And suddenly Mama would guess!

"Can't you see?" she would say. "Look at her! She's dead!"

Liza was now sitting quite still, sighing heavily with emotion, and looking at her thin legs in their "deathly blue" stockings. So, now she was dead. Dead.

But something was buzzing, buzzing, closer and closer... and then—bop!—it flew right into Liza's forehead. A fat May-bug, drunk on sunshine, had crashed into Lisa's forehead and fallen to the ground.

Liza jumped up and broke into a run.

"Nanny! Naaanny! A bug hit me! A bug attacked me!" Nanny took fright, then gave her an affectionate look.

"What's the matter, you silly little goose? There isn't even the least little mark on you. You just thought it was attacking you. Now sit down, my clever little thing, and I'll give you some foam, some lovely foam. Wouldn't you like that? Ahh?"

55

"Fo-oam! Fo-oam!" Liza began to laugh from a place deep down inside her soul that God's angels hadn't yet had time to whisk away.

"Nanny, I'll never die, will I? I'll eat lots of soup, and drink lots of milk, and I'll never die. That's right, isn't it?"

1916

THE QUIET BACKWATER

EVERY SEA, every large river and every stormy lake has its own quiet backwater.

The water there is clear and calm. No reeds rustle, no ripples disturb the smooth surface. Should anything touch this surface—a dragonfly's wing or the long leg of a dancing evening mosquito—now there's an event for you.

If you climb the steep bank and look down, you'll see right away where this quiet backwater begins. It's as if it's been marked off by a ruler.

Out there, beyond this line, waves toss and turn in anguish. They rock from side to side, as if from madness and pain, and suddenly, in a last despairing leap, they throw themselves towards the heavens, only to crash back down into the dark water, leaving the wind to snatch at clumps of wild, helpless foam.

But in the backwater, this side of the sacred line, it is quiet. Instead of waves rising in mutiny and flinging themselves at the heavens, the heavens themselves come down to the backwater, in clear azure and little puffs of cloud in the daytime, and garbed in all the mystery of the stars at night.

The estate is called Kamyshovka.

You can see that it once stood on the very edge of the river. But the river retreated and left behind it, as a forget-me-not, a little blue-eyed lake—a joy to ducks—and masses of stiff reeds growing in the front garden.

The main house is abandoned; the doors and windows are boarded up.

Life lingers on only in the lodge—a cross-eyed, lopsided little building.

Here live a retired laundress and a retired coachman. They are not doing nothing; they are looking after the estate.

In her old age the laundress has sprouted a beard, while the coachman, yielding to her more powerful personality, has turned into such an old woman's blouse that he calls himself Fedorushka.

They live righteously. They speak little, and because both are hard of hearing, both always have their say. If one actually manages to hear the other, they understand only hazily, so they keep to what is near and dear, what they lived through long ago, what they know all about and have already recalled many a time.

Besides the coachman and the laundress there are other souls living on the estate: a cunning mare who thinks only about oats and how she might work less, and a glutton of a cow. There are chickens too, of course, though it's hard to say how many—you can't say there are four, but neither can you say there are five. If you throw them some grain and are careful to say, "Come and get it, God bless!", then four chickens come running. But just you forget that blessing and along comes a fifth. Where it's come from no one knows—and it gobbles up all the seed and bullies the other hens. It's big and grey, and evidently it likes seed that hasn't been blessed.

What a worry it all is! The grain belongs to the master and mistress. Sooner or later the mistress will come and ask, "Who's been pecking at my grain? Four beaks or five?"

How will they answer that?

They are afraid they'll be called to account. It's been a hard winter. They've got through firewood aplenty. Fear sets them thinking: across the river lie piles of state-owned wood ready for the spring floating. They harness the mare, cross the river and bring back a load. When they've used it all up they go back for more. How glorious it is having such fine wood right there on your doorstep. Even the mare, sly though she is, doesn't pretend to be tired. She hauls the wood with pleasure.

And then comes—would you believe it?—a summons from the magistrate.

The magistrate asks, "Why did you steal the wood?"

"What do you mean, 'why'? To heat the stove. We've burnt all our own wood already. When her ladyship comes, she'll give us what for."

The magistrate could have been worse. He doesn't shout at them—but he does tell them to put the wood back. Why did he have to be so stingy? Yes, he'd brought them nothing but trouble.

And how had he found out, this magistrate? They hadn't seen anyone when they were fetching the wood. Apparently it was the tracks from their sled—going across the river to the piles of wood and back to their door again.

Tracks? Weren't people cunning nowadays? The things they could figure out!

It's a warm day. Four red hens are pecking at scattered, properly blessed crusts of bread.

The table has been brought out onto the porch for tea. There's company today. The coachman's kinswoman has come from the village—his grand-niece, a girl called Marfa. It's Marfa's name day and she has come here to celebrate.

She's a large girl, white, big-boned and slack-jawed. Her name-day dress is of such an intolerably bright pink that it even verges on blue. The day is clear and golden—the grass is young and garish green, the sky's the bluest of blues, and the yellow flowers in the grass are like little suns—but before the girl's dress they all seem dim and faded.

The old laundress looks at the dress. She squints and screws up her eyes. She feels that the girl's bearing lacks dignity.

"Why do you keep fidgeting?" the old woman grumbles. "Where's your manners? It's your name day, your patron saint is looking down at you from on high, but you—you're like a heifer with your tail swishing this way and that."

"What's that, Granny Pelageya?" the girl asks in surprise. "I haven't wiggled a finger since I sat down."

The old woman screws up her eyes at the bright, bright dress and can't understand what's the matter, what can be making her eyes so cloudy.

"Why don't you go and fetch the samovar?"

Along comes the old coachman. His face is anxious, his brows knitted together—evidently he has been having to deal with the cunning mare.

"She's eaten all the oats again. No matter how much you give her, she cleans up every last grain. The cunning creature! She's got more tricks than many a man. She could outwit more than a few of us, I tell you. I'll be in for it when the mistress comes."

"Yes, you'll be in for it all right," echoes the laundress. "Look! Her stores are nearly all gone! But it's her own fault. How does she expect me to feed a man—a peasant—all winter long? You think it's cheap feeding a peasant? Give him a potato and he wants butter too. Give him porridge and he's got to have broth as well. Is a peasant ever going to try and eat less? All he cares about is stuffing his belly."

The coachman nods sympathetically and even heaves a sigh, although he does half sense that the "peasant" in question might be himself. But that's the way things are. Deep in his soul he feels a certain awe before this peasant nature of his.

"Yes, peasants are peasants. Is a peasant going to try and eat less?"

Then the slack-jawed girl brought out a samovar with green stains down its side.

"Come and have yourselves some tea!" she said.

The old woman began blinking and screwing up her eyes again.

"Who's that you're talking to? Who is it you're calling to the table?"

"Why, you, Granny. And you, Grandpa."

"Then that's what you should say. There was a woman who called everyone to dinner with the words: 'Come and sit yourselves down.' But she didn't say, 'Let the baptized souls come and sit themselves down.' So anyone who felt like it came to dinner: they crawled out from on top of the stove, from behind the stove, from the sleeping shelf, from the bench and from under the bench, all the unseen and unheard, all the unknown and undreamt of. Great big eyes peering, great big teeth clacking. 'You called us,' they said. 'Now feed us.' But what could she do? She could hardly feed such a crowd."

"What happened? What did they all do?" asked the girl, goggle-eyed.

"What do you think?"

"What?"

"Well, they did what they do."

"What did they do?"

"They all did what they had to do."

"But what was it they had to do, Granny?"

"Ask too many questions—there's no knowing who'll answer."

The girl hunched herself up in fright and looked away to one side.

"Why do you keep fidgeting?" The old woman was squinting at the girl's bright pink skirt. "And you the name-day girl! Your name day is your saint's feast day—it's a holy day. The name day of the bee is the day of Saints Zosima and Savvaty. The bee may be a simple, humble creature—but all the same, on her name day she doesn't buzz, she doesn't sting. She just settles on a little flower and thinks about her guardian angel."

"We pay our respects to the mare on the day of Saints Frolus and Laurus," said the coachman, blowing on the tea he had poured out into his chipped saucer.

"The Feast of the Annunciation is the bird's name day. She doesn't weave her nest or peck for grain. She sings, but only softly and respectfully."

"On Saint Vlas's Day we pay our respects to the cattle," said the coachman, still trying to get a word in.

"And the Feast of the Holy Spirit is the earth's name day. On this day no one dares to trouble the earth. No one burrows or digs or picks flowers—none of that is allowed. Burying the dead is not allowed. It's a great sin to insult the earth on her name day. The beasts understand this too—and on the Day of the Holy Spirit no beast will scratch the earth with a claw, or stamp it with a hoof, or strike it with a paw. It's a great sin. Every beast knows about feast days. The glow-worm celebrates on St John the Baptist's Day. He blows on his little flames and prays to his angel. Then it's Saint Aquilina's Day—the name day of red berries—that's when your strawberries and raspberries and currants and brambles and cranberries and cowberries and all the other little forest berries celebrate their name day. On Saint

63

Aquilina's Day there's not a wolf, fox or hare will lay a paw on a red berry. Even the bear's afraid: why would he want to make trouble for himself? He doesn't take a single step until he's sniffed around and made sure he won't be trampling on any berries."

The girl seemed frightened again. She was looking away to one side, tucking her flat feet under her pink skirt. Snuffling and sighing.

The coachman also wanted to have his say.

He might not know many things. He had been in the army. A long time ago. They had had to push back the enemy. Then they had had to push on somewhere else. And somewhere else. Where? Who knows? No one can remember everything.

"Three years I was away. Then I came back home. 'Hello, Fedorushka,' says the wife, and the youngsters, too. And there in the corner, I see a cradle. And in the cradle a nursling. All right, I think, if it's a nursling it's a nursling. The next day I ask my eldest, 'Who's that there in the cradle?' 'That,' she says, 'is a little 'un.' All right, if it's a little 'un then it's a little 'un. The day after that I ask my eldest, 'So, where'd you get this little 'un?' 'Grandma,' she says, 'brought it.' Well, if it was Grandma then it was Grandma. The child began to grow. I heard him being called Petka. All right then, Petka. He grew big. And last year Petka's son got married. But I never did find out where this Petka came from. And now? Well, I doubt anyone can remember any more."

"I can't remember," murmured the old woman. "I can't remember the cow's name day. It's vexing not to know. I've grown old and forgetful. And it's a sin to hurt someone's feelings."

They shut the gate behind the pink girl. The day was over. It was time to go to sleep.

It had been a difficult day. You can't fall asleep straight away after a day like that. After guests have been round you always sleep poorly. The tea, and the talk, and the finery, and all the fuss.

"So when is the cow's name day? Unless you know, you might say an unkind word to her on her name day—and that's a sin. But the cow can't say anything. She'll keep her mouth shut. While up on high an angel will begin to weep…"

It's hard being old! Hard!

Beyond the window the night is a deep blue. It calls something to mind—but just what, it is impossible to remember.

Softly rustle the reeds forgotten by the river.

The river has gone away; it has left the reeds behind.

1916

DUTY AND
HONOUR

MARIA PAVLOVNA was an energetic woman who wore green neckties and told it like it was.

She called on Medina at eleven in the morning, before Medina had time to do her face and hair and when her defences would be at their weakest.

"Well, well," said Maria Pavlovna, looking straight at the curling paper on top of her friend's head. "This all looks very sweet. But perhaps I could trouble you to explain just who was walking you arm in arm across the street last night. Hmm?"

Medina widened her eyes, arched her naked brows and threw up her hands—that is, she drew upon all the meagre resources at her disposal to express surprise.

"Me? Last night? Arm in arm? I don't understand!"

"You don't understand? She doesn't understand! Just wait until Ivan Sergeyevich gets back from his business trip—he'll understand for you!"

Medina made to throw up her hands and widen her eyes again, but somehow this failed to achieve the desired effect, so she decided to look aggrieved instead.

"No, Maria, I well and truly don't understand—whatever are you talking about?"

"I'm talking about the way you're taking advantage of your husband's absence to run around with that clown Fasolnikov. Oh yes! Worse still—the two of you were talking together by the front door for a whole hour and a half. Very clever!"

"I assure you…" Medina stammered. "I assure you that I didn't notice him in the least."

"You didn't notice that you were walking arm in arm with him? Heavens above! Save that for someone else!"

"I swear it's true. I'm ever so scatterbrained!"

"Next time you should keep an eye on what's happening right there by your own elbow. You were talking at the door for two whole hours. The porter is sniggering. The drivers are sniggering. Anna Nikolayevna was going past and she saw everything. She says that she could see from a whole block away that Medina was in love. Now she's spreading the news—all over town."

Medina threw up her hands in horror.

"Me? In love? What nonsense!"

"Save that for someone else," said Maria Pavlovna matter-of-factly. Lighting a cigarette, she asked, "Is he coming to your party tomorrow?"

"Of course not. Although I did invite him. How could I not invite him? So, it's possible, after all, that he might come. He was at my name-day party, so why would he suddenly, now… Of course he'll come."

"Well done! Now you'll have all your guests winking at one another behind your back. Extraordinarily clever! And you know what will happen next? As soon as Ivan Sergeyevich gets back, people will be sending him anonymous letters."

Medina went quiet. "What do you mean?"

"Simple enough. Anna Nikolayevna will be the first to write. She'll open his eyes for him."

"What should I do?"

"I'm afraid that's your problem. You must obey the voice of duty and honour."

"And what does this voice say?"

"It says that you must write to your Fasolnikov and tell him that, first of all, you are a respectable woman, and, second, he must not call on you again."

"Somehow that doesn't sound right. 'You see, I'm a respectable woman, so please don't call on me any more…' That makes it sound like he should only keep disreputable company!"

"Don't try to wriggle out of it. You'll be only too happy to write such a letter when Ivan Sergeyevich comes home, but by then it will be too late. As for me, I really don't care one way or the other."

Maria Pavlovna stood up, eloquently shook the creases from her dress and straightened her green necktie.

Now very agitated, Medina said, "Stop, Maria, for heaven's sake! Tell me what to write!"

Maria Pavlovna sat down and lit another cigarette.

"Write: 'Dear sir!'"

"You know best, but I can't write 'Dear sir' to someone I've been on friendly terms with."

"Well, then write: 'Esteemed Nikolai Andreyich'."

"Address a boy like that as 'esteemed'? Heaven only knows what he'd make of it. In my opinion it would be better simply to write 'Dear'."

"Do you think so? Well, all right then. That will do. So then: 'Dear Nikolai Andreyich! I have the honour of informing you that I am an honourable woman...'"

"You know best, but I can't write like that. It sounds like an official document!"

"Then simply write: 'I am an honourable woman, and I request that you...'"

"You know best, but it still doesn't sound right."

"Well, then write: 'I hasten to inform you that I am an honourable woman.'"

"And he'll say, 'She kept silent for four months, but now, suddenly, she hastens to...' Maria, my dear, don't be angry! But perhaps we can put that at the end? Then, I assure you, it will carry even more of a punch!"

"Fine. Now write this: 'Please do not take this wrong, but I beg you—do not come over tomorrow.'"

"You know best, but that sounds terribly crude. Maybe I should just call the whole thing off after all."

"Do what duty and honour tell you to do."

"And what *do* they tell me to do? Should I call the party off?"

"Certainly, call it off. In that case, write: 'Please do not take this wrong, but I beg you, please, not to come over tomorrow, as the evening has been called off, and there will not be anyone here. Do not ask me to explain. Your sense of delicacy will help you to understand.' That's it. Sign it: 'At your service' and send it."

"You know best, but somehow it's a bit crude. What if I make it a little bit softer?"

"Go ahead—make it softer! And when Ivan Sergeyevich comes home, he'll soften you up all right."

"Really! You always see the worst in everything. The letter is, of course, very good, except… Please don't be offended, but you have no sense of style. Sometimes it's enough simply to move—or remove—even the simplest, least meaningful word, and the whole letter will begin to sound special. Yours somehow sounds common—but please don't be offended."

"What a fool you are! You can't string two words together, but the way you go on about *style*!"

"Maybe I am a fool, and maybe I can't string two words together, but are *you* really so very smart? See for yourself—the word 'not' is repeated four times in four lines. Do you really call that good style?"

"Four? Are you sure about that?"

"Yes, four."

"Then take out one 'not' and we're done. Now I really must run. I hope you'll heed the voice of duty and honour. Send the letter right away."

Maria Pavlovna patted her friend's cheek indulgently and left. Medina sighed heavily and sat down to write a fair copy.

"Take out one 'not' and we're done."

She crossed out one 'not', copied the letter, and reread it:

Dear Nikolai Andreyich!

Please do not take this wrong, but I beg you, please, to come over tomorrow, as the evening has been called off, and there will not be anyone here. Do not ask me to explain. Your sense of delicacy will help you to understand.

At your service,

V. Medina.

She read it once again and was slightly taken aback.

"How strange! It doesn't sound quite the same now, but Maria herself said to take out one 'not'. In any case, it's certainly improved the style."

She perfumed the letter with Astris, put it in the post, and smiled an enlightened smile at herself in the mirror.

"How easy, really, it is to obey the voice of duty and honour!"

1913

PART II

1916–19: Rasputin, Revolution and Civil War

PETROGRAD MONOLOGUE

No! No more! I've promised myself not to say another word about the question of food. Enough is enough! It's become downright unbearable! No matter what one is talking about, one always ends up on the subject of food. As if there's nothing else in the world of any interest.

What about beauty? What about art? What, for goodness' sake, about love?

I ran into Michel recently. People always used to go on about him being such an aesthete; they used to say his soul was a sugared violet. Some violet! I was talking to him about *Parsifal*, but all *he* wanted to talk about was horse meat! Meat, meat, meat—a fine *meeting* of minds, I call it! It was dreadful. And I adore *Parsifal*! Have you seen the new production? It's wonderful! I seem to have forgotten the name of the fellow with the big belly who sang Parsifal himself... But he was wonderful. Ah, how I love art! Not long ago I was at a World of Art[1] exhibition. Have you ever seen Boris Grigoriev? Ah, what an artist! Subtle, piquant, delicious! Aesthetic erotica and erotic aesthetics! You know, whenever I look at his paintings, I feel he's moving his brush not over the canvas, but over my body and soul. Honest to God. So there I was at the exhibition, standing in front of his painting. I closed my eyes so I could take it in better. Suddenly someone was grabbing hold of my arm. Madam Bunova! "Hurry!" she said. "Let's go to the next room. An artist has painted these enormous apples. We must get his address and find out which cooperative he belongs to. There's no way he could have conjured up something this wonderful just from his imagination!"

And do you know? They really were remarkable apples. I haven't seen apples like that for a long time. Great big red apples. I wonder how much they would cost. I saw an apple a little like them at Yeliseyev's,[2] but it wasn't the same—nothing like as big. But the way they pamper that apple you'd think it was Lina Cavalieri[3]—they bathe it and tart it up, and every morning the shop assistants give it a manicure. Although, wouldn't you know it, apparently that apple isn't even for sale. The proprietors are waiting for the value of the rouble to go up.

And yesterday the Bolonkins' cooperative was distributing rice… Oh, don't say I've got back onto the subject of food! Well, I won't do it again, I really won't. I swear I won't. One must take spiritual respite in beauty, in art.

Speaking of which, being beautiful these days is so difficult it's just dreadful.

Can you imagine, even good face powder is impossible to get your hands on. Oh yes, it's just dreadful! Madam Bolonkina says you can use face powder to make flatbread.

You just mix it with either cold cream or lipstick. And it's very tasty, only you feel sick for a long time afterwards. These days, we can take it that people are making flatbread from anything and everything. Madam Bunova's brother says he's made flatbread from window putty, and the recipe is ever so simple: you just pick it out of the window frame and eat it… Ah, goodness gracious, I'm going on about food again! I beg your pardon, it's just a nervous tic—it will pass. After all, I gave you my word. One must take spiritual respite. These are such trying times. Yesterday I ran into a certain composer—such talent, such beauty! And can you imagine, *he* doesn't have any money either. "I'm selling my entire collection of Persian rugs one by one," he said. "That's how I'm feeding myself. I'm like a moth, feeding on rugs." Well, if you ask me, better rugs than horse meat. I'm so sick and tired of this horse meat that I can't even bear to hear about it. But Madam Bolonkina eats it. She may pretend she doesn't, but she certainly does. She recently invited us all over for roast beef. "I've got some wonderful roast beef," she said. But when the maid was bringing it out to the table, instead of saying, "Your first course is ready," she said, "Your horses are ready." So much for her roast beef! Oh dear, have I done it again? Good heavens, forgive me—I gave my word, after all. We shall talk about love, about art.

Now, what was I going to say? Oh yes, Merkin the dentist makes flatbread from fillings and cardamom. He sings its praises. "It's got a lot going for it," he says. "If it gets stuck in your teeth, it'll do you nothing but good." Oh, but what am I saying? Not again! Oh, goodness gracious! But I do love art, I really do!

1918

ONE DAY IN THE FUTURE

I F A STONE thrown in the air meets no resistance, it will describe an arc as dictated by the laws of physics and fall to the ground.

Right?

The foggy morning sky was suddenly cleft by a little pale-gold ray. The ray seemed to spurt out, as though bursting through sturdy grey fabric, but once it had escaped to freedom, it wasn't sure what to do with itself. In the thrill of excitement it slid along the deep snow and the stone walls, sprang up and struck the great Venetian window of the count's house. It struck the glass, then fled in alarm. But this quick strike was enough to wake Terenty Gurtsov, the broad-shouldered, heavy-bearded drayman (number plate 4511), who was sleeping there in the bedchamber.

Terenty stretched, grunted and rang for the servant.

At his summons a woman came to the door. Straightening her pince-nez, she respectfully enquired, "How may I be of assistance, sir?"

Terenty was not very fond of this woman.

"What took you so long?"

Even so, he appreciated her cleanliness and punctilious-ness—matters which, as a former lady-doctor, she took very seriously.

"A vice admiral is here to see you, Terenty Sidorych. He's brought you a notice."

"Eh? A notice? Well, let 'im in."

In walked a man of middling years, dressed in a shabby naval uniform, without epaulettes, braid or buttons.

"Sir, I'm a courier. I've brought you a notice."

"Whaddaya mean, 'a notice'?"

"Here it is, sir, you can read it. And would you sign for receipt, please."

He held out a sheet of paper and the delivery book.

Terenty twirled the paper around, then lost his temper. "Whaddaya doin', shovin' it at me like that? Read it to me, don't stick it in my face! You're here now—so read it!"

The vice admiral looked uncomfortable, and, with a glance at the notice, he said, "It's an order for you to give a lecture today at the university."

"Whaddaya mean a 'lekcher'?"

"It says 'in the philology faculty'."

"Phila-what?"

"Philology."

"Philala, philala—why don't you philala yourself!… And what do they want me for? I'm done with draying, I'm a man of leisure now. What? Can't they find another drayman?"

"Evidently it's your turn to occupy the chair, sir."

"Hock me pie what?"

"The chair, sir."

"I hain't never hocked a pie in me life. Gimme the book, where do I sign?"

"Right here, sir."

Terenty sucked the tip of the pencil and drew an 'X'.

"That'll do. I'm too busy now to write my whole fambly name."

The vice admiral departed. Terenty got dressed and left the house.

His doorman had once been a singer at the Imperial Theatre. With the graceful magnificence of Verdi's Don Carlos, he flung the doors open before Terenty.

The cabby was a good one, even if he was a former botany professor. Though that may have been why he talked with such enthusiasm about oats.

They even turned out to have acquaintances in common. The professor's brother, a famous surgeon in his day, was Terenty's junior doorman.

The conversation was so interesting that Terenty didn't notice they had arrived.

Wanting to look smart, he had stopped on the way to buy a newspaper from a former lieutenant general. Fanning himself languidly, as though it were hot, he made his way up the stairs.

In one of the halls a lecture on the history of philosophy had just finished. The lecture had been given by Semyon Lazdryga, a former watchman. Evidently the students had enjoyed the lecture: they were enthusiastically throwing the lecturer up in the air.

"What do you want?" one of these students politely enquired.

"I'm s'posed to give a lekcher. On philala. They seem to think us draymen are thin on the ground, so they've asked me along."

"All right then, give it to us."

"Just don't go on too long," said another student. "It's not our idea of fun, either."

Terenty cleared his throat, stroked his beard, and began.

"Comrades in university! Here I was a drayman, and now I'm come a... come a... philala. Because you here need this higher ejucation. And them capitalists aren't allowed at you. They'd teach you things you can't even pernounce. They'd even make you use hypostrophies. Isn't that right?"

"Right!" replied the students.

"We need to do away with all that stuff. Isn't that right?"

"All right! Come on, guys, let's toss him!"

And they spent a long time throwing him up in the air. They were even going to send a telegram to the Minister of Enlightenment, but it turned out none of them knew how to write. Then they remembered the Minister couldn't read or write either, so they decided it was probably better not to bother him.

Instead of sending the telegram, they tossed Terenty a bit longer, then let him go.

On his return journey he overtook several carts loaded with firewood. Their drivers had the most improbable backgrounds: one had been a tenor with the Mariinsky Theatre, another an academician, the third a staff captain, the fourth a gynaecologist. Terenty watched them for a while, then turned and shook his head.

"Yes, a drayman's work is harder than a philala's."

At home he had an unpleasant surprise. In the dining room his ten-year-old son was studiously learning the alphabet.

Terenty tore the book out of the boy's hands and ripped it to shreds.

"You mangy pup!" he yelled. "So you thought you'd start readin' books, eh? Learn the sciences, eh? So you wanna end up a goatherd?"

Angrily banging the door behind him, he went to his study to eat cabbage soup.

The little boy sobbed and sobbed as he gathered up the shredded pages. The lady-doctor cleared the dishes away, tiptoed up to the crying boy, and tentatively stroking his head, she whispered, "Don't cry, my child. One day we shall see the heavens glittering like diamonds."[1]

1918

ONE OF US

THE THEATRE was half empty and very cold.

To warm themselves a little, or maybe just so they wouldn't miss the tram, many people put on their fur coats during the interval and then wore them all through the last act.

Mrs Kudakina, the wife of a general, couldn't bear these ways. They struck her as vulgar and uncouth.

She hadn't been to the opera for a long time and now she felt like a fish out of water.

"Where's Ardanova? Where's the Princess? Where's Levam-Tamurayeva? *Nobody* is here!"

Les nôtres—people like us—had disappeared. They had been replaced by *les autres*—people not at all like us—who had come in smocks, blacked boots and woollen jumpers. Perched on the box ledges, they were laughing boisterously, crunching into apples, applauding in all the wrong places and making loud curtain calls for the wrong performers.

It was all just dreadful.

In the foyer where the general's wife always went to powder her nose and see what the other ladies were wearing, *les autres* were loitering in a dense, drab crowd, stamping their boots and pressing up against one another like sardines.

Mrs Kudakina, the general's wife, was very put out.

To make matters worse, she would have to walk home alone, down dark and frightening streets packed with highway robbers. No, this game certainly wasn't worth the candle.

The nearer they got to the end of the performance, the more frightened she felt by the prospect of the dark street and the dark figures lurking in it.

Literally not one of *les nôtres* was present. She really would have to walk home alone.

The performance finished. She hurriedly put on her coat and rushed outside, doing up the buttons on the way. She just needed to stay with the crowd. That would be less frightening.

On the square right in front of the theatre were mounds of packed snow. In her hurry to get across the street, the general's wife found herself standing on one such mound and didn't know what to do. Her feet were slipping and there was nothing to hold on to.

"Good heavens! Am I going to have to get down on my hands and knees?"

"Madam, please allow me to assist you!" came a mild bass from behind her.

She turned round.

Before her stood an elderly gentleman of medium height, perhaps a civil servant from the old days. He was clean-shaven, with short, greying side whiskers and a respectful manner.

"One of *les nôtres*!" thought the general's wife, holding out her hand to him with a certain grace. "*Merci!* How kind of you!"

"The snow is piled so high here that one could easily break a leg," said the civil servant, supporting her by the arm. "Let's cross to the other side where it's less slippery."

The general's wife brightened. Obviously he was going in her direction. Thank heavens! Now there was nothing to be afraid of.

"Hmm!" said the civil servant with a disapproving shake of his head. "These new ways! Have you just attended the theatre, madam?"

"Yes, I was at the opera."

"And who was singing this evening?"

She told him.

"But that's dreadful!" replied the old gentleman indignantly. "Roles like those are beyond them. This wouldn't have happened in the old days!"

"It seems you spend a lot of time at the theatre?"

"Nowadays I don't set foot in it. Why would I? It's too distressing. Have you realized what kind of people go there now?"

The general's wife grew animated. "Indeed! Indeed!" she said. "It's simply dreadful. Today there was literally not a single one of *les nôtres*."

"Precisely! They just sit there blinking—they don't

understand anything at all. As for the ballet—I went once for old times' sake. I wanted to see old friends. You know, I almost wept from rage. Makletsova was dancing—and there they all were yelling, 'Bravo, Krasavina!' Just because someone had made a mistake and put her name in the programme notes. Just imagine: they've got their eyes wide open, but they still can't see who's dancing. There was a performance of *The Barber of Seville* a while back, and at the end they called for the composer! How do you like that?"

"*C'est affreux! C'est affreux!*"[1] said the general's wife, truly upset.

"Remember the gala performances in the old days! The glitter, the gold, the crowds of generals! The fine ladies, all their diamonds and feathers! And their stoles! Sables! Furs so thick that your hand sank right into them. All perfumed and soft."

"Oh!" said the general's wife with a playful laugh. "I see you're well versed in ladies' attire?"

"Oh yes! And everything was so beautiful! Countess Westen, parterre box, left-hand side—what tiny feet she had! Always in white-satin slippers. And her tiny feet always had to be wrapped in tissue before she could put her boots on."

"Zizi? You know Zizi?"

"She dressed beautifully. A patron, first class."

"Tell me, did you ever visit the Westens at home?"

"I only saw them at the theatre."

"Do you know her sister too?"

"Yes, I did once go to her house. She asked me to come round. I called in with a ticket for her."

The general's wife was happy. The walk wasn't frightening at all; it was even rather enjoyable. What was most pleasing of all was that she'd immediately recognized her amiable companion as one of *les nôtres*. She was already imagining telling all this to her husband.

Boldly she grasped her companion's arm and said, coquettishly, "Forgive me for being so *sans façon*,[2] but it's terribly slippery here!"

"It's my pleasure, madam."

"What a shame," thought the general's wife, "that I can't really ask him who he is. It would seem rude. He might be a former minister. How very droll! What a romantic encounter! I wonder if there's some way I can get him to say…"

"Yes, what trying times these are…" the civil servant said with a sigh, and fell silent.

"It must be terribly dull for you now that… now that everyone from the old regime is sitting at home without anything to do…"

"Well, yes, of course it's dull for someone who's used to working. But our time will come again. For now I'm living at my daughter's. But our time will come! They'll remember us yet! They certainly will! And they'll want us back! They won't get by for long without us. They'll be begging us to come back!"

The general's wife recalled a dignitary of her acquaintance, who, when speaking of his own hopes, had used these very same words. Literally, the very same words.

"You didn't happen to know Ostryatinov, did you?" she asked.

"No, I never had occasion to meet him."

"He used to say exactly the same thing. And my husband—I'll be sure to introduce you—he would agree with you completely… Although these days he steers clear of politics altogether. It was terrible when his department was closed down—it really affected his nerves. I suppose you shun politics, too? Or have you still not lost hope? You can tell me everything, it's all right. We belong to the same world. You know that as well as I do."

"No, I stay out of politics. I leave politics to the boys."

"Oh, the next entrance is mine," said the general's wife. Surely he would introduce himself before he went on his way?

"The Chagins' house. I know it," said the bureaucrat. "I know all the houses round here. I most certainly do! Twenty-six years I used to go down this road on my way to the theatre."

"You really went as often as that?"

"Oh yes, nearly every day."

"Goodness, you really are a man of the theatre!" the general's wife said in astonishment. She guessed at once: he must have been having some kind of ballet liaison.

"Yes, madam! Twenty-six years—I'm not making it up."

"But how can a man get as impassioned about the theatre as that? I think there must be some very special reason," she said with a little giggle.

And she playfully wagged a gloved finger at him.

But he didn't smile. He tipped his hat, wiped his large, bald head and, with a sigh, replied, "No, passion didn't come into it. I was working. Madam, for twenty-six years I was an usher at that very theatre. Indeed I was!"

The general's wife didn't say a word to her husband about her instinctive ability to recognize *les nôtres*.

Feeling badly out of sorts, she went straight to bed, without even having some tea.

1918

RASPUTIN

THERE ARE PEOPLE who are remarkable because of their talent, intelligence, or public standing, people whom you often meet and whom you know well. You have an accurate sense of what these people are like, but all the same they pass through your life in a blur, as if your psychic lens can never quite focus on them, and your memory of them always remains vague. There's nothing you can say about them that everyone doesn't already know. They were tall or they were short; they were married; they were affable or arrogant, unassuming or ambitious; they lived in some place or other and they saw a lot of so-and-so. The blurred negatives of the amateur photographer. You can look all you like, but you still can't tell whether it's a little girl or a ram...

The person I want to talk about flashed by in a mere two brief encounters. But how firmly and vividly his character is etched into my memory, as if with a fine blade.

And this isn't simply because he was so very famous. In my life I've met many famous people, people who have truly earned their renown. Nor is it because he played such a tragic role in the fate of Russia. No. This man was unique, one of a kind, like a character out of a novel; he lived in legend, he died in legend, and his memory is cloaked in legend.

A semi-literate peasant and a counsellor to the Tsar, a hardened sinner and a man of prayer, a shape-shifter with the name of God on his lips.

They called him cunning. Was there really nothing to him but cunning?

I shall tell you about my two brief encounters with him.

1

The end of a Petersburg winter. Neurasthenia.

Rather than starting a new day, morning is merely a continuation of the grey, long-drawn-out evening of the day before.

Through the plate glass of the large bay window I can see out onto the street, where a warrant officer is teaching new recruits to poke bayonets into a scarecrow. The recruits have grey, damp-chilled faces. A despondent-looking woman with a sack stops and stares at them.

What could be more dismal?

The telephone rings.

"Who is it?"

"Rozanov."[1]

In my surprise, I ask again. Yes, it's Rozanov.

He is very cryptic. "Has Izmailov[2] said anything to you? Has he invited you? Have you accepted?"

"No, I haven't seen Izmailov and I don't know what you're talking about."

"So he hasn't yet spoken to you. I can't say anything over the telephone. But please, please do accept. If you don't go, I won't either."

"For heaven's sake, what are you talking about?"

"He'll explain everything. It's not something we can talk about on the telephone."

There was a click on the line. We had been disconnected.

This was all very unexpected and strange. Vasily Rozanov was not someone I saw a lot of. Nor was Izmailov. And the combination of Rozanov and Izmailov also seemed odd. What was all this about? And why wouldn't Rozanov go to some place unless I went too?

I rang the editorial department of the *Stock Exchange News*, where Izmailov worked. It was too early; no one was there.

But I didn't have to wait long. About two hours later Izmailov rang me.

"There is the possibility of a very interesting meeting… Unfortunately, there's nothing more I can say over the telephone… Maybe you can guess?"

I most certainly could not guess. We agreed that he should come round and explain everything.

He arrived.

"Have you still not guessed who we're talking about?"

Izmailov was thin, all in black, and in dark glasses; he looked as if he had been sketched in black ink. His voice was hollow. It was all rather weird and sinister.

Izmailov really was a rather weird figure. He lived in the grounds of the Smolensk cemetery, where his father had once been a priest. He practised black magic, loved telling stories about sorcery, and he knew charms and spells. Thin, pale and black, with a bright-red strip of thin mouth, he looked like a vampire.

"So you really don't understand?" he asked with a grin. "You don't know who it is we can't discuss over the telephone?"

"Kaiser Wilhelm perhaps?"

Izmailov looked through his dark glasses at the two doors into my study—and then, over his glasses, at me.

"Rasputin."

"Ah!"

"Here in Petersburg there's a publisher. Filippov—perhaps you've heard of him? No? Well, anyway, there is. Rasputin goes to see him quite often. He dines with him. For some reason Rasputin is really quite friendly with him. Filippov also regularly entertains Manuilov, who has a certain reputation in literary circles. Do you know him?"

Manuilov was someone I had come across a few times. He was one of those "companion fish" that are part of the entourage of great writers or artistic figures. At one point he'd worshipped Kuprin,[3] then he moved over to Leonid Andreyev.[4] Then he'd quietened down and seemed to disappear altogether. Now he had resurfaced.

"This Manuilov," said Izmailov, "has suggested to Filippov that he should ask round some writers who'd like to get a glimpse of Rasputin. Just a few people, carefully chosen so there's no one superfluous and no chance of any unpleasant surprises. Only recently a friend of mine happened to be in the company of Rasputin—and someone covertly took a photograph. Worse still—they sent this photograph to a magazine. 'Rasputin,' the caption read, 'among his friends and admirers.' But my friend is a prominent public figure; he's a serious man, absolutely respectable. He can't stand Rasputin and he feels he'll never get over the disgrace of this photograph—of being immortalized amid this picturesque crowd. Which is why, to avoid any unpleasantness of this kind, I've made it a condition that there should be no superfluous guests. Filippov has given his promise, and this morning Manuilov came over and showed me the guest list. One of the writers is Rozanov, and Rozanov insists that you absolutely must be there. Without you, he says the whole thing will be a waste of time. Evidently he has a plan of some kind."

"What on earth can this plan be?" I asked. "Maybe I should stay at home. Although I would, I admit, be curious to get a glimpse of Rasputin."

"Precisely. How could anyone not be curious? One wants to see for oneself whether he really is someone significant in his own right or whether he's just a weapon—someone being exploited by clever people for their own ends. Let's take a chance and go. We won't stay long and we'll keep together. Like it or not, he's someone who'll be in the history books. If we miss this chance, we may never get another."

"Just so long as he doesn't think we're trying to get something out of him."

"I don't think he will. The host has promised not to let on that we're writers. Apparently Rasputin doesn't like writers. He's afraid of them. So they won't be telling him this little detail. This is in our interests too. We want Rasputin to feel completely at ease—as if among friends. Because if he feels he's got to start posturing, the evening will be a complete waste of time. So, we'll be going, will we? Tomorrow late—not before ten. Rasputin never turns up any earlier. If he's held up at the palace and can't come, Filippov promises to ring and let us all know."

"This is all very strange. And I've never even met the host."

"I don't know him either, not personally—nor does Rozanov. But he's someone well known. And he's a thoroughly decent fellow. So, we're agreed: tomorrow at ten."

2

I had glimpsed Rasputin once before. In a train. He must have been on his way east, to visit his home village in Siberia. He was in a first-class compartment. With his entourage: some little man or other who might have been his secretary, a woman of a certain age with her daughter, and Madame V——, a lady-in-waiting to the Tsaritsa.[5]

It was very hot and the compartment doors were wide open. Rasputin was presiding over tea—with a tin teapot, small dried bagels and lumps of sugar on the side. He was wearing a pink calico smock over his trousers, wiping his forehead and neck with an embroidered towel and talking rather peevishly, with a broad Siberian accent.

"Dearie! Go and fetch us some more hot water! Hot water, I said, go and get us some. The tea's right stewed but they didn't even give us any hot water. And where is the strainer? Annushka, where've you gone and hidden the strainer? Annushka! The strainer—where is it? Oh, what a muddler you are!"

In the evening of the day Izmailov had come round—that is, the day before I was due to meet Rasputin—I went to a rather large dinner party at the home of some friends.

The mirror above the dining-room fireplace was adorned with a sign that read: "In this house we do not talk about Rasputin."

I'd seen signs like this in a number of other houses. But this time, because I was going to be seeing him the next day, there was no one in the world I wanted to talk about more than Rasputin. And so, slowly and loudly, I read out: "In this house we do not talk about Ras-pu-tin."

Sitting diagonally across from me was a thin, tense,

angular lady. She quickly looked round, glanced at me, then at the sign, then back at me again. As if she wanted to say something.

"Who's that?" I asked my neighbour.

"Madame E——," he replied. "She's a lady-in-waiting. Daughter of *the* E——" He named someone then very well known. "Know who I mean?"

"Yes."

After dinner this lady sat down beside me. I knew she'd been really wanting to talk to me—ever since I'd read out that sign. But all she could do was prattle in a scatterbrained way about literature. Clearly she didn't know how to turn the conversation to the subject that interested her.

I decided to help her out.

"Have you seen the sign over the fireplace? Funny, isn't it? The Bryanchaninovs have one just like it."

She immediately came to life.

"Yes, indeed. I really don't understand. Why shouldn't we talk about Rasputin?"

"Probably because people are talking about him too much. Everyone's bored with the subject…"

"Bored?" She seemed almost scared. "How could anyone find him boring? You're not going to say that, are you? Don't you find Rasputin fascinating?"

"Have you ever met him?" I asked.

"Who? Him? You mean—Rasputin?"

And suddenly she was all fidgety and flustered. She was gasping. Red blotches appeared on her thin, pale cheeks.

"Rasputin? Yes… a very little… a few times. He feels he absolutely *has* to get to know me. They say it's very interesting, very interesting indeed. Do you know, when he stares at me, my heart begins to pound in the most alarming way… It's astonishing. I've seen him three times, I think, at friends'. The last time he suddenly came right up close and said: 'What is it, you little waif? You be sure to come and see me—yes, mind you do!' I was completely at a loss. I said I didn't know, that I couldn't… And then he put his hand on my shoulder and said, 'You shall come. Understand? Yes, you absolutely shall!' And the way he said 'shall' so commandingly, with such authority, it was as if this had already been decided on high and Rasputin was in the know. Do you understand what I mean? It was as if, to him, my fate were an open book. He sees it, he knows it. I'm sure you understand I would never call on him, but the lady whose house I met him at said I really must, that plenty of women of our station call on him, and that there's nothing in the least untoward about it. But still… I… I shan't…"

This "I shan't" she almost squealed. She looked as if she were about to give a hysterical shriek and start weeping.

I could hardly believe it! A mild-mannered lady, mousy and thin, and she looked as if she were at least thirty-five. And yet she had suddenly, shamelessly, lost all self control at the mere mention of Rasputin, that peasant in a pink calico smock whom I had heard ordering "Annushka" to look for the tea strainer…

The lady of the house came over to where we were sitting and asked us a question. And without replying, probably without even hearing her, Madame E—— got up and with a jerky, angular gait went over to the mirror to powder her nose.

3

All the next day I was unable to put this twitching, bewitched lady-in-waiting out of my mind.

It was unnerving and horrible.

The hysteria around the name of Rasputin was making me feel a kind of moral nausea.

I realized, of course, that a lot of the talk about him was petty, foolish invention, but nonetheless I felt there was something real behind all these tales, that they sprang from some weird, genuine, living source.

In the afternoon Izmailov rang again and confirmed the invitation. He promised that Rasputin would definitely be there. And he passed on a request from Rozanov that I should wear something "a bit glamorous"—so Rasputin would think he was just talking to an ordinary "laydee" and the thought that I might be a writer wouldn't so much as enter his head.

This demand for "a bit of glamour" greatly amused me.

"Rozanov seems determined to cast me in the role of some Biblical Judith or Delilah. I'll make a hash of it, I'm afraid—I haven't the talents of either an actor or an agent provocateur. All I'll do is mess things up."

"Let's just play it by ear," Izmailov said reassuringly. "Shall I send someone over to fetch you?"

I declined, as I was dining with friends, and was going to be dropped off after the meal.

That evening, as I was dressing, I tried to imagine a peasant's idea of "a bit of glamour". I put on a pair of gold shoes, and some gold rings and earrings. I'd have felt embarrassed to deck myself out any more flashily. It wasn't as if I was going to be able to explain to all and sundry that this was glamour on demand!

At my friends' dinner table, this time without any wiles on my part, the conversation turned to Rasputin. (People evidently had good reason to put injunctions up over their fireplaces.)

As always, there were stories about espionage, about Germans bribing Russian officials, about sums of money finding their way via the elder[6] into particular pockets and about court intrigues, the threads of which were all in Rasputin's hands.

Even the "black automobile" got linked with the name of Rasputin.

The "black automobile" remains a mystery to this day. Several nights running this car had roared across the Field of Mars, sped over the Palace Bridge and disappeared into the unknown. Shots had been fired from inside the car. Passers-by had been wounded.

"It's Rasputin's doing," people were saying. "Who else?"

"What's he got to do with it?"

"He profits from everything black, evil and incomprehensible. Everything that sows discord and panic. And there's nothing he can't explain to his own advantage when he needs to."

These were strange conversations. But these were strange times, and so no one was especially surprised. Although the events soon to unfold swept the "black automobile" right out of our minds. All too soon we would have other things to think about.

But at the time, at dinner, we talked about all these things. First and foremost, people were astonished by Rasputin's extraordinary brazenness. Razumov, who was then the director of the Department of Mines, indignantly related how one of his provincial officials had come to him with a request for a transfer. And to support his case, he had held out a piece of paper on which Rasputin—whom Razumov had never even met—had scrawled:

Dearie, do wot the barer asks and you'll have no caws for regret. Grigory.

"Can you imagine? The cheek of it! The brazen cheek of it! And there are a great many ministers who say they've received little notes like this. And all too many of them just do as he asks—though they don't, of course, admit as much. I've even been told I was reckless to be getting so angry, because *he* would hear about it. It was vile. Can you imagine it? 'Dearie'! As for the fine fellow who turned up with the note, I showed him what a 'Dearie' I can be! Apparently he flew down the stairs four at a time. And he had seemed like such a respectable man—as well as being a rather eminent engineer."

"Yes," said someone else, "I've heard about any number of these 'Dearie' recommendations, but this is the first time I've heard about one not being granted. People get all indignant, but they don't feel able to refuse the man. 'He's vindictive,' they say, 'a vindictive peasant.'"

4

Some time after ten o'clock I arrived at Filippov's.

Our host greeted me in the hall. After saying in a friendly way that we'd already met once before, he showed me into his study.

"Your friends arrived long ago."

In the small, smoke-filled room were some half a dozen people.

Rozanov was looking bored and disgruntled. Izmailov appeared strained, as if trying to make out that everything was going fine when really it wasn't.

Manuilov was standing close to the doorway, looking as if he felt entirely at home. Two or three people I didn't know were sitting silently on the divan. And then there was

Rasputin. Dressed in a black woollen Russian kaftan and tall patent-leather boots, he was fidgeting anxiously, squirming about in his chair. One of his shoulders kept twitching.

Lean and wiry and rather tall, he had a straggly beard and a thin face that appeared to have been gathered up into a long fleshy nose. His close-set, piercing, glittering little eyes were peering out furtively from under strands of greasy hair. I think these eyes were grey. The way they glittered, it was hard to be sure. Restless eyes. Whenever he said something, he would look round the whole group, his eyes piercing each person in turn, as if to say, "Have I given you something to think about? Are you satisfied? Have I surprised you?"

I felt at once that he was rather preoccupied, confused, even embarrassed. He was posturing.

"Yes, yes," he was saying. "I wish to go back as soon as possible, to Tobolsk. I wish to pray. My little village is a good place to pray. God hears people's prayers there."

And then he studied each of us in turn, his eyes sharply and inquisitively piercing into each one of us from under his greasy locks.

"But here in your city nothing's right. It's not possible to pray in this city. It's very hard when you can't pray. Very hard."

And again he looked round anxiously, right into everyone's faces, right into their eyes.

We were introduced. As had been agreed, my fellow scribes did not let on who I really was.

He studied me, as if thinking, "Who *is* this woman?"

There was a general sense of both tedium and tension—not what we wanted at all. Something in Rasputin's manner— maybe his general unease, maybe his concern about the impression his words were making—suggested that somehow he knew who we were. It seemed we might have been given away. Imagining himself to be surrounded by "enemies from the press", Rasputin had assumed the posture of a man of prayer.

They say he really did have a great deal to put up with from journalists. The papers were always full of sly insinuations of every kind. After a few drinks with his cronies, Rasputin was supposed to have divulged interesting details about the personal lives of people in the very highest places. Whether this was true or just newspaper sensationalism, I don't know. But I do know that there were two levels of security around Rasputin: one set of guards whom he knew about and who protected him from attempts on his life; another set whom he was supposed not to know about and who kept track of whom he was talking to and whether or not he was saying anything he shouldn't. Just who was responsible for this second set of guards I can't say for certain, but I suspect it was someone who wanted to undermine Rasputin's credibility at court.

He had keen senses, and some animal instinct told him he was surrounded. Not knowing where the enemy lay, he was on the alert, his eyes quietly darting everywhere…

I was infected by my friends' discomfort. It felt tedious and rather awkward to be sitting in the house of a stranger and listening to Rasputin straining to come out with spiritually edifying pronouncements that interested none of us. It was as if he were being tested and was afraid of failing.

I wanted to go home.

Rozanov got to his feet. He took me aside and whispered, "We're banking on dinner. There's still a chance of him opening up. Filippov and I have agreed that you must sit beside him. And we'll be close by. You'll get him talking. He's not going to talk freely to us—he's a ladies' man. Get him to speak about the erotic. This could be really something—it's a chance we must make the most of. We could end up having a most interesting conversation."

Rozanov would happily discuss erotic matters with anyone under the sun, so it was hardly a surprise that he should be so eager to discuss them with Rasputin. After all, what didn't they say about Rasputin? He was a hypnotist and a mesmerist, at once a flagellant and a lustful satyr, both a saint and a man possessed by demons.

"All right," I said. "I'll do what I can."

Turning around, I encountered two eyes as sharp as needles. Our surreptitious conversation had obviously disturbed Rasputin. ·

With a twitch of the shoulder, he turned away.

We were invited to the table.

I was seated at one corner. To my left sat Rozanov and Izmailov. To my right, at the end of the table, Rasputin.

There turned out to be around a dozen other guests: an elderly lady with a self-important air ("She's the one who goes everywhere with him," someone whispered to me); a harassed-looking gentleman, who hurriedly got a beautiful young lady to sit on Rasputin's right (this young lady was dressed to the nines—certainly more than "a bit glamorous"—but the look on her face was crushed and hopeless, quite out of keeping with her attire); and at the other end of the table were some strange-looking musicians, with a guitar, an accordion and a tambourine—as if this were a village wedding.

Filippov came over to us, pouring out wine and handing round hors-d'oeuvres. In a low voice I asked about the beautiful lady and the musicians.

The musicians, it turned out, were a requirement—Grisha sometimes liked to get up and dance, and only what *they* played would do. They also played at the Yusupovs'.

"They're very good. Quite unique. In a moment you'll hear for yourself." As for the beautiful lady, Filippov explained that her husband (the harassed-looking gentleman) was having a difficult time at work. It was an unpleasant and complicated situation that could only be sorted out with the help of the elder. And so this gentleman was seizing every possible opportunity to meet Rasputin, taking his wife along with him and seating her beside Rasputin in the hope that sooner or later he would take notice of her.

"He's been trying for two months now, but Grisha acts as if he doesn't even see them. He can be strange and obstinate."

Rasputin was drinking a great deal and very quickly. Suddenly he leant towards me and whispered, "Why aren't you drinking, eh? Drink. God will forgive you. Drink."

"I don't care for wine, that's why I'm not drinking."

He looked at me mistrustfully.

"Nonsense! Drink. I'm telling you: God will forgive you. He will forgive you. God will forgive you many things. Drink!"

"But I'm telling you I'd rather not. You don't want me to force myself to drink, do you?"

"What's he saying?" whispered Rozanov on my left. "Make him talk louder. Ask him again, to make him talk louder. Otherwise I can't hear."

"But it's nothing interesting. He's just trying to get me to drink."

"Get him to talk about matters erotic. God Almighty! Do you really not know how to get a man to talk?"

This was beginning to seem funny.

"Stop going on at me! What am I? An agent provocateur? Anyway, why should I go to all this trouble for you?"

I turned away from Rozanov. Rasputin's sharp, watchful eyes pierced into me.

"So you don't want to drink? You are a stubborn one! I'm telling you to drink—and you won't."

And with a quick and obviously practised movement he quietly reached up and touched my shoulder. Like a hypnotist using touch to direct the current of his will. It was as deliberate as that.

From his intent look I could see he knew exactly what he was doing. And I remembered the lady-in-waiting and her hysterical babbling: *And then he put his hand on my shoulder and said so commandingly, with such authority…*

So it was like that, was it? Evidently Grisha had a set routine. Raising my eyebrows in surprise, I glanced at him and smiled coolly.

A spasm went through his shoulder and he let out a quiet moan. Quickly and angrily he turned away from me, as if once and for all. But a moment later he was leaning towards me again.

"You may be laughing," he said, "but do you know what your eyes are saying? Your eyes are sad. Go on, you can tell me—is he making you suffer badly? Why don't you say anything? Don't you know we all love sweet tears, a woman's sweet tears. Do you understand? I know everything."

I was delighted for Rozanov. The conversation was evidently turning to matters erotic.

"What is it you know?" I asked loudly, on purpose, so that Rasputin, too, would raise his voice, as people often unwittingly do.

Once again, though, he spoke very softly.

"I know how love can make one person force another to suffer. And I know how necessary it can be to make someone suffer. But I don't want *you* to suffer. Understand?"

"I can't hear a thing!" came Rozanov's cross voice, from my left.

"Be patient!" I whispered.

109

Rasputin went on.

"What's that ring on your hand? What stone is it?"

"It's an amethyst."

"Well, that'll do. Hold your hand out to me under the table so no one can see. Then I'll breathe on the ring and warm it… The breath of my soul will make you feel better."

I passed him the ring.

"Oh, why did you have to take it off? That was for me to do. You don't understand…"

But I had understood only too well. Which was why I'd taken it off myself.

Covering his mouth with his napkin, he breathed onto the ring and quietly slid it onto my finger.

"There. When you come and see me, I'll tell you many things you don't know."

"But what if I don't come?" I asked, once again remembering the hysterical lady-in-waiting.

Here he was, Rasputin in his element. The mysterious voice, the intense expression, the commanding words—all this was a tried and tested method. But if so, then it was all rather naive and straightforward. Or, perhaps, his fame as a sorcerer, soothsayer and favourite of the Tsar really did kindle within people a particular blend of curiosity and fear, a keen desire to participate in this weird mystery. It was like looking through a microscope at some species of beetle. I could see the monstrous hairy legs, the giant maw—but I knew it was really just a little insect.

"Not come to me? No, you shall come. You shall come to me."

And again he quickly reached up and quietly touched my shoulder. I calmly moved aside and said, "No, I shan't."

And again a spasm went through his shoulder and he let out a low moan. Each time he sensed that his power, the current of his will, was not penetrating me and was meeting resistance, he experienced physical pain. (This was my impression at the time and it was confirmed later.) And in this there was no pretence, as he was evidently trying to conceal both the spasms in his shoulder and his strange, low groan.

No, this was not a straightforward business at all. Howling inside him was a black beast… There was much we did not know.

5

"Ask him about Vyrubova"[7] whispered Rozanov. "Ask him about everyone. Get him to tell you everything. And *please* get him to speak up."

Rasputin gave Rozanov a sideways look, from under his greasy locks.

"What's that fellow whispering about?"

Rozanov held his glass out towards Rasputin and said, "I was wanting to clink glasses."

Izmailov held his glass out, too.

Rasputin looked at them both warily, looked away, then looked back again.

Suddenly Izmailov asked, "Tell me, have you ever tried your hand at writing?"

Who, apart from a writer, would think to ask such a question?

"Now and again," replied Rasputin without the least surprise. "Even quite a few times."

And he beckoned to a young man sitting at the other end of the table.

"Dearie! Bring me the pages with my poems that you just tapped out on that little typing machine."

"Dearie" darted off and came back with the pages.

Rasputin handed them around. Everyone reached out. There were a lot of these typed pages—enough for all of us. We began to read.

It turned out to be a prose poem, in the style of the 'Song of Songs' and obscurely amorous. I can still remember the lines: "Fine and high are the mountains. But my love is higher and finer yet, because love is God."

But that seems to have been the only passage that made any sense. Everything else was just a jumble of words.

As I was reading, the author kept looking around restlessly, trying to see what impression his work was making.

"Very good," I said.

He brightened.

"Dearie! Give us a clean sheet, I'll write something for her myself."

"What's your name?" he asked.

I said.

He chewed for a long time on his pencil. Then, in a barely decipherable peasant scrawl, he wrote:

To Nadezhda
  God is love. Now love. God wil forgive yu.
                                            Grigory

The basic pattern of Rasputin's magic charms was clear enough: love, and God will forgive you.

But why should such an inoffensive maxim as this cause his ladies to collapse in fits of ecstasy? Why had that lady-in-waiting got into such a state?

This was no simple matter.

6

I studied the awkwardly scrawled letters and the signature below: "Grigory".

What power this signature held. I knew of a case where this scrawl of seven letters had rescued a man who had already been sentenced to forced labour and sent off to Siberia.

And it seemed likely that this same signature could just as easily get someone sent off to Siberia…

"You should hang on to that autograph," said Rozanov. "It's quite something."

It did in fact stay in my possession for a long time. In Paris, some six years ago, I found it in an old briefcase and gave it to J.W. Bienstock, the author of a book about Rasputin in French.

Rasputin really was only semi-literate; writing even a few words was hard work for him. This made me think of the forest warden in our home village—the man whose job had been to catch poachers and supervise the spring floating of timber. I remembered the little bills he used to write: "Tren to dacha and bak fife ru" (five roubles).

Rasputin was also strikingly like this man in physical appearance. Perhaps that's why his words and general presence failed to excite the least mystical awe in me. "God is love, you *shall* come" and so on. That "fife ru", which I couldn't get out of my head, was constantly in the way…

Suddenly our host came up, looking very concerned.

"The palace is on the line."

Rasputin left the room.

The palace evidently knew exactly where Rasputin was to be found. Probably, they always did.

Taking advantage of Rasputin's absence, Rozanov began lecturing me, advising me how best to steer the conversation on to all kinds of interesting topics. The main thing was to get him to talk about the Khlysts[8] and their rites. Was it all true? And if so, how was it all organized and was it possible, say, to attend?

"Get him to invite you, and then you can bring us along, too."

I agreed willingly. This truly would be interesting.

But Rasputin didn't come back. Our host said he had been summoned urgently to Tsarskoye Selo—even though it was past midnight—but that, as he was leaving, Rasputin had asked him to tell me he would definitely be coming back.

"Don't let her go," said Filippov, repeating Rasputin's words. "Have her wait for me. I'll be back."

Needless to say no one waited. Our group, at least, left as soon as we had finished eating.

7

Everyone I told about the evening showed a quite extraordinary degree of interest. They wanted to know the elder's every word, and they wanted me to describe every detail of his appearance. Most of all, they wanted to know if they could get themselves invited to Filippov's, too.

"What kind of impression did he make on you?"

"No very strong impression," I replied. "But I can't say I liked him."

People were advising me to make the most of this connection. One never knows what the future holds in store, and Rasputin was certainly a force to be reckoned with. He toppled ministers, and he shuffled courtiers as if they were a pack of cards. His displeasure was feared more than the wrath of the Tsar.

There was talk about clandestine German overtures being made via Rasputin to Alexandra Fyodorovna. With the help of prayer and hypnotic suggestion he was, apparently, directing our military strategy.

"Don't go on the offensive before such and such a date—or the Tsarevich will be taken ill."

Rasputin seemed to me to lack the steadiness needed to manage any kind of strategy. He was too twitchy, too easily distracted, too confused in every way. Most likely he accepted bribes and got involved in plots and deals without really thinking things through or weighing up the consequences. He himself was being carried away by the very force he was trying to control. I don't know what he was like at the beginning of his trajectory, but by the time I met him, he was already adrift. He had lost himself; it was as if he were being swept away by a whirlwind, by a tornado. As if in delirium, he kept repeating the words: "God... prayer... wine". He was confused; he had no idea what he was doing. He was in torment, writhing about, throwing himself into his dancing with a despairing howl—as if to retrieve some treasure left behind in a burning house. This satanic dancing of his was something I witnessed later...

I was told he used to gather his society ladies together in a bathhouse and—"to break their pride and teach them humility"—make them bathe his feet. I don't know whether this is true, but it's not impossible. At that time, in that atmosphere of hysteria, even the most idiotic flight of fancy seemed plausible.

Was he really a mesmerist? I once spoke to someone who had seriously studied hypnotism, mesmerism and mind control.

I told him about that strange gesture of Rasputin's, the way he would quickly reach out and touch someone and how a spasm would go through his shoulder when he felt his hypnotic command was meeting resistance.

"You really don't know?" he asked in surprise. "Mesmerists always make that kind of physical contact. It's how they transmit the current of their will. And when this current is blocked, then it rebounds upon the mesmerist. The more powerful a wave the mesmerist sends out, the more powerful the current that flows back. You say he was very persistent, which suggests he was using all his strength. That's why the return current struck him with such force; that's why he was writhing and moaning. It sounds as if he was suffering real pain as he struggled to control the backlash. Everything you describe is entirely typical."

8

Three or four days after this dinner, Izmailov rang me a second time.

"Filippov is begging us to have dinner with him again. Last time Rasputin had to leave almost straight away; he'd barely had time to look about him. This time Filippov assures us that it will all be a great deal more interesting."

Apparently Manuilov had dropped in on Izmailov. He'd been very insistent (almost like some kind of impresario!) and had shown Izmailov the final guest list: all respectable people who knew how to behave. There was no need to worry.

"Just once more," Izmailov said to me. "This time our conversation with him will be a lot more fruitful. Maybe we'll get him to say something really interesting. He truly *is* someone out of the ordinary. Let's go."

I agreed.

This time I arrived later. Everyone had been at the table for some time.

There were many more people than the first time. All of the previous guests were there—as were the musicians. Rasputin was sitting in the same place. Everyone was talking politely, as if this were just an ordinary dinner. No one was looking at Rasputin; it was as if his presence were of no consequence to them at all. And yet the truth was all too obvious: most of the guests did not know one another and, although they now seemed too timid to do anything at all, there was only one reason why they had come. They wanted to have a look at Rasputin, to find out about him, to talk to him.

Rasputin had removed his outer garment and was sitting in a taffeta shirt, worn outside his trousers. It was a glaring pink, and it had an embroidered collar, buttoned on one side.

His face was tense and tired; he looked black. His piercing eyes were deeply sunken. He'd all but turned his back on the lawyer's glamorously dressed wife, who was again sitting next to him. My own place, on his other side, was still free.

"Ah! There she is," he said with a sudden twitch. "Well, come and sit down. I've been waiting. Why did you run off last time? I came back—and where were you? Drink! What's the matter? I'm telling you—drink! God will forgive you."

Rozanov and Izmailov were also in the same places as before.

Rasputin leant over towards me.

"I've missed you. I've been pining after you."

"Nonsense. You're just saying that to be nice," I said loudly. "Why don't you tell me something interesting instead? Is it true you organize Khlyst rituals?"

"Khlyst rituals? Here? Here in the city?"

"Well, don't you?"

"Who's told you that?" he asked uneasily. "Who? Did he say he was there himself? Did he see for himself? Or just hear rumours?"

"I'm afraid I can't remember who it was."

"You can't *remember*? My clever girl, why don't you come along and see me? I'll tell you many things you don't know. You wouldn't have English blood, would you?"

"No, I'm completely Russian."

"There's something English about your little face. I have a princess in Moscow and she has an English face, too. Yes, I'm going to drop everything and go to Moscow."

"What about Vyrubova?" I asked, rather irrelevantly—for Rozanov's sake.

"Vyrubova? No, not Vyrubova. She has a round face, not an English one. Vyrubova is my little one. I'll tell you how it is: some of my flock are little ones and some are something else. I'm not going to lie to you, this is the truth."

Suddenly Izmailov found his courage. "And... the Tsaritsa?" he asked in a choked voice. "Alexandra Fyodorovna?"

The boldness of the question rather alarmed me. But, to my surprise, Rasputin replied very calmly, "The Tsaritsa? She's ailing. Her breast ails her. I lay my hand upon her and I pray. I pray well. And my prayer always makes her better. She's ailing. I must pray for her and her little ones." And then he muttered, "It's bad... bad..."

"What's bad?"

"No, it's nothing... We must pray. They are good little ones..."

I recall reading in the newspapers, at the beginning of the revolution, about the "filthy correspondence between the elder and the depraved princesses"—correspondence that it was "quite inconceivable to publish". Some time later, however, these letters *were* published. And they went something like this: "Dear Grisha, please pray that I'll be a good student." "Dear Grisha, I've been a good girl all week long and obeyed Papa and Mama..."

"We must pray," Rasputin went on muttering.

"Do you know Madame E——?" I asked.

"The one with the little pointed face? I think I've glimpsed her here and there. But it's you I want to come along and see me. You'll get to meet everyone and I'll tell you all about them."

"Why should I come along? It'll only make them all cross."

"Make who cross?"

"Your ladies. They don't know me; I'm a complete stranger to them. They're not going to be pleased to see me."

"They wouldn't dare!" He beat the table with his fist. "No, not in *my* house. In *my* house everyone is happy—God's grace descends on everyone. If I say 'bathe my feet', they'll do as I say and then drink the water! In my house everything is godly. Obedience, grace, humility and love."

"There, you see? They bathe your feet. No, you'll be better off without me."

"You shall come. I'll send for you."

"Has everyone really come when you've sent for them?"

"No one's refused yet."

9

Apparently quite forgotten, the lawyer's wife sitting on the other side of Rasputin was hungrily and tenaciously listening to our conversation.

From time to time, noticing me looking at her, she would give me an ingratiating smile. Her husband kept whispering to her and drinking to my health.

"You ought to invite the young lady to your right," I said to Rasputin. "She's lovely!"

Hearing my words, she looked up at me with frightened, grateful eyes. She even paled a little as she waited for his response. Rasputin glanced at her, quickly turned away and said loudly, "She's a stupid bitch!"

Everyone pretended they hadn't heard.

I turned to Rozanov.

"For the love of God," he said, "get him to talk about the Khlysts. Try again."

But I'd completely lost interest in talking to Rasputin. He seemed to be drunk. Our host kept coming up and pouring him wine, saying, "This is for you, Grisha. It's your favourite."

Rasputin kept drinking, jerking his head about, twitching and muttering something.

"I'm finding it very hard to talk to him," I said to Rozanov. "Why don't you and Izmailov try? Maybe we can all four of us have a conversation!"

"It won't work. It's a very intimate, mysterious subject. And he's shown he trusts you…"

"What's him over there whispering about?" interrupted Rasputin. "Him that writes for *New Age*?"

So much for our being incognito.

"What makes you think he's a writer?" I asked. "Someone must have misinformed you… Before you know it, they'll be saying I'm a writer, too."

"I think they said you're from *The Russian Word*," he replied calmly. "But it's all the same to me."

"Who told you that?"

"I'm afraid I can't remember," he said, pointedly repeating my own words when he'd asked who had told me about the Khlysts.

He had clearly remembered my evasiveness, and now he was paying me back in kind: "I'm afraid I can't remember!"

Who had given us away? Hadn't we been promised complete anonymity? It was all very strange.

After all, it wasn't as if we'd gone out of our way to meet the elder. We had been invited. We had been offered the opportunity to meet him and, what's more, we'd been told to keep quiet about who we were because "Grisha doesn't like journalists"—because he avoids talking to them and always does all he can to keep away from them.

Now it appeared that Rasputin knew very well who we were. And not only was he not avoiding us but he was even trying to draw us into a closer acquaintance.

Who was calling the shots? Had Manuilov orchestrated all this—for reasons we didn't know? Or did the elder have some cunning scheme of his own? Or had someone just blurted out our real names by mistake?

It was all very insalubrious. What was truly going on was anyone's guess.

And what did I know about all these dinner companions of ours? Which of them was from the secret police? Which would soon be sentenced to forced labour? Which might be a German agent? And which of them had lured us here? Which member of this upright company was hoping to use us for their own ends? Was Rasputin the weaver of this web—or the one being caught in it? Who was betraying whom?

"He knows who we are," I whispered to Rozanov.

Rozanov looked at me in astonishment. He and Izmailov began whispering together.

Just then the musicians struck up. The accordion began a dance tune, the guitar twanged, the tambourine jingled. Rasputin leapt to his feet—so abruptly that he knocked his chair over. He darted off as if someone were calling to him. Once he was some way from the table (it was a large room), he suddenly began to skip and dance. He thrust a knee forward, shook his beard about and circled round and round. His face looked tense and bewildered. His movements were frenzied; he was always ahead of the music, as if unable to stop...

Everyone leapt up. They stood around him to watch. "Dearie", the one who had gone to fetch the poems, turned pale. His eyes bulged. He squatted down on his haunches and began clapping his hands. "Whoop! Whoop! Whoop! Go! Go! Go!"

And no one was laughing. They watched as if in fear and—certainly—very, very seriously.

The spectacle was so weird, so wild, that it made you want to let out a howl and hurl yourself into the circle, to leap and whirl alongside him for as long as you had the strength.

The faces all around were looking ever paler, ever more intent. There was a charge in the air, as if everyone was expecting something... Any moment!

"How can anyone still doubt it?" said Rozanov from behind me. "He's a Khlyst!"

Rasputin was now leaping about like a goat. Mouth hanging open, skin drawn tight over his cheekbones, locks of hair whipping across the sunken sockets of his eyes, he was dreadful to behold. His pink shirt was billowing out behind him like a balloon.

"Whoop! Whoop! Whoop!" went "Dearie", continuing to clap.

All of a sudden Rasputin stopped. Just like that. And the music broke off, as if the musicians were quite used to this.

Rasputin collapsed into an armchair and looked all around. His piercing eyes now seemed bewildered, vacant.

"Dearie" hastily gave him a glass of wine. I went through into the drawing room and told Izmailov I wanted to leave.

"Sit down for a moment and get your breath back," Izmailov replied.

The air was stifling. It was making my heart pound and my hands tremble.

"No," said Izmailov. "It's not hot in here. It's just your nerves."

"Please, don't go," begged Rozanov. "Now you can get him to invite you to one of his rituals. There'll be no difficulty now!"

The guests had moved into the salon and were sitting around the edges of the room, as if in anticipation of some sort of performance. The beautiful woman came in, too, her husband holding her by the arm. She was walking with her head bowed; I thought she was weeping.

I stood up.

"Don't go," said Rozanov.

I shook my head and went out towards the hall. Out of the dining room came Rasputin. Blocking my path, he took my elbow.

"Wait a moment and let me tell you something. And mind you listen well. You see how many people there are all around us? A lot of people, right? A lot of people—and no one at all. Just me and you—and no one else. There isn't anyone else standing here, just me and you. And I'm saying to you: come to me! I'm pining for you to come. I'm pining so badly I could throw myself down on the ground before you!"

His shoulder went into spasms and he let out a moan.

And it was all so ludicrous, both the way we were standing in the middle of the room together and the painfully serious way he was speaking…

I had to do something to lighten the atmosphere.

Rozanov came up to us. Pretending he was just passing by, he pricked up his ears. I started to laugh. Pointing at him, I said to Rasputin, "But he won't let me."

"Don't you listen to that madman—you come along. And don't bring him with you, we can do without him. Rasputin may only be a peasant, but don't you turn up your nose at him. For them I love I build stone palaces. Haven't you heard?"

"No," I replied, "I haven't."

"You're lying, my clever girl, you *have* heard. I can build stone palaces. You'll see. I can do many things. But for the love of God, just come to me, the sooner the better. We'll pray together. Why wait? You see, everyone wants to kill me. As soon as I step outside, I look all around me: where are they, where are their ugly mugs? Yes, they want to kill me. Well so what! The fools don't understand who I am. A sorcerer? Maybe I am. They burn sorcerers, so let them burn me. But there's one thing they don't understand: if they kill me, it will be the end of Russia. Remember, my clever girl: if they kill Rasputin, it will be the end of Russia. They'll bury us together."

He stood there in the middle of the room, thin and black—a gnarled tree, withered and scorched.

"And it will be the end of Russia… the end of Russia…"

With his trembling hand crooked upwards, he looked like Chaliapin singing the role of the miller in Dvořák's *Rusalka*.

At this moment he appeared dreadful and completely mad.

"Ah? Are you going? Well if you're going, then go. But just you remember… Remember."

As we made our way back from Filippov's, Rozanov said that I really ought to go and visit Rasputin: if I refused an offer coveted by so many, he would almost certainly find it suspicious.

"We'll all go there together," he assured me, "and we'll leave together."

I replied that there was something in the atmosphere around Rasputin I found deeply revolting. The grovelling, the collective hysteria—and at the same time the machinations of something dark, something very dark and beyond our knowledge. One could get sucked into this filthy mire—and never be able to climb out of it. It was revolting and joyless, and the revulsion I felt entirely negated any interest I might have in these people's "weird mysteries".

The pitiful, distressed face of the young woman who was being thrust so shamelessly by her lawyer husband at a drunken peasant—it was the stuff of nightmares, I was seeing it in my dreams. But he must have had many such women—women about whom he shouted, banging his fist on the table, that "they wouldn't dare" and that they were "happy with everything".

"It's revolting," I went on. "Truly horrifying! I'm frightened! And wasn't it strange, later on, how insistent he was about my going to see him?"

"He's not accustomed to rejection."

"Well, my guess is that it's all a lot simpler. I think it's because of *The Russian Word*. He may make out that he doesn't attach any significance to my work there, but you know as well as I do how afraid he is of the press and how he tries to ingratiate himself with it. Maybe he's decided to lure me into becoming one of his myrrh-bearing women.[9] So that I'll write whatever he wants me to write, at his dictation. After all, he does all of his politicking through women. Just think what a trump card he would have in his hands. I think he's got it all figured out very well indeed. He's cunning."

10

Several days after this dinner I had a telephone call from a lady I knew. She reproached me for not coming to a party she had given the evening before and that I'd promised to attend.

I had completely forgotten about this party.

"Vyrubova was there," said the lady. "She was waiting for you. She very much wants to meet you, and I had promised her you would be there. I'm terribly, terribly upset you couldn't come."

"Aha!" I thought. "Messages from the 'other world'. What can she want of me?"

That she was a messenger from that "other world" I didn't doubt for a moment. Two more days went by.

An old friend dropped in on me. She was very flustered.

"S—— is going to have a big party. She's called round a couple of times in person, but you weren't at home. She came to see me earlier today and made me promise to take you with me."

I was rather surprised by S——'s persistence, as I didn't know her so very well. She wasn't hoping to get me to give some kind of a reading, was she? That was the last thing I wanted. I expressed my misgivings.

"Oh no," my friend assured me. "I promise you that she has no hidden designs. S—— is simply very fond of you and would like to see you. Anyway, it should be a very enjoyable evening. There won't be many guests, just friends, because they can't put on grand balls now, not while we're at war. That would be in poor taste. There will be no one there who shouldn't be there—no one superfluous. They're people who know how to give a good party."

11

We arrived after eleven.

There were a lot of people. Among the tail coats and evening dresses were a number of figures in identical black or light-blue domino masks. They were the only ones in fancy dress; it was clear they had come as a group.

My friend took me by the arm and led me to our hostess: "Well, here she is. See? I've brought her with me."

A Gypsy was singing in the large ballroom. Short and slight, she was wearing a high-necked dress of shining silk. Her head was thrown back and her dusky face an emblem of suffering as she sang the words:

> In parting she said:
> "Don't you forget me in foreign lands…"

"Just wait a moment," the hostess whispered to me. "She's almost finished."

And she went on standing beside me, evidently looking around for someone.

"Now we can go."

She took my hand and led me across the ballroom, still looking.

Then we entered a small, dimly lit sitting room. There was no one there. The hostess seated me on a sofa.

"I'll be back in a moment. Please don't go anywhere."

She did indeed come back in a moment, together with a figure in a black mask.

"This mysterious figure will keep you entertained," said S—— with a laugh. "Please wait for me here."

The black figure sat down beside me and looked silently at me through narrow eye-slits.

"You don't know me," it murmured at last, "but I desperately need to speak to you."

It was not a voice I had heard before, but something about its intonations was familiar. It was the same quivering, hysterical tone in which that lady-in-waiting had spoken of Rasputin.

I peered at the woman sitting beside me. No, this wasn't Madame E——. Madame E—— was petite. This lady was very tall. She spoke with a faint lisp, like all of our high society ladies who as children begin speaking English before Russian.

"I know everything," the unknown woman began edgily. "On Thursday you're going to a certain house."

"No," I replied in surprise. "I'm not going anywhere."

She grew terribly flustered. "Why don't you tell me the truth? Why? I know everything."

"Where is it you think I'm going?" I asked.

"There. His place."

"I don't understand a thing."

"Do you mean to test me? All right, I'll say it. On Thursday you're going to… to… Rasputin's."

"What makes you think that? No one has asked me."

The lady fell silent.

"You may not have received the invitation yet… but you soon will. It's already been decided."

"But why are you so upset about all this?" I asked. "Perhaps you could tell me your name?"

"I haven't put on this idiotic mask only to go and tell you my name. And as far as you're concerned, my name is of no importance. It doesn't matter. What matters is that on Thursday you're going to be there."

"I have no intention of going to Rasputin's," I replied calmly. "Of that I can assure you."

"Ah!"

She suddenly leant forward and, with hands tightly encased in black gloves, seized hold of my arm.

"No, you're joking! You will be going! Why wouldn't you?"

"Because it's of no interest to me."

"And you won't change your mind?"

"No."

Her shoulders began to tremble. I thought she was weeping.

"I thought you were someone sincere," she whispered.

I was at a loss.

"What is it you want from me? Does it upset you that I won't be going? I don't understand a thing."

She seized hold of my arm again.

"I implore you by everything you hold sacred—please refuse this invitation. We have to get him to cancel this evening. He mustn't leave Tsarskoye on Thursday. We mustn't let him—or something terrible will happen."

She muttered something, her shoulders quivering.

"I don't see what any of this has to do with me," I said. "But if it will make you feel any better, then please believe me: I give you my word of honour that I won't go. In three days' time I'm going to Moscow."

Again her shoulders began to tremble, and again I thought she was weeping.

"Thank you, my dear one, thank you…"

She quickly bent over and kissed my hand.

Then she jumped up and left.

"No, that can't have been Vyrubova," I thought, remembering how Vyrubova had wanted to see me at that party I hadn't gone to. "No, it wasn't her. Vyrubova is quite plump, and anyway, she limps. It wasn't her."

I found our hostess.

"Who was that masked lady you just brought to me?"

The hostess seemed rather put out.

"How would I know? She was wearing a mask."

While we were at dinner the masked figures seemed to disappear. Or perhaps they had all just taken off their fancy dress.

I spent a long time studying the faces I didn't know, looking for the lips that had kissed my hand...

Sitting at the far end of the table were three musicians: guitar, accordion and tambourine. The very same three musicians. Rasputin's musicians. Here was a link... a thread.

12

The next day Izmailov came over. He was terribly upset.

"Something awful has happened. Here. Read this." And he handed me a newspaper.

In it I read that Rasputin had begun frequenting a literary circle where, over a bottle of wine, he would tell entertaining stories of all kinds about extremely high-ranking figures.

"And that's not the worst of it," said Izmailov. "Filippov came over today and said he'd had an unexpected summons from the secret police, who wanted to know just which literary figures had been to his house and precisely what Rasputin had talked about. Filippov was threatened with exile from Petersburg. But the most astonishing and horrible thing of all is that, there on the interrogator's desk, he could clearly see the guest list, in Manuilov's own hand."

"You're not saying Manuilov works for the secret police, are you?"[10]

"There's no knowing whether it was him or another of Filippov's guests. In any case, we've got to be very careful. Even if they don't interrogate us, they'll be following us. No doubt about that. So if Rasputin writes to you or summons you by telephone, you'd better not respond. Although he doesn't know your address, and he's unlikely to have remembered your last name."

"So much for the holy man's mystical secrets! I feel sorry for Rozanov. What a dull, prosaic ending…"

13

"Madam, some joker's been telephoning. He's rung twice, wanting to speak to you," said my maid, laughing.

"What do you mean, 'some joker'?"

"Well, when I ask, 'Who's calling?', he says, 'Rasputin.' It's somebody playing the fool."

"Listen, Ksyusha, if this man carries on playing the fool, be sure to tell him I've gone away, and for a long time. Understand?"

14

I soon left Petersburg. I never saw Rasputin again.

Later, when I read in the papers that his corpse had been burnt, the man I saw in my mind's eye was that black, bent, terrible sorcerer:

"Burn me? Let them. But there's one thing they don't know: if they kill Rasputin, it will be the end of Russia.

"Remember me then! Remember me!"

I did.

1932

PART III

1920s and 1930s in Paris

QUE FAIRE?

I HEARD TELL of a Russian general, a refugee, who went out onto the Place de la Concorde and looked around. He looked up at the sky and round at the square, the houses, the shops and the colourful, chattering crowd. He scratched the bridge of his nose and said, with feeling:

"All this, ladies and gentlemen, is well and good. Even very well and good, all this. But, well… *que faire*? What *is* to be done? Fair's fair, but *que* bloody *faire* with it all?"

The general was by way of an appetizer. The meat of the story is still to come…

We—*les russes*, as they call us—live the strangest of lives here, nothing like other people's. We stick together, for example, not like planets, by mutual attraction, but by a force quite contrary to the laws of physics—mutual repulsion. Every *lesrusse* hates all the others—hates them just as fervently as the others hate him.

This general antipathy has given rise to several neologisms. Hence, for example, a new grammatical particle, "that-crook", placed before the name of every *lesrusse*

139

anyone mentions: "that-crook Akimenko", "that-crook Petrov", "that-crook Savelyev".

This particle lost its original meaning long ago and now equates to something between the French *le*, indicating the gender of the person named, and the Spanish honorific *don*: "don Diego", "don José".

You'll hear conversations like this:

"Some of us got together at that-crook Velsky's yesterday for a game of bridge. There was that-crook Ivanov, that-crook Gusin, that-crook Popov. Nice crowd."

A chat between business people might go like this:

"I'd advise you to get that-crook Parchenko in on this deal. Very useful chap."

"But isn't he, er... Can he be trusted?"

"Good Lord, yes! That-crook Parchenko? Trust him with my life! He's pure as the driven snow."

"Wouldn't we be better off with that-crook Kusachenko?"

"Oh no. He's a great deal crookeder."

New arrivals are startled to begin with, even alarmed, by this prefix.

"Why a crook? Who said so? Have they got proof? What did he do? Where?"

And they're even more alarmed by the nonchalant reply.

"What... Where... Who knows? They call him a crook and that's fine by me."

"But what if he isn't?"

"Get away with you! Why ever wouldn't he be?"

And that's right—why wouldn't he?

The *lesrusses* sticking together here by mutual repulsion fall into two distinct categories: those selling Russia and those saving Russia.

The sellers lead a merry life. They frequent theatres, dance the foxtrot, have Russian cooks and invite the saviours of Russia over to share their Russian borscht. In the midst of all this frivolity, they don't neglect their main occupation, but if you should ask how much they're selling Russia for these days, and with what conditions attached, you're unlikely to get a straight answer.

The saviours are a very different kettle of fish. They're hard at it day and night—constantly on the move, always ensnared in political intrigues and forever denouncing each other.

They rub along quite happily with the sellers and get money from them to save Russia. But they loathe one another, with a white-hot passion.

"Did you hear about that-crook Ovechkin? What a snake he's turned out to be! He's selling Tambov."

"Well, I never! Who to?"

"What do you mean 'who to'? To the Chileans."

"What?"

"To the Chileans—that's what!"

"What do the Chileans want with Tambov?"

"What a question! They want a Russian base!"

"But Tambov doesn't belong to Ovechkin. How can he be selling it?"

"I told you, he's a snake. He and that-crook Gavkin

played a really dirty trick on us: can you imagine, they took—they lured—our young lady over to them with her typewriter, at the very moment when we should have been supporting the government of Ust-Sysolsk."

"Does Ust-Sysolsk have a government?"

"Did have. But not for long, it seems. There was a lieutenant colonel—can't remember his name—who proclaimed himself its government. He managed to hold out for a day and a half. If we'd come to his aid in time we could have saved the situation. But how can you get anywhere without a typewriter? That's how we let the whole of Russia slip through our fingers. And all because of him—because of that-crook Ovechkin. And what about that-crook Korobkin—have you heard? That's pretty rich, too. He accredited himself as ambassador to Japan."

"Who appointed him?"

"No one knows. He's making out it was some kind of government of Tiraspol Junction station. That existed for all of fifteen or twenty minutes… through some misunderstanding. Then it got embarrassed and dissolved itself. But that Korobkin, he didn't waste a moment—in those fifteen minutes he managed to wangle the whole thing."

"But does anyone recognize him?"

"Oh, he doesn't mind about that. All he wanted out of it was a visa—that's why he accredited himself. It's a disgrace!"

"But did you hear the latest news? They say Bakhmach has been taken!"

"Who by?"

"No one knows."

"Who from?"

"We don't know that either. It's disgraceful!"

"Where on earth did you find all this out?"

"On the radio. We get the Kiev Telegraft and listen to Bullshevik Broadcasting from Moscow – and now we're got our own pan-European station, Eurogarble News!"

"What does Paris make of it?"

"Paris? We all know Paris won't lift a finger. Like dogs in their cosy French manger! Makes no difference to them."

"Now tell me—does *anyone* understand any of this?"

"Not really. You must know what Tyutchev said all those years ago: 'You cannot understand Russia with your mind.'[1] And since the human body has no other organ of understanding, all we can do is throw up our hands in despair. They say one of our public figures was starting to understand with his stomach. So they sent him packing."

"Hmm…"

"Hmm…"

So anyway… this general looked around and said, with feeling:

"All this, ladies and gentlemen, is well and good. Even very well and good. But *que faire*? Fair's fair, but *que* bloody *faire*?"

Que indeed.

1923

SUBTLY WORDED

L ETTERS BEGAN TO APPEAR from the Soviet Union.
More and more often.

Strange letters.

The kind of letter that lends strength and credence to the
rumour that everyone in the Soviet Union has gone crazy.

Journalists and public figures trying to draw conclusions
from these letters about the economic and political situation
in Russia—or even just everyday life there—got caught in
such dense thickets of nonsense as to arouse scepticism even
among those whose faith in the infinite nature of Russia's
potential was usually unshakeable.

Several such letters have come my way.

One of them, addressed to a lawyer by his doctor brother,
began with the words: *Dear Daughter!*

"Ivan Andreyevich, how come you've ended up as the
daughter of your own brother?"

"I've no idea. I'm scared to think."

The letter contained the following news: *Everything's
splendid here. Anyuta has died from a strong appetite…*

"He must mean appendicitis," I guessed.

And the whole Vankov family have also died from appetite.

"Hmm, something's not right."

Pyotr Ivanovich has been leading a secluded life for four months now. Koromyslov began leading a secluded life eleven months ago. His fate is unknown.

Misha Petrov led a secluded life for only two days, then there was a careless incident with a firearm he happened to be standing in front of. Everyone feels awfully delighted.

"Dear God! What is all this? They're not people but beasts. A man perishes in an unfortunate accident and they feel delighted!"

We went round to your apartment. There's a lot of air there now…

"What on earth! What's that meant to mean?"

"I'm scared to think. I don't want to know."

The letter finished with the words:

I write little because I want to continue to mix with society and not to lead a secluded life.

This letter weighed on me for a long time.

"What a tragedy," I said to people I knew. "The brother of our Ivan Andreyevich has lost his mind. He calls Ivan Andreyevich his daughter, and he writes such nonsense I'd be embarrassed to repeat it."

I felt very sorry for the poor fellow. He was a good man.

Then I heard there was some Frenchman offering to take a letter right into Petrograd.

Ivan Andreyevich was delighted. I decided to add a few words too. Maybe the man wasn't yet quite off his rocker, maybe he'd understand a few simple words.

Ivan Andreyevich and I agreed to compose the letter

together. So it would be clear and simple and not too much for a mind whose powers were failing.

We wrote:

Dear Volodya!

We received your letter. What a pity everything is so terrible for you. Is it really true that people have now begun eating human flesh? How horrific! What's got into you? They say your death rate is terribly high. All this worries us like crazy. Life's going well for me. If only you were here, too, everything would be quite wonderful. I've married a Frenchwoman and I'm awfully happy.

Your brother Ivan.

At the end of the letter I added:

My warmest greetings to all of you,

Teffi

The letter was ready when a mutual friend dropped in, a worldly-wise and experienced barrister.

Learning what we had been doing, he looked very thoughtful and said in a serious tone, "But did you write the letter correctly?"

"Er, what do you mean, 'correctly'?"

"I'm asking if you can guarantee that your correspondent will not be arrested and shot because of this letter of yours."

"Heavens! What do you mean? It just says the simplest things, nothing dangerous."

"May I have a quick look?"

"Please do. There's nothing secret."

He took the letter. Read it. Sighed.

"Just as I thought. A firing squad within twenty-four hours. That's what happens."

"For the love of God! What's wrong with the letter?"

"Everything. Every sentence. First, you should have written as a woman. Otherwise, your brother will be arrested as the brother of a man who has evaded military conscription. Second, you shouldn't mention having received a letter, since correspondence is forbidden. And then you shouldn't let on that you understand how awful things are there."

"But then what should I do? What should I write?"

"Allow me. I'll reword your letter in the appropriate style. Don't worry—they'll understand."

"All right then. Reword it."

The barrister did a little writing, a little crossing out, then read out the following:

Dear Volodya!

I didn't receive your letter. How good that everything is going so well for you. Is it really true that now people have stopped eating human flesh? How truly delightful! What's got into you? They say your birth rate is terribly high. All this calms us like crazy. Life's going badly for me. If only you were here, too, everything would be quite terrible. I've married a Frenchman and I'm awfully unhappy.

Your sister Ivan.

The postscript:

> *To hell with the lot of you.*
> *Teffi.*

"There," said the barrister, grimly admiring his composition and adding commas in appropriate places. "Now the letter can be sent with no risk at all. You're safe and sound, and the recipient will remain alive. And the letter will reach him. Everything in order and subtly worded."

"I'm just worried about the postscript," I remarked timidly. "It does somehow seem a bit rude."

"That's as it should be. We don't want people getting themselves shot because of you and your endearments."

"All this is quite brilliant," Ivan Andreyevich said with a sigh. "The letter and everything. But then what are people there going to think of us? After all, the letter is, if you don't mind my saying so, idiotic."

"It's not idiotic, it's subtle. And even if they do think we've become idiots, who cares? At least they'll still be alive. Not everyone today can boast of having living relatives."

"But what if it frightens them?"

"Well, if you're scared of wolves, don't go into the forest. It's no good being frightened if you want to receive letters."

The letter was sent.

Lord, have mercy on us. Lord, save and preserve us.

1920

MARQUITA

THERE WAS a suffocating smell of chocolate, tobacco and warm silk.

Flushed ladies were powdering their noses, haughtily and languidly surveying the clientele, as if to say, "We're certainly a cut above you, but we won't make a thing of it."

And then, suddenly, forgetting their haughty languor, they were bending down over their plates and hurriedly, sincerely and greedily munching their pastries.

The waitresses, all of them daughters of provincial governors (did we ever imagine our governors could end up with so many daughters?), pulled in their stomachs as they squeezed between the tables, abstractedly repeating, "One chocolates, two pastry and one milk…"

The café was Russian, which is why it offered music and "entertainments".

First came a genial, lanky fellow with blue eyes—one of the seminarians who had been sent into exile. Sticking out his Adam's apple, he danced an Apache dance together with a skinny little woman whose bow legs were like sticks of macaroni. He hurled her around with fierce abandon, but the look on his face was good-natured and rather abashed.

"What else can I do?" his face was saying. "We've all got to eat."

Next was the "Gypsy singer Raisa Tsvetkova"—that is, Raichka Blum.[1] She curled back her upper lip, like a yawning horse, and then, in a nasal voice, burst out with:

> Fanweell, fanweell, my deear frieend!
> Fanweell, fanweell—my geepsy femeelee!…

But she couldn't help it. Raichka thought this was how Gypsies sang.

Sashenka was next.

As always, she had stage fright. She crossed herself inconspicuously and, looking around the café, wagged a finger at her little Kotka, so he would sit still.

Kotka was very small, but with a large head. His round nose was only just above the table top, almost touching the pastry on his plate. He was sitting very still.

Sashenka put her hands on her hips, proudly stuck out her own nose—which was every bit as round as Kotka's—raised her eyebrows Spanish-style and began to sing 'Marquita'.

She had a pure voice, and she enunciated the words simply and with conviction. The clientele loved it.

Sashenka turned pink. Returning to her seat, she kissed Kotka with still trembling lips. "You've been a good boy, you sat nice and still—now you can have your pastry!"

Raichka was sitting at the same table. She whispered, "Get him out of the way. The owner's looking at you. He's by the door. There's a Tatar with him. There, with the black nose. He's rich. Smile, for the love of God! Smile when someone's looking at you! Heavens—men look at her, and she hasn't even got the sense to smile!"

As they were leaving, the cashier looked pointedly at Sashenka and handed Kotka a box of sweets.

"I was asked to give this to the young gentleman."

The cashier, too, was the daughter of a provincial governor.

"Who by?"

"How should I know?"

Raichka took Sashenka's arm and whispered, "These, of course, are for you. And I really must give you some advice: don't drag that brat around with you. Believe me—I know everything. I can assure you—it really does put men off. A little child, some sweets—and there's the end of it! A woman must be a mysterious flower (honest to God!) and not give anything away about her domestic arrangements. Men all have domestic arrangements of their own—and that's what they want to get away from. Or do you want to go on singing *romances russes* in this teashop until you're an old woman? Until either you or the teashop come to the end of your days?"

Sashenka listened with fear and respect.

"But what do you want me to do with Kotka?"

"Oh, get an aunty of yours to sit with him!"

"What aunty? I haven't got any aunties."

"I can't believe the way Russian families always manage not to have any aunties!"

Sashenka at once felt very guilty.

"And you must learn to be a bit more fun! Last week Schnutrel came to listen to you twice. Yes, and he applauded, and he came and sat down at your table. And what did you do? Probably you told him your husband had abandoned you!"

"I did nothing of the kind," Sashenka insisted, blushing deeply and guiltily.

"As if your husband is of any interest to him! No, a woman must be like Carmen. Cruel and fiery. Now, when I was a young girl back in Nikolayev…"

And Raichka launched into her stories about the wonders of Nikolayev, that luxurious Babylon of passions, where she herself, though she had barely started at secondary school, managed at once to be Carmen, Cleopatra, Madonna and milliner.

The following day the black-nosed Tatar said to the owner of the café, "Please introduce mee, Greegory, to young lady. She take my heart. She keess her leettle boy—she have soul. I wild and shy man—she now like my fameely, like my own tribe. Introduce mee."

The Tatar's small, bright eyes blinked, and his nose swelled with tender emotion.

"Yes, all right. But what are you getting so worked up about? I'll introduce you. She really does seem very nice— though one never can tell."

The owner took the Tatar over to Sashenka. "This is my friend, Asayev. He wishes to be introduced to you, Alexandra Petrovna."[2]

Asayev shifted his weight from one foot to the other and gave an embarrassed smile. Sashenka stood there, looking red and frightened.

"We could have supper…" Asayev said all of a sudden.

"We, we don't do suppers here. Only tea, *faif-of-clok tea* until half past six."

"No, I want you go have supper with me some place. Shall we-e?"

Sashenka took fright even more. "*Merci*… Another time… I'm in a hurry… My little boy… at home."

"Your leettle boy. Then I come tomorrow."

He bowed crookedly, quickly and mechanically, as if this were some formal occasion, and went off on his way.

Raichka grabbed Sashenka by the arm.

"I really can't bear it. That was plain lunacy. An extremely rich man falls in love with her—and what does she do? Thrusts her little brat at him. Look, tomorrow I shall give you my black hat and you must buy yourself some new shoes. Yes, you really must—it's important."

"I don't want to be a kept woman," said Sashenka, and let out a sob.

"You what?" said Raichka in astonishment. "Who's making you do anything? And where's the harm in having a rich man pining for you? Where's the harm in having him send you flowers? Of course, if all you do is sigh and dandle children in front of him, then he won't hang about for long. He's an Oriental—and they like their women fiery. Believe me—I know everything."

"He seems… very sweet," said Sashenka, smiling.

"Play your cards right—and he'll marry you. So, come round this evening for the hat. And what about perfume? Have you got some?"

Sashenka slept badly that night. She kept thinking about the Tatar, moved by his ugliness.

"Poor man. He needs affection and love, but that's not allowed. I have to be proud and burning and altogether a real Carmen. Tomorrow I have to buy patent-leather shoes. His nose is all pitted and he keeps puffing and snorting. It's a shame. He's lonely, I know it. He's got no one to look after him."

She thought about her husband—who was handsome and no good.

"What does he care about Kotka? All he does is go dancing in nightclubs. And someone just saw him with a sallow Englishwoman—and in a car of his own."

She had a little cry.

She bought the shoes first thing, which got the day off to a Carmenesque start.

"Tra-la-la-la!"

And—better still—her neighbour had developed another gumboil. This meant she'd be staying at home for the next three or four days. The neighbour promised to keep an eye on Kotka.

In Raichka's hat, and with a rose pinned at her waist, Sashenka felt she was a real demonic woman.

"So you think I'm a simpleton, do you?" she said to

Raichka. "Ha! You don't know me yet. I can wrap any man round my little finger. And you don't really think this Armenian is of any importance to me, do you? I could have dozens like him if I felt like it."

Raichka looked at her sceptically and suggested she put on more lipstick.

The Tatar arrived in the evening and went straight over to Sashenka.

"Let's go. For supper."

And while she was putting her coat on, he hung about just beside her, almost touching her with his nose.

His own private car was waiting outside. This was beyond Sashenka's wildest imaginings. She almost lost her nerve, but her patent-leather shoes ran up to the car and jumped into it of their own accord—as if this were what they'd been made for.

In the car, the Tatar took her by the hand and said, "You be like my fameely, like my own tribe. I want tell you something. Veree soon."

They went into an expensive Russian restaurant. The Tatar abstractedly ordered some shashlik. He kept looking at Sashenka and smiling.

Thinking it would help with her demonism, Sashenka downed a glass of port. The Tatar began to sway about and the lamp careered to one side.

She seemed to have overdone it.

"I wild and shy," said the Tatar, looking into her eyes. "I sad and lonelee. I all alone. You too onlee one?"

Sashenka wanted to say something about her husband but remembered Raichka.

"Onlee one," she repeated robotically.

"One and one make two!" said the Tatar, suddenly laughing and taking her by the hand.

Sashenka failed to understand, but she didn't let on. Instead, she tossed her head back and laughed provocatively.

The Tatar let go of her hand in surprise.

"Carmen," thought Sashenka. "I've got to be a real Carmen."

"Are you capable of madness?" she asked, languidly narrowing her eyes.

"Don't know. Never opportunitee. I from small town."

Not knowing what to say next, Sashenka unpinned her rose, and, twirling it about next to her cheek, began singing, "Marquita! Marquita, my beauty!" The Tatar watched sadly.

"You be bored, you must sing? Is hard for you?"

"Ha-ha! I adore singing, dancing, wine, revelry. Ha! You don't know me yet!"

Rose-tinted lamps, a soft sofa, flowers on the tables, the languid wails of a jazz band, wine in a silver bucket. Sashenka felt she was a beautiful señorita, with huge black eyes and imperious eyebrows. Yes, she was the beautiful Marquita.

"Your son be veree good leettle boy," the Tatar said softly.

Sashenka knitted her imperious brows. "Oh, please! We're not going to talk about children, nappies and semolina, are we? To the wondrous strains of this tango and while wine sparkles in our glasses, we must speak of beauty, of life's poetry, not of its prose… I love beauty, madness, all that dazzles. I have the soul of Carmen. I am Marquita… My past seems so far from me now that I can't even see that child as my own…"

She threw her head back bacchante-style and pressed her wine glass to her lips. But then her soul quietly started to weep. "I've disowned him! I've disowned my little Kotka! My poor, skinny, blue-eyed little Kotka…"

The Tatar silently downed two glasses of wine—and down drooped his black nose.

Sashenka wasn't sure what to do next. She too fell silent.

The Tatar asked for the bill and got up.

On the way back they sat in the car in silence. Sashenka couldn't think how to start up another dazzling conversation. The Tatar was still letting his nose droop, as if he were dozing.

"He's had too much to drink," she decided. "And he was over-excited. There's something rather sweet about him. I think I'm going to end up really loving him."

As they were saying goodbye, she squeezed his hand with feeling.

"Until tomorrow, yes?"

She wanted to add something Carmenesque, but she couldn't think what.

At home, she was greeted by the fellow tenant with the gumboil. "All your son does is whine and throw tantrums.

There's nothing I can do with him. This is the last time you'll catch *me* looking after him!"

And there was her little Kotka—shivering on a huge sofa bed in a half-dark room, under a light bulb shaded by newspaper. Seeing his mother, he shook even more and wailed, "Where've you been, thtupid?"

Sashenka took the angry, whining little boy in her arms and slapped him—but before he could start bawling, she started to cry herself. She hugged her little Kotka closer.

"Never mind… be patient, my darling little chap. Just bear up a little longer. It'll be our turn soon. Someone's going to love us, someone's going to be looking after us both. It won't be long now."

The next morning, the owner of the café happened to run into Asayev. The Tatar was trudging along despondently, his cheeks blue and unshaven, one eye a little swollen.

"Why so down in the dumps? Will we be seeing you this evening?"

The Tatar looked away blankly.

"No. All ended."

"What do you mean? You're not saying Sashenka's given you the push, are you?"

The Tatar shrugged his shoulders.

"She… you not know… She be demon. I make meestake. No. I not come this evening. All ended!"

1924

MY FIRST TOLSTOY

I REMEMBER... I'm nine years old.

I'm reading *Childhood and Boyhood* by Tolstoy. Over and over again.

Everything in this book is dear to me.

Volodya, Nikolenka and Lyubochka are all living with me; they're all just like me and my brothers and sisters. And their home in Moscow with their grandmother is our Moscow home; when I read about their drawing room, morning room or classroom, I don't have to imagine anything—these are all our own rooms.

I know Natalya Savishna, too. She's our old Avdotya Matveyevna, Grandmother's former serf. She too has a trunk with pictures glued to the top. Only she's not as good-natured as Natalya Savishna. She likes to grumble. "Nor was there anything in nature he ever wished to praise." So my older brother used to sum her up, quoting from Pushkin's 'The Demon'.

Nevertheless, the resemblance is so pronounced that every time I read about Natalya Savishna, I picture Avdotya Matveyevna.

Every one of these people is near and dear to me.

159

Even the grandmother—peering with stern, questioning eyes from under the ruching of her cap, a bottle of eau de Cologne on the little table beside her chair—even the grandmother is near and dear to me.

The only alien element is the tutor, Saint-Jérôme, whom Nikolenka and I both hate. Oh, how I hate him! I hate him even more and longer than Nikolenka himself, it seems, because Nikolenka eventually buries the hatchet, but I go on hating him for the rest of my life.

Childhood and Boyhood became part of my own childhood and girlhood, merging with it seamlessly, as though I wasn't just reading but truly living it.

But what pierced my heart in its first flowering, what pierced it like a red arrow was another work by Tolstoy— *War and Peace.*

I remember...

I'm thirteen years old.

Every evening, at the expense of my homework, I'm reading one and the same book over and over again—*War and Peace.*

I'm in love with Prince Andrei Bolkonsky. I hate Natasha, first because I'm jealous, second because she betrayed him.

"You know what?" I tell my sister. "I think Tolstoy got it wrong when he was writing about her. How could anyone possibly like her? How could they? Her braid was 'thin and short', her lips were puffy. No, I don't think anyone could have liked her. And if Prince Andrei was going to marry her, it was because he felt sorry for her."

It also bothered me that Prince Andrei always shrieked when he was angry. I thought Tolstoy had got it wrong here, too. I felt certain the Prince didn't shriek.

And so every evening I was reading *War and Peace*.

The pages leading up to the death of Prince Andrei were torture to me.

I think I always nursed a little hope of some miracle. I must have done, because each time he lay dying I felt overcome by the same despair.

Lying in bed at night, I would try to save him. I would make him throw himself to the ground along with everyone else when the grenade was about to explode. Why couldn't just one soldier think to push him out of harm's way? That's what I'd have done. I'd have pushed him out of the way all right.

Then I would have sent him the very best doctors and surgeons of the time.

Every week I would read that he was dying, and I would hope and pray for a miracle. I would hope and pray that maybe this time he wouldn't die.

But he did. He really did! He did die!

A living person dies once, but Prince Andrei was dying forever, forever.

My heart ached. I couldn't do my homework. And in the morning... Well, you know what it's like in the morning when you haven't done your homework!

Finally, I hit upon an idea. I decided to go and see Tolstoy and ask him to save Prince Andrei. I would even allow him to marry the Prince to Natasha. Yes, I was even prepared to agree to that—anything to save him from dying!

I asked my governess whether a writer could change something in a work he had already published. She said she thought he probably could—sometimes in later editions, writers made amendments.

I conferred with my sister. She said that when you called on a writer you had to bring a small photograph of him and ask him to autograph it, or else he wouldn't even talk to you. Then she said that writers didn't talk to juveniles anyway.

It was very intimidating.

Gradually I worked out where Tolstoy lived. People were telling me different things—one person said he lived in Khamovniki, another said he'd left Moscow, and someone else said he would be leaving any day now.

I bought the photograph and started to think about what to say. I was afraid I might just start crying. I didn't let anyone in the house know about my plans—they would have laughed at me.

Finally, I took the plunge. Some relatives had come for a visit and the household was a flurry of activity—it seemed a good moment. I asked my elderly nanny to walk me "to a friend's house to do some homework" and we set off.

Tolstoy was at home. The few minutes I spent waiting in his foyer were too short to orchestrate a getaway. And with my nanny there it would have been awkward.

I remember a stout lady humming as she walked by. I certainly wasn't expecting that. She walked by entirely naturally. She wasn't afraid, and she was even humming. I had thought everyone in Tolstoy's house would walk on tiptoe and speak in whispers.

Finally *he* appeared. He was shorter than I'd expected. He looked at Nanny, then at me. I held out the photograph and, too scared to be able to pronounce my "R"s, I mumbled, "Would you pwease sign your photogwaph?"

He took it out of my hand and went into the next room.

At this point I understood that I couldn't possibly ask him for anything and that I'd never dare say why I'd come. With my "pwease" and "photogwaph" I had brought shame on myself. Never, in his eyes, would I be able to redeem myself. Only by the grace of God would I get out of here in one piece.

He came back and gave me the photograph. I curtsied.

"What can I do for you, madam?" he asked Nanny.

"Nothing, sir, I'm here with the young lady, that's all."

Later on, lying in bed, I remembered my "pwease" and "photogwaph" and cried into my pillow.

At school I had a rival named Yulenka Arsheva. She, too, was in love with Prince Andrei, but so passionately that the whole class knew about it. She, too, was angry with Natasha Rostova and she, too, could not believe that the Prince shrieked.

I was taking great care to hide my own feelings. Whenever Yulenka grew agitated, I tried to keep my distance and not listen to her so that I wouldn't betray myself.

And then, one day, during literature class, our teacher was analysing various literary characters. When he came to Prince Bolkonsky, the class turned as one to Yulenka. There she sat, red faced, a strained smile on her lips and her ears so suffused with blood that they even looked swollen.

Their names were now linked. Their romance evoked mockery, curiosity, censure, intense personal involvement— the whole gamut of attitudes with which society always responds to any romance.

I alone did not smile—I alone, with my secret, "illicit" feeling, did not acknowledge Yulenka or even dare look at her.

In the evening I sat down to read about his death. But now I read without hope. I was no longer praying for a miracle.

I read with feelings of grief and suffering, but without protest. I lowered my head in submission, kissed the book and closed it.

There once was a life. It was lived out and it finished.

1920

HEART OF A VALKYRIE

SOMETHING WAS GOING ON in the apartment block at No. 43. Monsieur Vitrou had died.

Many of those who heard the sad news could not immediately understand who was being spoken of. While he was alive, Monsieur Vitrou had never actually been called "Monsieur Vitrou".

He had been called "the concierge's husband", or sometimes "that sot" or "that good-for-nothing"—which was how they all saw him. He was always spoken of with some degree of dissatisfaction.

Monsieur had never performed a single real deed—only misdeeds. Not real crimes, of course, but, literally, misdeeds.

He would forget to stoke the boiler for the central heating, or, on a warm day, he would so overheat the building that you could scarcely breathe. He would forget to take round the morning post, or else he would muddle up the letters and newspapers and then go back round the apartments pestering everyone to hand over letters already opened "by mistake".

After all these misunderstandings, he'd take refuge in the bistro for days on end.

"Puisqu'on est toujours mécontent!"[1]

His appearance did not inspire respect. He was square and red, and he always looked embarrassed. This was because when he ran into people it was always either on his way to the bistro or on his way back home again. Whichever way he was headed, there was scant cause for celebration.

Everyone felt sorry for the concierge. She was a fine woman, reservedly affable and with elegantly greying hair.

"She has to support him. If only he'd pop his clogs, the old sot."

She did not complain, nor did she quarrel with him, but her contempt was silent and fastidious to the point of disgust. She tolerated him like a mangy dog that you can't quite bring yourself to put down.

And then he grew ill. Almost overnight he went from square and red to white and skinny.

He would sit at the door, no longer embarrassed but reproachful.

Then he took to his bed.

"Now all he does is lie about in bed!" people said at No. 43.

"He's only getting what he deserves," they said at No. 45, where the bistro was situated.

And then he died.

He died at dawn. The first to learn of his death were the *femmes de ménage*,[2] who delivered the news to every floor along with the milk and brioches.

Groups began to gather at the baker's, the butcher's and the Italian's little shop, the women huddling in knitted shawls and swinging their string bags of provisions.

"He's died, the husband of the concierge at No. 43. Monsieur Vitrou."

They were like a gaggle of geese as they hissed and whispered their expressions of surprise and sympathy.

There was something frightening about the very unfamiliarity of the sentence "Monsieur Vitrou is dead."

The words "Monsieur Vitrou" instead of "the concierge's old sot" invited people to recognize this man as a human being, endowed, like everyone else, with a name of his own and not just an abusive enumeration of misdeeds. This person, evidently, had achieved something consequential and even lofty: he had died.

To think he'd been capable of such a deed!

The residents of No. 43 all became rather quiet. They closed the front door gently and darted quickly towards the stairs, casting sidelong glances at the concierge's window.

The actress on the second floor performed in farces but was tragic by nature. She was constantly tormented by the thought that some role or other was passing her by. Now, too, on the death of Monsieur Vitrou, she felt forgotten in the wings. She would have been surprised if someone had explained to her that her despondency sprang from jealousy of the concierge's husband, that she didn't like being upstaged in the minds of her fellow tenants at No. 43. But in the evening she came up with a solution that soothed her nerves. A friend had brought her a basket of orchids; she ordered him to go down at once and place the flowers on the coffin of poor Monsieur Vitrou.

And while her aggrieved friend pursed his lips and carried his sumptuous gift slowly down the stairs, and as the ladies going the other way stood reverentially to one side, the actress leant over the balustrade and rapidly stamped her heels in sheer delight. In the concierge's room, they would go "ooh" and "ah" in amazement. Yes, indeed, in this production she had ended up with a splendid role!

The sickly sweet smell of chlorine and formaldehyde rose up the stairs, slipped under doors and into people's thoughts and dreams.

The elderly gentleman from the third floor suffered an asthma attack and made his daughter play cards with him until morning.

The actress from the second floor would not allow her friend to leave. She had a feeling that she was going to die soon, very soon. Smiling meekly, she closed her eyes.

The two old women from the ground floor wandered from room to room, startling one another, until late into the night.

The children on the first floor cried and wouldn't let anyone put the light out.

In the morning the concierge's son went round delivering invitations to the funeral. The invitation was an enormous sheet with a black border. There it was—on the pillow of the old man with asthma, on the actress's lace-covered table, on the two elderly women's chest of drawers, on the tablecloth on the first floor. Eyelashes fluttered over it; eyes came to rest upon it.

For the first time, the concierge, Madame Vitrou, saw her husband's name in print and in the place of honour. For the first time, he had performed a socially acceptable, bourgeois deed that inspired everyone's interest and even reverence. They were talking about him, asking about him, thinking about him on all five floors, and in the building next door, and across the street, and at the bakery, and on the corner.

He was Monsieur Vitrou. To be his wife was now an honour. For the first time, it was she who belonged to him, and not the other way around. She was his widow, rather than him being "the concierge's husband". And the priest, with whom she had discussed the funeral service, consoled her by saying, "Don't cry. Think instead that you will soon be meeting him again." It was as though even the priest recognized the contribution of Monsieur Vitrou, as if his status were somehow greater than hers.

Those profane thoughts that had plagued her when she realized her husband was dying—she now banished them from her mind. Thoughts that he was dying too late, when she had already grown old. Thoughts that, had this happened fifteen years earlier, when the widowed plumber had taken such an interest in the building, coming to check the taps as often as twice a day—then it would have been another matter altogether. That plumber now had his own shop in Rouen…

But after Vitrou's death, now that life had taken such a solemn turn, she forgot all about the plumber.

The smell of chlorine and formaldehyde intensified and spread ever further, reverberating like a deep chord on the organ.

The terrifying words "Monsieur Vitrou has died" were alive and, before them, the whole of everyday life was dying. These words had a sound, a six-syllable descending melody. They had a colour—a broad black band around a white rectangle. And there was a smell—a terrible, heavy, sweet scent. The tenants of No. 43 did not want to eat; they were unable to sleep, to read, to converse. They were dying from the sound, from the colour, from the smell of "Monsieur Vitrou has died".

The funeral was a solemn affair. The residents clubbed together to buy flowers—two vast wreaths made up of immortelles, hinting at immortality here on earth and saying that Monsieur le concierge would not be forgotten. And, in the place of honour, quivering at the head of the coffin, were the orchids, poisonously corrupt and gluttonous, beings from another world, paying a visit here, in the midst of bourgeois pink carnations, like a beguiling lady benefactress descending into a cellar to call on a sick laundress.

The widow Vitrou stood right at the front, but, turning slightly towards the coffin, she could see through her mourning veil how solemnly and sorrowfully the crowd of worshippers was listening to the *De Profundis*.

And many of them were weeping.

The old man from the third floor was shaking his head, as if to say he did not approve of this prank by old Monsieur le concierge. He would have preferred to be sleeping, but he had dragged himself along in the hope of somehow propitiating the nasty, frightening thing that had crept into the apartment building.

Bitterly weeping beside him was his daughter, who was thinking about how she was never going to get married. Her father had ruined her life, while he himself enjoyed a life of leisure, pretending to suffer from asthma and making her get up at six in the morning to brew his coffee.

Also weeping was the lilac-powdered actress from the second floor. She was imagining that she herself was lying there in the coffin, as if understudying the concierge in his magnificent starring role.

"Flowers and tears," she was whispering. "Flowers and tears, but we, the dead, we no longer have need of anything."

The old women from the ground floor also had a little cry. They never missed a funeral, if they could help it, because for them this was the most relevant of everyday events—the most pertinent, you might say, to the agenda of the day.

The widow Vitrou saw all this—all this sorrow and reverence for her husband. She heard the incomprehensible, wise and mysterious Latin words that the priest was speaking to him—to Monsieur Vitrou. And when the church warden thumped the ground with his mace and began slowly letting people come up to her to express their condolences; when, one after another, these people reached out to her and to her stocky sons Pierre and Jules; when she saw these people shaking her sons' hands in their black Lisle gloves, which were all new and squeaky, she suddenly began to weep, loudly, sincerely and bitterly.

She was weeping for her husband, now majestic and proud and crowned with everlasting flowers; she was weeping for the "Monsieur Vitrou" before whom everyone was bowing and thanks to whom they were pressing her gloved hand with such respect. She was weeping for Monsieur Vitrou; she took pride in him and loved him.

And when, after the funeral, the family members crowded into her small apartment began to relax and have something to eat, with a few sighs, yet not without appetite—what can one do, after all *he* may have departed to a better world, but *we* still have to nourish ourselves in order to keep going a little longer in this worse world—then the widow Vitrou said as she poured out the coffee:

"My dear André often used to say that coffee should be drunk very hot and with cognac."

This was scarcely a pearl of wisdom, but she pronounced it with the restrained prophetic zeal with which one repeats the words of the great and the mighty.

And so it was understood. There was a meaningful hush and deep sighs. And these words were repeated with reverence to someone who had not quite been able to hear them.

1931

ERNEST WITH THE LANGUAGES

T HE STORY I'm about to tell you I didn't witness first-hand, although some of the *dramatis personae* are people I used to know, some are people I've at least seen around, and the story itself is one I've heard so many times that I can vouch for the truth of it.

The main character was a tutor on a country estate. His name was Ernest Ivanovich. His last name I don't remember—they just called him "Ernest with the languages". And not without good reason.

First I must set the scene that prepares for the first appearance of Ernest Ivanovich. It was a hot summer's day. In the drawing room, its blinds drawn to keep out the heat, sat the lady of the house, Alexandra Petrovna Dublikatova, wearing a fine cambric dressing gown. A widow of middling years, she was middling, too, in appearance, although the story does not require us to dwell on this. There she sat, sewing lace trim onto a blouse. She was in good spirits, humming something to herself as she examined her handiwork.

Sitting in the room with her were her children, twelve-year-old Vanya, ten-year-old Liza and eight-year-old

Varenka, as well as a visitor—Verochka, the young lady from next door.

"Well, then," said Alexandra Petrovna, continuing their conversation, "to order fish or not to order?"

And she added, "'Toe bee ore note toe bee?' as Hamlet once said."

She pronounced this sentence—one that the whole world is by now heartily sick of—in her own peculiar way, using only long vowel sounds.

Verochka from next door smirked and corrected her. "It's 'too bee', not 'toe bee'."

"Oh, really?" said Dublikatova nonchalantly. Turning to her son, she said, "You're studying Latin, Vanya. Is it 'toe bee' or 'too bee'?"

Vanya looked away and answered glumly, "I don't know. We haven't yet got that far."

But Verochka from next door was not discouraged.

"Oh, Alexandra Pavlovna, how funny you are! That's not Latin, it's English! It's Hamlet!"

But the widow wasn't going to surrender either.

"Well, what if it *is* Hamlet? I have an excellent knowledge of Hamlet. He was a Danish prince. But I can't see why you think that a highly educated man like Hamlet, from the upper crust of society, couldn't dash off a sentence in Latin. And why would he speak English when he's from Denmark? Most likely, he spoke Danish."

Just then Verochka remembered that her daddy had borrowed a thresher from Dublikatova and fell silent. But

Dublikatova took the conversation to heart, and, as a dutiful mother, began mulling it over.

"We *do* need to hire a tutor. Liza needs to resit German, Vanya needs to resit German, French and Latin, and Varenka needs to prepare for gymnasium. We need to take on a tutor with languages anyway, so he may as well teach them English, too. Otherwise they'll think the same as that idiot Verochka—that Hamlet cock-a-doodle-dooed in some barnyard language. I'll write to Madame Chervinaya in Moscow—she'll be able to find us something suitable."

No sooner said than done.

Madame Chervinaya wrote back, and, two weeks later, sitting before the widow Dublikatova was a neatly combed and shaved gentleman with a chin that he kept thrusting forward and bulging eyes.

"Indeed," the gentleman was saying, looking sternly at Dublikatova, who kept tucking her fingers into her palms to hide her nails, which were stained by the juice of the black-currants she had been sorting through all morning to make jam. "Indeed," he was saying, "languages are indispensable. I'll endeavour to teach the children French and German."

"And English," added the widow. "I must insist on English."

The gentleman pressed his lips together, thought for a moment, then said sternly, "Three languages at once. That is not pedagogical, methodological or—most importantly—didactical. On this last point I particularly insist, while nevertheless emphasizing the first two."

After saying this, he pursed his lips and thrust his head forward, furrowing his brow and rolling his pale eyes.

But this did not trouble the widow.

"Yes, indeed, I understand all that perfectly well," she replied, although she had not understood any of it. "All the same, I absolutely must insist. To be quite frank, when I invited you here, it was, first and foremost, English that I had in mind. Or do you not have a command of English?"

To this the gentleman replied, "What a peculiar question."

And he even turned red. Evidently he was offended.

Thus the question of English was resolved, and established as a priority.

On the whole Dublikatova liked the new tutor. He wore clean clothes. He spoke little and very sternly. He was serious about the children's lessons. And he was perfectly well mannered, even if he was in the habit of wiping his mouth with a quick, circular movement of his index finger. But even the way he did *that* seemed perfectly well mannered.

Her mind now at ease as regards the tutor, the widow Dublikatova busied herself with another matter—the preparations necessary for the imminent visit of her sister Lizaveta. Lizaveta was the most important person in the whole family—or so she had managed to establish herself. As a young woman she had married a rich merchant. In order to pre-empt any slight to her noble heritage, she had immediately begun putting on airs and graces. She instructed her nephews and nieces to call her "Tante Lili" and sprinkled her conversation with French *mots*. She took umbrage at everything and was affronted by everyone. And on becoming a rich, childless widow, she was once and for all elevated to the position of head of the entire family. For she had three sisters and two brothers, who between them had produced a further eleven potential heirs. And if she should form a particularly strong attachment to one of them, then she might neglect the other ten.

It was precisely in the hope of such neglect on her part that her brothers and sisters alike enticed her to their homes with the most ardent of familial hospitality.

So it was that having persuaded "Tante Lili" to come and stay for the summer, Dublikatova was bustling about, trying to ensure that everything met her sister's refined standards. She put up fresh wallpaper in two rooms so that her sister could choose the room she preferred. She arranged for the planting of roses of the most delicate shades, and for milk to be given to the suckling pigs. She had the piano tuned and she got rid of the mice. What more could a loving sister do?

Finally Lili arrived.

She was thin, sallow, draped in diaphanous scarves of muted hues and smelt sickeningly of cloves.

Everything left her simply aghast. Of the little boy she said in a loud whisper, like an actor in an old-fashioned theatre, "Mercy! What a monster!"

Of the girls she exclaimed, "Mercy! Why have you dressed them like that?"

And to Dublikatova herself, she said, "Really! Aren't you letting yourself go, rather?"

And even though she kissed everyone, she did so with visible repulsion.

Breakfast left her supremely dissatisfied.

"What is this ghastly thing?" she asked.

"Jacket potato," replied Dublikatova, turning red.

"How can you serve such stuff?" said Tante Lili indignantly, helping herself to a second portion.

All in all, despite her indignation, she ate like a trencherman.

To the tutor she paid absolutely no attention at all.

So the days went by. Dublikatova was bending over backwards in her attempts to please her rich sister, who for her part did nothing but grumble and act bored.

"What about your spiritual needs?" she would lament towards the end of the day. "You vegetate—like beasts. You have no sense of self sacrifice, no hunger for great deeds."

"But what do you want from us, Lili dear," asked an anguished Dublikatova. "The children are still little. Just wait and see, they'll grow up and begin to, erm… sacrifice."

"Oh, you don't understand a thing!" Lily lamented. "You live like a vegetable—you live the life of an animal."

Then one morning Lili set off on a dreamy stroll. Passing the tutor's wing, she heard a loud male voice, saying in a pleasant tone and with great firmness, "Happiness is life's pudding, not its bread."

The voice said this, then dreamily said it again.

Lili was rooted to the spot.

"How intriguing! He's sitting there and philosophizing."

After a brief pause the voice rang out again.

"Tears are the pearls of the soul," it pronounced firmly. "Don't cast them before swine."

Then it added, "That's enough!"

At breakfast Lili kept a close eye on the tutor and realized that he was no ordinary man.

"He was born to be a leader," she said that evening to her surprised sister. Surprised as she was, Dublikatova felt no need to ask any questions. Thank heavens there was at least one thing her sister was happy with!

The next morning Lili went back to the wing of the house where the tutor lived. This time she came from the opposite direction and was able to see the tutor. He was sitting in an armchair beside the window. Looking up at the clouds, he said, "Measure twice, cut once."

Lili was a little surprised by the mismatch between his words and his posture, but she continued to observe him.

"Do unto others as you would have them do unto you. As you would have them do unto you. As you would have them do unto you," repeated this remarkable person, who then got to his feet and moved away from the window.

At breakfast the children were astonished. Tante Lili's cheeks were as pink as blotting paper and she had a rose pinned to her waist. She asked the tutor, "Ernest Ivanovich, do you like veal?"

To which he replied with some reserve, "Yes, I like eating meat."

And he wiped his mouth with his index finger.

The next morning she went once again to the wing and heard that "the glory of beauty withers and dies, but the glory of wisdom lives forever".

She couldn't see the tutor, but she could hear his voice coming closer to the window, then moving away again. Evidently he was pacing around the room in thought.

Then his voice rang out again, even more intensely: "The strong suffer in silence."

Lili's heart clenched tight.

He was strong, and he was suffering in silence. Was he being paid enough for his lessons? Sasha was so vulgar that she could easily be short-changing him. What a man! What wisdom! What strength! What a pity their paths had crossed so late in her life...

And she began standing outside the wing every morning and listening. Sometimes there wasn't a sound; at other times she seemed to hear children's voices. Perhaps the children were going to his room to study and were distracting him from his meditations?

Once she heard the stern admonishment: "Those who adorn their body deserve contempt. Those who adorn their soul are worthy of admiration."

After this she stopped wearing her brooch.

One day, at lunch, the little girl Varenka was chattering away about how she would like to trip some Seryozha or other so that he would fall over and smash his nose. On hearing this, Lili grew red and agitated and said, "Varya!

You must do unto others as you would have them do unto you!"

And in a trembling voice, she asked, "Isn't that right, Ernest Ivanovich?"

The tutor stared at her. He wiped his mouth with his finger and said, with a shrug of the shoulders, "As an ideal, it's excellent. But if, for example, you're playing cards, you can hardly wish for your opponent to win."

"Oh, I would never dream of playing cards!" exclaimed Lili. "Cards are dreadful."

He shrugged his shoulders again.

On another occasion, when she saw Dublikatova straightening a bow on the little girl's dress, Lili exclaimed, "Sasha, you shouldn't be encouraging her to adorn her body! Isn't that right, Ernest Ivanovich?"

Ernest Ivanovich was taken aback.

"What do you mean? I think it's nice. Yes, I think it's very nice indeed, as I must emphasize."

It was Lili's turn to be taken aback. She even seemed scared.

"*You* are saying that? *You?*"

"Well, yes, I am. Why are you so surprised? I attach a great deal of importance to one's appearance."

But then she realized he was being ironic, and she laughed tenderly.

An overflowing heart finds relief through words. One fine evening, her cheeks aflame, Lili said to her sister, "What a wonderful person Ernest Ivanovich is! Sometimes in the morning, when I happen to be passing the wing, I hear him talking to himself. Everything he says is so deep and meaningful."

"When does he... I don't know what you're... Ah, yes, I see... It's when he's dictating—dictating translation to the children. I hired him with languages."

"Don't be so ridiculous!" said Lili angrily. "It's nothing to do with translation! Why do you always have to cheapen everything?"

And she left the room.

She left the room, but only after exciting considerable alarm in Dublikatova's heart. Dublikatova was now repeating to herself the well-worn phrase: "The silly woman's gone and fallen in love."

But what if things progressed further? What if that goose Ernest grasped that Lili was a woman with money? What if he ended up marrying her?

Dublikatova thought and thought. She thought until her heart was pounding and she had to take valerian. She didn't sleep a wink.

In the morning she made up her mind.

"I'll sack him—I'll sack him along with his languages. But how?"

Here she got lucky. Lili caught a cold and took to her bed. Seeing that she was going to be in bed for at least another three days, Dublikatova summoned Ernest Ivanovich. She said she was sorry but that she was going to have to let him go—she was going away with the children the day after next and, well, there was nothing that could be done about it.

"What a pity," said Ernest Ivanovich. "The children have been making great strides, and particularly in English, as I must emphasize."

Dublikatova hemmed and hawed, but in the end she said a resolute farewell to the tutor.

Tante Lili was dumbfounded.

"But you must understand," said Dublikatova, trying to placate her, "you must understand that this had nothing to do with me. He'd received news from home, he said that his wife or some other member of his family had fallen ill…"

"His *wife*!" exclaimed Tante Lili. "Men like that don't have wives. He… he's… too great a man… Too tall, I mean."

She didn't survive the blow. That is, she didn't survive in the village. She went away to suffer abroad.

As for the tutor, Ernest Ivanovich, he may have disappeared from Dublikatova's life, but not without a trace. A trace remained, and quite an amusing one at that. When the children were taken to school in Moscow, it turned out that they knew no English whatsoever. They translated and spoke quite briskly in some other strange language, but just what language that was—no one had a clue. Dublikatova was appalled.

"He must have been the Devil himself!"

Much later it was established that the language the tutor had foisted upon his young charges instead of English was

Estonian. And he had drummed it into their heads so well that, despite their mother's pleading and their own suffering, they were never able to forget it.

As for the widow Dublikatova, she conceived an intense loathing of Shakespeare. Because, strictly speaking, it had all started with him.

But, as Shakespeare never found out, there's no need to dwell on this any further.

1936

PART IV

1930s: Magic Tales

"THE KIND THAT WALK"

F IRST TO RAISE THE ALARM would be the two young pointers that were always playing by the gate.

They would begin baying a peculiar warning bay—a dog's way of saying "Bewa-a-a-re! Bewa-a-a-re!"

At this, the entire pack of village dogs slumbering by our front door would jump to their feet—big dogs, little dogs, pedigree, half-breed and stray mutts with no breeding whatsoever.

From the kennel would emerge a great shaggy dog named Watcher, who looked like an old man wearing a sheepskin coat inside out. He would fly into a rage, barking himself hoarse, jumping up on his hind legs and tugging at his chain.

This entire canine concert marked an event that was rather straightforward and by no means unusual: Moshka the carpenter coming in through the gate.

Why the dogs grew so agitated at the sight of him I can't understand even now.

Moshka was old, very thin, long and stooped. On his head he wore a yarmulke and he had side-locks, a long black rekel coat and galoshes. For those parts, in short, he looked entirely ordinary.

What was remarkable about him was not his appearance but other things—which the dogs could hardly have known about.

First, he had a reputation as an unswervingly honest man. He carried out every job well, on time and at a fair price, and without asking for a deposit.

Second, and this, too, the dogs couldn't have known, he was a man of few words. I don't know whether he ever spoke at all. Maybe he only winked and shook his side-locks.

But what was truly remarkable about him was a legend that shed some light on his strange ways. Apparently, one Yom Kippur, some thirty years ago, while he and his fellow believers were praying and repenting of their sins in the synagogue, there was an incident that Jewish folk belief saw as unusual, but not beyond the bounds of possibility: poor Moshka was dragged off by a devil.

There were, naturally, people who had seen with their very own eyes how Moshka flew up into the air and was carried off by some foul being who looked like nothing so much as a ram. They'd wanted to help Moshka out by making the sign of the cross over the devil, but then they had thought better of it: the cross might get Moshka even deeper into trouble.

One old woman didn't see a ram but "somefink like a ball with flames comin' out its nose".

What kind of nose a ball has this old woman did not try to explain; she just spat over her shoulder.

Whatever the truth, Moshka disappeared for the better

part of thirty years. Then he reappeared—from heaven knows where—settled down beyond the cemetery in an abandoned bathhouse and began going from one landowner to another doing carpentry jobs. His work was good. How he'd learnt his trade during his years with the devil was hard to imagine.

There were, as always, clever people to be found who said with a little smirk that Moshka had simply been dodging military service and must have spent all those years in America.

This reasonable explanation was to no one's liking; some people even found it offensive.

"What far-fetched stories people come up with! When with our very own eyes we saw the devil drag him away. Besides, if Moshka was in America, don't you think he'd be telling us about it? People are real loudmouths when they come back from America. If you don't tell tales when you come back from America, when *are* you going to tell tales? But he just holds his tongue. Why? Why do you think? It's because he's bound by a vow of silence! Maybe he has to atone for some kind of sin. And why's he so honest? Don't tell me *that's* from being in America! Ha ha! And as for him not wanting to be paid in advance, well, that's because he's afraid the devil might drag him off again and money that belonged to others would simply be wasted."

I remember those "Moshka days" well.

An outbuilding; a small, empty, whitewashed room; planks, boards and sawdust.

A long black figure would be bent over a wide board and running a little box along it. From under the box cascaded delicate, silky curls of fragrant shavings.

My sister and I would stand in the doorway, holding our breath, watching Moshka. I think we stood there for hours at a time.

Moshka said nothing; he paid no attention to us at all. He would plane and saw and chisel. His movements were slow, as if unconscious, his eyes half closed. His movements lulled us into a kind of hypnotic trance. We would start breathing deeply and evenly, as if we were asleep. Our eyes, too, were half closed and rolled back. Something strange, pleasant and irresistible would come over us, enchanting us, bewitching us, taking away our strength and will.

At a call from our elders we would make an effort to rouse ourselves and then run back into the house. At table, our mother would say how pale we looked.

But the moment we were left to our own devices, we would run off to watch Moshka. This quiet, dark man held an inexplicable attraction for us.

Many years later, a landowner from Simbirsk told me how a Kalmyk had cured his six-year-old son of childhood epilepsy. The Kalmyk asked for a pound of pure silver, took a little hammer and began beating out a hollow cone. For nine days he shaped the silver, tapping with the hammer, slowly rotating the shining chunk of metal and humming very softly. The sick boy was told to stand beside him and watch. The boy turned calm and sleepy. After nine days the cone was finished, and the boy was cured.

In old Moshka's movements, too, there must have been something that had a hypnotic effect upon us.

But in the meantime, the legends around Moshka couldn't but inflame people's imaginations.

Just think—a man who has been carried off by the devil! How often in our humdrum world do you come face to face with something like that?

Once the story of his disappearance had been thoroughly picked over, it began to feel unsatisfying. It was hard to leave it at that. And so people's minds set to work.

The housekeeper kept bustling in; the laundress kept saying things in a whisper.

"Why are you always running off to see Moshka?" Nanny would grumble. "You shouldn't look at him. His kind bring harm—you mustn't look at them for long."

"What 'kind'? What kind is Moshka?"

"The kind that walk."

How mysterious and macabre the words sounded.

"Where does he walk, Nanny?"

"Here. He ought to stay *there*, but he comes and walks *here*. No good will come of it."

"But where's *there*?"

"Where he's bur-r-r-ried!"

The way she said the word, we didn't dare ask more. Evidently, Moshka had been buried somewhere and then got out…

In the evening the housekeeper was whispering something about the cemetery. It was scary. We understood that Moshka had been buried there—and now here he was, coming *here* from *there*.

There was another Jew working on our estate at the time. He was a sociable, talkative fellow. He was making bricks for the barn and he kept promising to build a little house for me and my sister. Knowing he had a loose tongue, we decided to ask him about Moshka.

Thanks to our house-building plans we were on the friendliest of terms: yes, he was sure to tell us everything.

And so off we went.

"Itska, tell us about Moshka. Is it true he's already been buried?"

Our question didn't surprise Itska, although I suspect now that he simply didn't understand us. But his response was so eloquent that it's stayed with me throughout all my long life:

"Moshka? Why does everyone keep on about Moshka? And why Moshka? Why not not-Moshka? Let me tell you once and for all—Moshka is simply Moshka."

And that was that.

That evening, in the nursery, there was an entire assembly. It was attended not only by the housekeeper, but also by the laundress, the kitchen woman and some witch in a brown headscarf whose connection to the household seemed rather distant; she might have been the coachman's mother-in-law.

Here we learnt—and deliberated upon—the most astonishing news. Moshka's carpentry work, we discovered, was just a cover. The cunning man was using it to divert attention from his real business: running a bathhouse for the dead.

Everything had been confirmed by statements from witnesses. Someone had a friend who had left town late on a Sunday evening. He'd had a bit too much to drink so he went the wrong way and ended up at Moshka's bathhouse. And then—heavens above! He heard a knocking and a crashing—like metal pails rolling about on the floor—and then it seemed as if lots of non-human voices were arguing. The man ran off in terror. But he went back the next morning and looked through the window: shelves had been overturned, boards were lying about on the floor and pails had been thrown all over the place. No doubt about it—something had been going on in the night. He told his friend—a clerk and a man of the world. This man of the world just grinned at him.

"What? Are you serious?" he asked. "Everyone's known for ages. Any fool could have told you that Moshka runs a bathhouse for the dead. Why else would the bathhouse be right next to the cemetery?"

"But… that bathhouse hasn't been used for years."

"Of course no one goes there," said the man of the world. "How many people are going to frequent a place like that? Only the kind that walk. Was all this on a Sunday?"

"Yes. It was Sunday."

"What Christian soul would go to the bathhouse on a Sunday? You know very well what I'm saying. You're not a child."

This entire story was narrated to the meeting in whispers, interspersed with little sobs.

Then we heard about the aunt of some woman who made communion bread. Her husband's brother had gone to the bathhouse one night on purpose. He'd looked through the window and seen two naked dead men sitting and steaming themselves with cold water. The brother-in-law took such a fright that he was struck dumb for the rest of his life.

And now the same mute brother-in-law was telling everyone to knock out the bathhouse windows, to take the door off its hinges and keep a good watch on the place. It was time to smoke Moshka out. Why should anyone round here give him work if he was *the kind that walk*?

Soon after this, Moshka disappeared. Some said he must have gone to find work in Kiev, others had seen with their very own eyes how he had been dragged off again by the devil.

Then it emerged that while Moshka was working for us in his usual way, planing his boards, someone had indeed gone to the trouble of smashing in the bathhouse windows and going off with the bathhouse door. And Moshka could hardly go on living there with no windows or doors. After all, his kind need to be able to hide away from people.

I may only have been little, but I could see that it was impossible to live without windows or doors. Although such things may not have mattered to Moshka. After all, he wasn't going to catch cold if he was *the kind that walk*.

But the story of him going to Kiev was, of course, no more than idle gossip. Because what did our herdsman find, on the nesting box next to the outbuilding, but an old galosh? Who did it belong to if not to Moshka? And how could it have got up there? It had fallen from the sky, of course, as Moshka was being carried off by the devil.

All in all, people felt a little regretful.

"He was a good sort. Quiet, hard-working, honest. The trouble is, he wasn't a human being. If he had been, none of this would have happened. It's a good thing he went away of his own accord. Otherwise... well, people were already beginning to talk about aspen stakes."

The galosh was solemnly burnt. Because people knew that if it wasn't destroyed Moshka was sure to come back for it. If not now—then in thirty years' time.

"It's better if he doesn't walk any more," said the kitchen woman. "Enough's enough."

1936

THE DOG
(A STORY FROM A STRANGER)

D O YOU REMEMBER that tragic death? The death of that artful Edvers? The whole thing happened right in front of my eyes. I was even indirectly involved.

His death was extraordinary enough in itself, but the strange tangle of events around it was still more astonishing. At the time I never spoke about these events to anyone. Nobody knew anything, except the man who is now my husband. There was no way I could have spoken about them. People would have thought I was mad and I would probably have been suspected of something criminal. I would have been dragged still deeper into that horror—which was almost too much for me as things were. A shock like that is hard to get over.

It's all in the past now. I found some kind of peace long ago. But, you know, the further my past recedes from me, the more distinctly I can make out the clear, direct, utterly improbable line that is the axis of this story. So, if I am to tell this story at all, I have to tell you all of it, the way I see it now.

If you want to, you can easily check that I haven't made any of this up. You already know how Edvers died. Zina

Volotova (née Katkova) is alive and well. And if you still don't believe me, my husband can confirm every detail.

In general, I believe that many more miracles take place in the world than we think. You only need to know how to see—how to follow a thread, how to follow the links in a chain of events, not rejecting something merely because it seems improbable, neither jumbling the facts nor forcing your own explanations on them.

Some people like to make every trivial event into a miracle. Where everything is really quite straightforward and ordinary, they introduce all kinds of personal forebodings and entirely arbitrary interpretations of dreams made to fit their stories. And then there are other, more sober, people who treat everything beyond their understanding with supreme scepticism, dissecting and analysing away whatever they find inexplicable.

I belong to neither of these groups. I do not intend to explain anything at all. I shall simply tell you everything truthfully, just as it happened, beginning at what I myself see as the story's beginning.

And I myself think the story begins during a distant and wonderful summer, when I was only fifteen.

It's only nowadays that I've become so quiet and melancholic—back then, in my early youth, I was full of beans, a real madcap. Some girls are like that. Daredevils, afraid of nothing. And you can't even say that I was spoilt, because there was no one to spoil me. By then I was already an orphan, and the aunt who was in charge of me, may she rest in peace, was simply a ninny. Spoiling me and disciplining me were equally beyond her. She was a blancmange. I now believe that she simply wasn't in the least interested in me, but then neither did I care in the least about her.

The summer I'm talking about, my auntie and I were staying with the Katkovs, who lived on a neighbouring estate, in the province of Smolensk.

It was a large and very sweet family. My friend Zina Katkova liked me a lot. She simply adored me. In fact the whole family were very fond of me. I was a pretty girl, good-natured and lively—yes, I really was very lively indeed. It seemed I was charged up with enough joy, enough zest for life to last me till the end of my days. As things turned out, however, that proved to be far from the case.

I had a lot of self-confidence then. I felt I was clever and beautiful. I flirted with everyone, even with the old cook. Life was so full it filled me almost to bursting. The Katkovs, as I've said, were a large family and—with all the guests who had come for the summer—there were usually about twenty people around the table.

After supper, we used to walk to a little hill—a beautiful, romantic spot. From it you could see the river and an old abandoned mill. It was a mysterious, shadowy place, especially in the light of the moon, when everything round about was bathed in silver, and only the bushes by the mill and the water under the mill wheel were black as ink, silent and sinister.

We didn't go to the mill even in daytime—we weren't

allowed to, because the wooden dam was very old and, even if you didn't fall right through it, you could easily sprain your ankle. The village children, on the other hand, went there all the time, foraging for raspberries. The canes had become dense bushes, but the raspberries themselves were now very small, like wild ones.

And so we would often sit in the evenings on the little hill, gazing at this old mill and singing all together, "Sing, swallow, sing!"

It was, of course, only us young who went there. There were about six of us. There was my friend Zina and her two brothers—Kolya, who was the elder by two years, and Volodya, who is now my husband. At the time he was twenty-three years old, already grown-up, a student. And then there was his college friend, Vanya Lebedev—a very interesting young man, intelligent and full of mockery, always able to come up with some witticism. I, of course, thought he was madly in love with me, only trying his best to hide it. Later the poor fellow was killed in the war... And then there was one more boy—red-haired Tolya, the estate manager's son. He was about sixteen years old and still at school. He was a nice boy, and even quite good-looking—tall, strong, but terribly shy. When I remember him now, he always seems to be hiding behind somebody. If you happened to catch his glance, he would smile shyly and quickly disappear again. Now, this red-haired Tolya really was head-over-heels in love with me. About this there could be no doubt at all. He was wildly, hopelessly in love with me, so hopelessly that no one even had the least wish to make fun of him or to try to laugh him out of it. No one teased him at all, though anyone else in his position would have been granted no mercy—especially with people like Vanya around. Vanya even used to make out that Fedotych, the old cook, was smitten with my charms: "Really, Lyalya, it's time you satisfied poor Fedotych's passion. Today's fish soup is pure salt.[1] We can't go on like this. You're a vain girl. *You* may enjoy his suffering—but what about *us*? Why should *we* be punished?"

Tolya and I often used to go out for walks together. Sometimes I liked to get up before dawn and go out to fish or pick mushrooms. I did this mainly in order to shock everyone. People would walk into the dining room in the morning for a cup of tea and say, "What's this basket doing here? Where have all these mushrooms come from?"

"Lyalya picked them."

Or some fish would suddenly appear on someone's plate at breakfast.

"Where's this come from? Who brought it?"

"Lyalya went fishing this morning."

I loved everyone's gasps of astonishment.

So, this red-headed Tolya and I were friends. He never spoke to me of his love, but it was as if there were a secret agreement between us, as if everything were so entirely clear and definite that there was no need to talk about it. Tolya was supposed to be a friend of Kolya Katkov's, although I don't really think there was any particular friendship between them. I think Tolya just wanted to be a part of our group; he just wanted the opportunity to stand behind someone and look at me.

And then one evening we all of us, including Tolya, went off to the hill. And Vanya Lebedev suddenly decided that each of us should tell some old tale or legend, whatever they could remember. The scarier, the better—needless to say.

We drew lots to decide who should begin. The lot fell to Tolya.

"He'll just get all embarrassed," I said to myself, "and he won't be able to think of any stories at all."

But, to our general astonishment, Tolya began straight away: "There's something I've been meaning to tell you all for a long time, but somehow I've never got round to it. A story about the mill. The story's quite true—only it's so strange you'd swear it was just a legend. I heard it from my own father. He used to live six miles away, in Konyukhovka. It was when he was a young man. The mill had been out of use for a long time even then. And then an old German with a huge dog suddenly came along and rented the mill. He was a very strange old man indeed. He never spoke to anyone at all; he was always silent. And the dog was no less strange; it would sit opposite the old man for days on end, never taking its eyes off him. It was only too obvious that the old man was terribly afraid of the dog, but there seemed to be nothing he could do about it. He seemed quite unable to get rid of the dog. And the dog just kept watching him, following the old man's every movement. Every now and then it would suddenly bare its teeth and growl. But the peasants who went there for flour said the dog never attacked any of them. All it ever did was look at the old man. Everyone found this very odd. People even asked the old man why he kept such a devilish creature. But there was no chance of getting any reply out of him. He simply never answered a word… And then it happened. All of a sudden this dog leapt on the old man and bit through his throat. Then the peasants saw the dog rushing away, as if someone were chasing it. No one ever saw the dog again. And the mill's been empty ever since."

We liked Tolya's old legend. Vanya Lebedev, however, said, "That's splendid, Tolya. Only you missed out a few things. And really, it should have been scarier. You should have added that the mill has been under a spell ever since. Whoever spends one whole night there will be able, if ever he wishes, to turn himself into a dog."

"But that's not true," Tolya replied shyly.

"How do you know? Maybe it *is* true. We simply don't know. I've got a feeling that's the way it is. It's just that no one's tested this out yet."

We all laughed. "But why? What's so special about turning into a dog? If one could turn oneself into a millionaire, that would be different. Or some hero or other, or a famous general—or a great beauty, for that matter. But who wants to turn into a dog? Where would that get you?"

No one told any more stories that evening. We talked about this and that, then went our separate ways.

The following morning Tolya and I went into the forest. We picked some berries, but there were too few to take back to the dining room so we decided I might as well eat them myself. We sat down beneath a fir tree, me eating berries and him just looking at me. Somehow this began to seem very funny.

"Tolya," I said, "You're staring at me the way that dog of yours looked at the miller."

"Really, I wish I could turn into a dog," he answered glumly, "because you're never going to marry me, are you?"

"No, Tolya, you know I'm not."

"You see, if I remain a man it'll be impossible for me to be near you all the time. But if I turn into a dog no one can stop me."

I had a sudden idea. "Tolya, darling! You know what? You could go to the mill and spend the night there. Please do! Turn into a dog, so that you can always be near me. You're not going to say you're scared, are you?"

He turned quite white—I was surprised, because all of this was just stuff and nonsense. I was joking. Neither of us, it went without saying, believed in that mysterious dog. But he, for some reason or other, turned pale and replied very gravely, "Yes, all right, I'll go and spend the night at the mill."

The day went by in its usual way and, after my morning walk, I didn't see Tolya at all. In fact, I didn't even think of him.

I remember some guests coming round—newlyweds from a neighbouring estate, I think. In short, there were lots of people—lots of noise and laughter. And it was only in the evening, when everyone except family had left and we youngsters had set out for our usual walk, that I began to think about Tolya again. It must have been when I saw the mill—and when someone said, "Doesn't the mill look dark and spooky this evening?"

"That's because we know the kind of things that go on there," replied Vanya Lebedev.

Then I started looking for Tolya. Turning round, I saw him sitting a little apart from the rest of us. He was completely silent, as if deep in thought.

Then I remembered what he'd said, and somehow this made me feel anxious. At the same time, I felt annoyed with myself for feeling anxious, and this made me want to make fun of Tolya.

"Listen, ladies and gentlemen!" I called out merrily. "Tolya's decided to conduct an experiment. Transformation into a dog. He's going to spend the night at the mill."

No one paid much attention to any of this. They probably thought I was joking. Only Vanya Lebedev answered, saying, "Yes, why not? Only please, dear Anatoly, be sure to turn into a hunting dog. That really would be a great deal more acceptable than a mere mongrel."

Tolya didn't say anything in reply. He didn't even move. When we were on our way home, I purposely lagged behind a little and Tolya joined me.

"Well, Lyalechka," he said. "I'm going. I'm going to the mill tonight."

Looking very mysterious, I whispered, "Go then. You must. But if, after this, you have the nerve *not* to turn into a dog, please never let me set eyes on you again!"

"I promise to turn into a dog," he said.

"And I will be waiting for you all night," I replied. "As soon as you've turned yourself into a dog, run straight back home and scratch on my shutter with your claws. I'll open the window, and then you can jump into the room. Understand?"

"Yes."

"Off you go then!"

And so I went to bed and began to wait. And just imagine—I couldn't get to sleep. Somehow I was terribly anxious.

There was no moon that night, but the stars were shining. I kept getting up, half-opening the window and looking out. I felt very scared of something. I felt scared even to open the shutters—I just looked out through a chink.

"Tolya's a fool," I said to myself. "What's got into him? Sitting on his own all night in a dead mill!"

I fell asleep just before dawn. And then, through my dreams, I hear a scratching sound. Somebody's scratching on the shutter.

I jump out of bed to listen better. Yes, I can hear the sound of claws against the shutter. I'm so scared I can hardly breathe. It's still dark, still night-time.

But I braced myself, ran to the window, flung open the shutters—and what do I see? Daylight! Sunshine! And Tolya's standing there laughing—only he's looking very pale. Overcome with joy, I grab him by the shoulders, then fling my arms round his neck.

"You scoundrel! How dare you not turn into a dog?"

He just kissed my hands, happy that I had embraced him.

"Lyalechka," he said, "can't you see? Or maybe you just don't know how to look properly. I *am* a dog, Lyalechka. I am your faithful hound forever. How can you not see it? I shall never leave you. But someone's put an evil spell on you that stops you from understanding."

I grabbed a comb from the table, kissed it and threw it out the window.

"Fetch!"

He rushed off, found the comb in the grass and brought it to me between his teeth. He was laughing, but there was something in his eyes that almost made me burst into tears.

All this happened as summer was drawing to a close.

Three or four days after that night, my aunt and I went back to our own village. We needed to get ready to return to Petersburg.

Volodya Katkov rather surprised me. He had got hold of a camera from somewhere, and during the days before our departure he kept on and on taking photographs of me.

Tolya kept at a distance. I barely saw him. And he left before me. For Smolensk. He was studying there.

Two years went by.

I only once saw Tolya during that time. He had come to Petersburg for a few days to attend to some practical matter, and he was staying with the Katkovs.

He had changed very little. He still had the same round, childish face, with grey eyes.

"Greetings, my faithful hound! Let me take your paw!"

He didn't know what to say. Terribly embarrassed, he just laughed.

Throughout his visit Zina Katkova kept sending me little notes: "You really must come round this evening. Your hound keeps howling." Or: "Come round as soon as you can. Your hound is wasting away. Cruelty to animals is a sin."

Everyone kept quietly making fun of him, but he behaved very calmly indeed. He didn't seek me out, and he went on hiding behind other people's backs.

There was just one occasion when Tolya seemed to go a bit wild. Zina was telling me that, since I had such a wonderful voice, I really must go and study at the conservatoire—and Tolya suddenly came out with, "Yes, I knew it! The stage! How utterly, utterly wonderful!"

Immediately after this little outburst, needless to say, he seemed terribly embarrassed again.

He was only in Petersburg for a few days. Soon after he had left, I received a huge bouquet of roses from Eilers'.[2] We were all racking our brains for a long time, wondering who on earth could have sent it, and it was only the following day, as I was changing the water in the vase, that I noticed a little cornelian dog tied to the bouquet by a thin gold thread.

I didn't tell anyone the flowers were from Tolya. I somehow started to feel awfully sorry for him. I even started to feel sorry for the dog. It had little shiny eyes, as if it were crying.

And how could someone as poor as Tolya have found the money for such an expensive bouquet? It was probably money his family had given him to go to the theatre with, or to buy things he really needed.

Expensive and splendid as they were, there was something tender and painful about these flowers. It was impossible to reconcile their air of sorrow with the impression created by Tolya's round, childishly naive face. I even felt glad when the flowers withered and my aunt threw them out. I somehow hadn't dared to throw them out myself. As for the little cornelian dog, I tucked it away in a drawer, to try and forget about it. And forget I did.

Then came a very chaotic period in my life. It started with the conservatoire, which disappointed me deeply. My professor was full of praise for my voice, but he said I needed to work on it. This, however, wasn't my way of doing things at all. I was used to doing nothing very much and receiving ecstatic praise for it. I would squeak out some little song and everyone would say, "Oh! Ah! Such talent!" As for systematic study, that was something entirely beyond me.

It also turned out that the generally held belief in my great talent was somewhat exaggerated. In the conservatoire I did not stand out in any way from the other girls. Or, if I did, it was only because I didn't even once bother to prepare properly for a lesson. This disappointment did, of course, have its effect on me. I became anxious and irritable. I found solace in flirtations, in pointless chatter and in endlessly rushing about. I was in a bad way.

I heard only once from Tolya. He sent me a letter from Moscow, where he had gone to continue his studies.

"Lyalechka," he wrote, "remember that you have a dog. If ever you are in need, just summon it."

He did not include his address, and I did not reply.

The war began.

The boys from my old circle all turned out to be patriots, and they all went off to the front. I heard that Tolya went too, but somehow I hardly thought about him. Zina joined the Sisters of Mercy, but I was still caught up in my mad whirl.

My studies at the conservatoire were going from bad to worse. And I'd fallen in with a wild, bohemian crowd. Aspiring poets, unrecognized artists, long evenings devoted to discussing matters erotic, nights at The Stray Dog.[3]

The Stray Dog was an astonishing institution. It drew in people from worlds that were entirely alien to it. It drew these people in and swallowed them up.

I shall never forget one regular visitor. The daughter of a well-known journalist, she was a married woman and the mother of two children.

Someone once happened to take her to this cellar, and one could say that she simply never left. A beautiful young woman, her huge black eyes wide open as if from horror, she would come every evening and remain until morning, breathing the alcoholic fumes, listening to the young poets howling out verses of which she probably understood not a word. She was always silent; she looked frightened. People said that her husband had left her and taken the children with him.

Once I saw a young man with her. He looked rather sickly. His dress and his general air were very sophisticated, "Wildean".

Looking cool and indifferent, he was sitting beside her at a table, and he seemed to be either writing or sketching something on a scrap of paper just under her nose. These words or signs evidently agitated her. She kept blushing and looking around: had anyone seen anything? She would grab the pencil from the young man and quickly cross out what he had written. Then she would wait tensely while he lazily scribbled something else. And then she would get agitated again and snatch back the pencil.

Something about this degenerate young man was so horrible, so deeply disturbing that I said to myself, "Can there, anywhere in the world, be a woman so idiotic as to allow that creature to come anywhere near her? A woman who would trust that man in any way, let alone be attracted to such a repulsive little reptile?"

In less than a fortnight I proved to be just such a woman myself.

I would prefer not to dwell on this disgusting chapter of my life.

Harry Edvers was a "poet and composer". He composed little songs, which he half-read, half-sang, always to the same tune.

His real name was Grigory Nikolayevich. I never discovered his surname. I remember I once had a visit from the police (this was later, under the Bolshevik regime) to ask if a certain Grigory Ushkin was hiding in my apartment. But I don't know for sure if it was him they were enquiring about.

This Harry entered my life as simply and straightforwardly as if he were just entering his room in a hotel, opening it with his own key.

Needless to say, it was in The Stray Dog that we first became acquainted.

I was on stage for part of that evening, and I sang Kuzmin's[4] little song, 'Child, don't reach out in spring for the rose'. At the time it was still very much in vogue. At the end of the first phrase someone in the audience sang out, "Rose lives in Odessa."

It had been someone sitting at the same table as Harry. As I was on my way back to my seat, Harry got to his feet and followed me. "Please don't take offence," he said. "That was Yurochka—he was just playing the fool. But you really shouldn't be singing Kuzmin. You should have been singing my 'Duchesse'."

And so it began.

Within two weeks I had had my hair cropped and dyed auburn, and I was wearing a black-velvet gentleman's suit. A cigarette between my fingers, I was singing the drivel Harry had made up:

> A pale boy composed of papier-mâché
> Was now the favourite of the blue princess.
> He had a certain *je ne sais quel* cachet
> Betokening voluptuous excess.

I would raise my eyebrows, shake the ash from my cigarette and go on:

> The princess had the bluest, sweetest soul,
> A dainty, pear-like soul—a true *duchesse*—
> A soul to savour, then to save and seal,
> A soul for lovers of *vraie délicatesse.*

And so on, and so on.

Harry listened, gave his approval, made corrections.

"You must have a rose in your buttonhole—some quite extraordinary, unnatural rose. A green rose. Huge and hideous."[5]

Harry had his retinue of followers, an entire court of his own. All of them green, unnatural and hideous. There was a green-faced slip of a girl, a cocaine addict. There was some Yurochka or other, "whom everybody knew". There was a consumptive schoolboy and a hunchback who played quite wonderfully on the piano. They all shared strange secrets that bound them together. They were all agitated about something or other, all suffering some kind of torment and, as I now realize, often just making mountains out of molehills.

The schoolboy liked to wrap himself up in a Spanish shawl and wear ladies' shoes with high heels. The green-faced girl used to dress as a military cadet.

It is not worth describing all this in detail. These people really don't matter; they're neither here nor there. I mention them merely to give you some idea of the circles into which I had descended.

At the time I was living in furnished accommodation on Liteyny Prospect. Harry moved in with me.

He latched on to me in a big way. I still don't know whether he truly fancied me or whether he just thought I was rich. Our relationship was very strange. Green and hideous. I don't propose to tell you about it now.

The strangest thing of all is that when I was with him I felt repelled by him. I felt a sharp sense of disgust, as if I were kissing a corpse. But I was unable to live without him.

Volodya Katkov came back on leave. He rushed into my apartment, full of joy and excitement. He exclaimed at my red hair: "Why on earth? What a one you are! Still, you really are awfully sweet!"

He turned me around, to look at me from all sides. It was clear that he really liked me. "Lyalechka, I'm only here for a week, and I'm going to spend every day of it with you. I've got a lot to say to you. It can't be put off any longer."

And then in came Harry. He didn't even knock. And I could see that he took an immediate dislike to Volodya. He must have felt jealous. And so he sprawled out in an armchair and began nonchalantly doing something he had never done before: addressing me with extreme familiarity, not as *vy* but as *ty*.

Volodya must have felt very confused indeed. For a long time he kept silently looking from me to Harry, and then from Harry to me again. Then he stood up decisively, straightened his field jacket and said goodbye.

It greatly upset me to see him leaving like this, but I too had been confused by Harry's rudeness. There was nothing I could think of to say, and I was unable to prevent Volodya from leaving. There had, I felt, been a terrible misunderstanding, but it seemed utterly impossible to do anything to put it right.

Volodya didn't call again. Nor did I expect him to. I felt that he had gone away, that his heart had gone away, forever.

Then came a period of isolation.

In spite of everything he had done to avoid this, Harry was about to be sent to the front. He went to Moscow to make representations.

I was on my own for more than a month.

It was an anxious time for me, and I had no money. I wrote to my aunt in Smolensk province, but I received no answer.

Eventually Harry returned. Entirely transformed. Tanned and healthy-looking, wearing a classy sheepskin coat, trimmed with astrakhan, and with a tall Caucasian hat, also astrakhan.

"Have you come from the front?"

"In a way," he answered. "Russia needs not only sacrificial cannon fodder, but also brains. I'm supplying the army with motorized vehicles."

Harry's brain may have been working magnificently, and it may have been needed by Russia, but he was still short of money.

"I need ready cash. Can you really not get hold of any for me? Are you really that lacking in patriotism?"

I told him about my misfortunes and about my aunt. He seemed interested and asked for her address. After hurrying about the city for a few days, he set off again. I had discovered by then that the secret of his new weather-beaten "soldierly" look was contained in two little pots of pink and ochre powder. To give him his due, this really did make him look very handsome.

By this time the mood of our little world of aesthetes had turned distinctly counter-revolutionary. Before leaving, Harry had composed a new little ditty for me:

> My heart hangs on a little white ribbon.
> White, white, white—remember the colour
>   white!

I was now wearing a white dress when I performed; we were all pretending to be countesses or marchionesses. The song was received well. So was I.

Soon after Harry had left, Zina Katkova came back unexpectedly from the front. She at once began telling me a story I found terribly upsetting.

"Our field hospital," she said, "had been set up on the edge of a forest. There was a great deal to do, but we had to leave the next morning. We were being rushed off our feet. At one moment I went out for a smoke—and suddenly there was a young soldier calling my name. Who do you think it was? It was Tolya. Tolya the dog. 'Forgive me, darling,' I say, 'I'm in a desperate rush.' 'But I just want to know how things are with Lyalechka,' he answers. 'She isn't in trouble, is she? For the love of God, tell me everything you know.' But just then I heard someone shouting for me. 'Wait, Tolya,' I say. 'The moment I've got this done I'll be straight back.' 'All right,' he says, 'I'll wait for you by this tree. We certainly won't be going anywhere before tomorrow.' And so I rushed back to my wounded. It was a terrible night. The Germans had got the range of our position, and at dawn we had to pack in a hurry. We didn't lie down for even a minute. I got a bit behind with everything and I had to run to get to our roll call. It was a miserable morning—endless grey drizzle. I'm running along—and suddenly—oh, Lord! What do I see? Tolya standing by a tree, all grey and ashen. He had been waiting for me all night long. He looked so pitiful. His eyes were sunken, as if staring out from under the earth.

And the man was smiling! Probably he'll be killed soon. Just think—he had been standing there all night long in the rain! Just to hear news of you! And I couldn't even stop for one moment. There was no time for anything. He thrust a slip of paper at me with his address. I shouted over my shoulder, 'Don't worry about Lyalya. I think she's getting married soon.' And then I worried I'd said the wrong thing. I might have upset him. Who knows?"

This story of Zina's greatly disturbed me. I was in a bad way and I needed the friendship of a good man. And where would I find a better man than Tolya? I felt moved. I even asked for his address and tucked the slip of paper away.

After that visit I really felt I didn't like Zina any longer. First, she had grown ugly and coarse. Second (and really, no doubt, I should have put this first), she treated me very coldly. More than that, she went out of her way to show her complete lack of interest in me and my whole manner of life. It was the first time, for example, that she had seen me with short red hair, but for some reason she behaved as if this wasn't in the least surprising or interesting. I naturally found this hard to believe. How could she not want to know why I had suddenly cut my hair short? It was obvious that her apparent lack of interest in how I looked was simply a way of expressing contempt for me and my dissipated life—as if from her exalted heights she barely even noticed my foolish antics.

She did not even ask whether I was still having singing lessons, or what I was up to in general. To get my own back,

I did my best to wound her: "I just hope the war comes to an end soon. Otherwise you'll lose every last semblance of humanity. You've become a real old harridan."

I then gave a mannered smile and added, "I, for my part, still acknowledge art alone. Your deeds will all pass away, since no one needs them. Art, however, is eternal."

Zina looked at me with a certain bewilderment and left soon afterwards. No doubt she wanted nothing more to do with me.

That evening I wept for a long time. I was burying my past. I understood for the first time that all the paths I had taken, all the paths I had followed to reach my present position, had been entirely destroyed—blown up like railway tracks behind the last train of a retreating army.

"And what about Volodya?" I thought bitterly. "Is that how a true friend behaves? He didn't ask any questions; he didn't find out anything for sure; he just took one look at Harry, turned round and left. If they all think I've gone mad, that I've lost my way, then why don't they come closer and help instead of just walking away? Why don't they support me and try to make me see reason? How can they be so cool and indifferent? How, at such a black and terrible time, can they abandon someone they were once close to?"

"Very virtuous they all are!" I carried on. "And they certainly make sure their virtue gets noticed. But is it really so very praiseworthy? How many temptations are there going to be for a woman with a face like Zina's? And Volodya's always been cold and narrow-minded. His petty little soul's as straight and narrow as they come. When did *he* last feel intoxicated by music or poetry? How much more I love my dear Harry, my dear and dissolute Harry, with his tender little song:

> My heart hangs on a little white ribbon.
> White, white, white—remember the colour
>   white!

"*They* would say this is rubbish. *They* would rather have Nekrasov—and his plodding, four-square poems in praise of civic virtue."

My green and hideous monsters now seemed nearer and dearer to me than ever.

They understood everything. *They* were my family.

But this new family of mine was now disappearing too. The cocaine addict was now fading away in a hospital. Yurochka had been packed off to the front. The consumptive schoolboy had volunteered for the cavalry because "he had fallen in love with a golden horse" and could no longer bear being with people.

"I've ceased to understand people or have any feelings for them," he kept saying.

From Harry's large retinue there remained only the hunchback.

He used to play 'The Waves of the Danube'[6] on a battered piano in a tiny cinema grandiloquently called The Giant of Paris—and he was slowly starving to death.

219

This was a very difficult time for me. I was kept going only by my anger towards those who had wronged me and by my overwrought and carefully nurtured tenderness towards my one and only Harry.

At last, Harry returned.

He found me in a very anxious state. I greeted him so joyfully that he was positively embarrassed. He hadn't realized I could be like this.

His behaviour was enigmatic. He kept disappearing for days on end. It seemed he really was buying and selling something.

After bustling about for a couple of weeks, he decided that we must move to Moscow: "Petersburg is a dead city. Moscow's seething with life. There are cafés springing up everywhere. You can sing there. You can read poems. One way or another you can earn a few roubles."

Moscow also apparently offered more scope for his own new commercial activities.

We packed up and moved.

Life in Moscow really did turn out to be more animated, more exciting and more fun. There were a lot of people I knew from Petersburg. It was a familiar world and I found my place in it easily.

Harry kept on disappearing somewhere or other. He seemed preoccupied and I saw very little of him.

And he forbade me, incidentally, to sing his 'Little White Ribbon'. Forbade me. He didn't *ask* me not to sing it—he *forbade* me. And he seemed very angry: "How can you not understand that that song has now become superfluous, superficial and utterly inappropriate?"

And he also happened to ask several times whether I knew the address of Volodya Katkov. I put this down to jealousy on his part.

"He's somewhere in the south, isn't he, with the Whites?"

"Of course."

"And he's not meaning to come here?"

"I don't know."

"And none of his family are here?"

"No."

He was strangely inquisitive.

Just what Harry was doing with himself was hard to understand. It seemed he was once again selling or supplying something. The good thing was that every now and then he would bring back some ham, flour or butter. Those were hungry days.

Once, as I was going down Tverskaya Street, I caught sight of a shabby figure that looked at me intently and then hurried across to the other side of the road. I felt I had seen this person before. I went on looking. It was Kolya Katkov! Volodya's younger brother, the comrade of my dog Tolya. Why hadn't Kolya said anything? He had clearly recognized me. Why had he been in such a hurry to slip away?

I told Harry about this encounter. For some reason my story made him very agitated. "How can you not understand?" he said. "He's a White officer. He doesn't want to be noticed."

"But what's he doing here in Moscow? Why isn't he with the White Army?"

"They must have sent him here on some mission. How stupid of you not to have stopped him!"

"But you just said he doesn't want to be noticed!"

"Makes no difference. You could have asked him back. We could have sheltered him here."

I was touched by Harry's generosity. "Harry, wouldn't you have felt scared to be sheltering a White officer?"

He blushed a little. "Not in the least," he muttered. "If you see him again, you really must bring him back with you. Yes, you really must!"

So Harry was capable of heroic deeds! More than that, he was even eager for a chance to prove his heroism!

It was a hot, sultry summer. A peasant woman who traded apples "from under her coat" suggested I go and live in her dacha just outside Moscow. I moved in with her.

Now and again Harry made an appearance. On one occasion he brought some of his new friends along too.

They were the same young Wildean poseurs as before. Green faces, the eyes of cocaine addicts. Harry too had recently taken to snorting a fair amount.

Most of his conversations with these new friends of his related to business.

Soon afterwards someone I knew showed up. He was from Smolensk province, from near our family home, and he brought me a strange little letter from my aunt.

"I've been carrying this letter around for the last two

months," he said. "I tried to find you in Petersburg, but I'd given up all hope. It seemed I was never going to find you. Then, quite by chance, I met an actress who told me your address."

"Evidently my letters aren't reaching you," my aunt wrote. "But at least the money is in your hands now, and it's a comfort to me to know this. I like your husband very much. He seems very enterprising—a man with a future."

What all this meant was quite beyond me. What husband? What money? And just what was it my aunt found so comforting?

Harry appeared.

"Harry," I said, "I've just received a letter from my aunt. She says she's glad the money is in my hands now."

I stopped, because I was struck by the look on his face. He was blushing so intensely that it had brought tears to his eyes. Finally I grasped what had happened: Harry had gone to see my aunt and had introduced himself as my husband—and the silly old woman had given him my money!

"How much did she give you?" I asked calmly.

"Around thirty thousand. Nothing much. I didn't want us to squander it all on trifles, and so I put the money into this automobile business."

"Mister Edvers," I said, "in the whole of this story there is only one thing I find truly surprising: the fact that you can still blush."

He shrugged his shoulders.

"What I find surprising," he said, "is that you haven't once wondered what we've been living on all this time and how we found the money to move here from Petersburg."

"So I've been paying my way, have I? Well, I'm glad to know that."

He left. A few days later, however, he made another appearance—as if this conversation hadn't happened at all. He even brought his friends again—two of the friends who had come the time before. They had brought with them some vodka and something to eat with it. One of them began making advances to me. They addressed each other—jokingly, I imagine—as "comrade". Edvers too was a "comrade". They asked me to sing. My admirer—whom I prefer not to mention by name—really appealed to me. There was something weary and depraved about him, something that reminded me of people from our "hideous green" Petersburg world. Without giving it any particular thought, I sang our 'Little White Ribbon': "My heart hangs on a…"

"It's a sweet tune, but the words are idiotic!" said Harry. "Wherever did you get hold of such antediluvian nonsense?"

And he quickly changed the subject, evidently afraid I would tell everyone he had written the words himself.

Three days later I was supposed to be singing in a café. Our manager got very embarrassed when he saw me and muttered something about it no longer being possible for me to sing that night. I was very surprised, but I didn't insist. I sat down in a corner. Somehow nobody seemed to notice me. The only person who did was Lucy Lyukor. In a poisonous tone of voice, the little poetess said, "Ah, Lyalya! I hear you haven't been wasting time. They say you've dyed your little white ribbon red!"

Sensing my bewilderment, she explained, "Only the other day you were singing for a group of Chekists.[7] I don't imagine you treated them to your 'Little White Ribbon'!"

"What Chekists?"

She gave me a sharp look, then named the comrade who had been making advances to me.

I did not reply. I just got up and left.

I was terribly frightened by what had happened. Harry had well and truly landed me in the dirt!

The incident with my aunt had not shocked me so very deeply. Nobody in our bohemian world was particularly scrupulous about money. Though it was unpleasant, of course, that he had kept the whole business a secret from me. This, however, was another matter altogether. How could I stay with him now? He was crazed with cocaine and in cahoots with the Cheka. No, I couldn't let Comrade Harry call the tune any longer. Had he not been trying to use me to lure White officers into a trap? It was not just out of the goodness of his heart, I now realized, that he had wanted me to invite Kolya Katkov to stay.

I was in despair. Where could I go? There was not a single close friend or relative I could turn to, no one I could count on to show me even just a little everyday kindness. My aunt? But I would have to obtain a travel permit, and besides, I didn't have a kopek to my name.

I went back home.

There was no sign of Harry. It was several days since I'd last seen him.

I did all I could. I made the rounds of different institutions. I wrote petitions and applications. I tried to get myself registered with the newly reconstituted Artists' Union. Then it would be easier for me to get a travel permit.

And then one day I was walking down the street and all of a sudden… You could have knocked me down with a feather. Kolya. Kolya Katkov. There he was—right in front of my eyes.

"Kolya!" I shouted.

He appeared not to see me and quickly turned down a side street. After a moment's thought, I followed him. He was waiting for me.

I now realized why I had been slow to recognize him the previous time. He had grown a beard.

"Kolya," I said. "What are you doing here? Why are you in Moscow?"

"I'm leaving today," he replied. "But you shouldn't have let it be seen that you know me. Isn't that obvious?"

"You're leaving today?" I exclaimed—and felt more despairing than ever. "Kolya!" I said, "for the love of God, save me! I'm lost."

He evidently began to feel pity for me.

"There's nothing I can do now, Lyalechka. I'm a hunted beast. And anyway, I'm leaving today. There really is nothing I can do. I'll ask someone to call round."

I remembered Harry and the people he now brought to my lair.

"No," I said. "You mustn't send anyone round."

And then I had another thought, a thought that brought warmth to my heart.

"Kolya," I said, "is there any chance you'll be seeing Tolya?"

"It's certainly possible," he answered.

"Tell him, for the love of God, that Lyalya is calling on her dog for help. Remember my words and repeat them exactly. Promise me. And tell him to leave a note for me in the café on Tverskaya Street."

"If all goes well," he said, "I'll be seeing him in about five days' time."

Kolya was in a great hurry. We parted. I was crying as I walked down the street.

Back home I thought everything over very carefully and decided not to say anything to Harry. Instead I would try to trick him into handing over some of the money—money that did, after all, belong to me!

My efforts to get hold of a permit met with success, and soon nearly everything was ready.

And then the day came…

I'm sitting in the dacha on my own, leafing through some papers in my desk, when I begin to feel that someone is looking at me. I turn around—a dog! Large, brownish red and thin, with matted fur—a German spitz or chien-loup. It's standing in the doorway and looking straight at me. "What's going on?" I think. "Where on earth's this dog come from?"

"Kapitolina Fedotovna!" I call out to my landlady. "There's a dog in here!"

Kapitolina Fedotovna comes in, very surprised. "But the doors are all shut," she says. "How did it get in?"

I wanted to stroke the dog—there was something so very expressive about the way it was looking at me—but it wouldn't allow me to. It wagged its tail and retreated into a corner. And just kept on looking at me.

"Maybe we should give it something to eat," I say to Kapitolina. In reply, she mutters something about there not being enough food any longer even for human beings, but she brings some bread anyway. She throws a piece to the dog. The dog doesn't touch it.

"Better throw the dog out!" I say. "It's acting strange. It might be sick."

Kapitolina flung the door open. The dog went out.

Afterwards we recalled that it never once let us touch it. Nor did it once bark, nor did it ever eat. We saw it—and that was all.

Later that day Harry appeared.

He looked awful—well and truly exhausted. His eyes were bulging and bloodshot, his face taut and sallow.

He walked in, with barely a word to me.

My heart was beating frantically. I had to speak to him—for the last time.

Harry slammed the door. He was terribly edgy. Something had happened to him—or else he had overdone the cocaine.

"Harry," I said finally. "We need to talk."

"Hang on a moment," he said confusedly. "What's the date today?"

"The twenty-seventh."

"The twenty-seventh! The twenty-seventh!" he muttered despairingly.

What was so astonishing about this I really don't know, but his repeated exclamation made the date stick in my mind. And subsequently this turned out to be important.

"What's that dog doing in here?" he shouted all of a sudden.

I turned round—there in the corner of the room was the dog. Taut, pointing, it was looking at Harry intently, as if it were nothing but eyes—as if its eyes were now its entire being.

"Get that dog out of here!" Harry screamed.

There was something excessive about his fear. He rushed to the door and flung it open. Slowly the dog began to move towards the door, not taking its eyes off Harry. It was slightly baring its teeth, its hackles raised.

Harry slammed the door after it.

"Harry," I began again. "I can see you're upset, but I just can't put this off any longer."

He looked up at me, and then his whole face suddenly twisted in horror. I could see he was now looking not at me but past me. He seemed to be looking at the wall behind me. I turned round: there outside the window, with both paws on the low sill, was the reddish-brown dog. It dropped back down at once, perhaps startled by my movement. But I managed to glimpse its raised hackles, the muzzle it had thrust alertly forward, its bared teeth, the terrible eyes it kept fixed on Harry.

"Go away!" Harry shouted. "Get rid of it! Drive it away!"

Trembling all over, he rushed into the hallway and bolted the door.

"This is terrible, terrible!" he kept repeating.

I sensed that I too was shaking all over, and that my hands had gone cold. And I understood that we were in the middle of something truly awful, that I ought to do something to calm Harry, to calm myself, that I had chosen a very bad moment indeed, but for some reason I was quite unable to stop and I hurriedly, stubbornly, went on:

"I've taken a decision, Harry."

His hands trembling, he struck a match and lit a cigarette.

"Oh, have you?" he said with a nasty smirk. "How very interesting."

"I'm leaving. I'm going to my aunt's."

"Why?"

"It's better not to ask."

A spasm passed across his face.

"And if I don't let you?"

"What right do you have to stop me?"

I was speaking calmly, but my heart was racing and I could hardly breathe.

"I have no right at all," he answered, his entire face trembling. "But I need you here now, and I won't let you go."

With these words he pulled out the drawer of my desk and immediately saw my new passport and papers.

"Ah! So it's like that, is it?"

He snatched the entire sheaf and began tearing the papers first lengthways and then crossways.

"For your dealings with the Whites I could easily..."

But I was no longer listening. I leapt on him like a madwoman. I was shrieking; I was clawing at him. I hit him on his hands and arms. I tried to tear the papers out of his hands.

"Chekist! Thief! I'll kill you! I'll kill you!"

He grabbed me by the throat. Really he was not so much strangling me as just shaking me; his bared teeth and staring eyes were wilder and more terrible than anything he actually did. And the loathing and hatred I felt for those wild eyes and that gaping mouth made me begin to lose consciousness.

"Somebody help me!" I gasped.

Then it happened—something truly weird. There was the sound of smashing glass, and something huge, heavy and shaggy jumped into the room and crashed down on Harry from one side, bringing him to the floor.

All I can remember is Harry's legs twitching. They were poking out from under the red, tousled mass that covered his body, which was almost completely still.

By the time I came to, it was all over. Harry's body had been removed; the dog had torn his throat out.

The dog had disappeared without a trace.

Apparently, some boys had seen a huge hound, leaping across fences as it ran past.

All this happened on the twenty-seventh. That is important; much later, when I was a free woman, in Odessa, I found out that Kolya Katkov had passed on to Tolya my appeal for help, and that Tolya had dropped everything and rushed to my rescue. That meant trying to slip through the Bolshevik front line. He was tracked down, caught and shot—all on the twenty-seventh. The twenty-seventh, that very day.

That's the whole story; that's what I wanted to tell you. I've made nothing up; I've added nothing, and there's nothing I can explain—or even want to explain. But when I turn back and consider the past, I can see everything clearly. I can see all the rings of events and the axis or thread upon which a certain force had strung them.

It had strung the rings on the thread and tied up the loose ends.

1936

PART V

Last Stories

THE BLIND ONE

THE DAY WAS WAN. Tear-stained.

The sea was grey and bled of colour. It was merging with the sky, yet that did not make it seem without boundaries. Rather, it seemed to be coming to an end somewhere very close, creeping dimly and hazily upwards and dying away in the heavy fog. It wasn't even lapping against the shore. It was utterly stagnant and dead.

The sea had died; it had come to an end.

On a bench at a right angle to the shore sat a lady in a hat and city clothes. She wasn't from anywhere nearby. The locals didn't dress like that.

She had turned away from the sea and was looking down the lane. Here the park came right up to the shore. On her face was an expression of boredom and displeasure. It was clear she was waiting. It was equally clear, from the movement of her lips and the nervous shifting of her brows, that she was mentally composing unpleasant comments.

Sitting on a bench somewhere off to the side, nearer the park, was another woman, somewhat older. On her knees was a board covered with a piece of paper, and she was pressing something into it with a little stick.

The first lady stood up and began to walk towards the shore. From somewhere to her right came the sound of voices. Holding one another tightly by the hand, three young women in coarse calico smocks were entering the water. They were taking awkward steps and letting out little squeals. From the shore an old woman was calling, "Don't let go! Don't go far! Have a dip and come back out again. I'm telling you—don't let go! You'll drown."

The old woman was sitting on a rock. She had a beaked nose and was wearing a white headscarf.

"Darya Petrovna!" the girls called back. "It's all right. We'll keep together."

"Who are these girls?" asked the first lady, now close to the sea.

"They're our blind lasses from the orphanage," replied the old woman. Then she started calling again: "I'm telling you, come back towards the shore. No one's going to be dragging you out of the water."

From behind the bushes emerged another three girls. In grey chintz dresses with short calico capes, they too were walking along hand in hand. They were walking awkwardly, stumbling and needing one another's support. Suddenly they began to sing:

> Oh, open up! Oh, open up
> The joyous doors to our bright heaven!

They sang simply and earnestly, in the manner of Russian laundresses and other working women. Two of them were singing in unison; the third was singing a very beautiful accompaniment.

> Oh, won't you shine! Oh, won't you shine
> A friendly light on my dark land!

The sorrowful sky, and the wan sea, and this cheerless blind song were so perfectly in harmony, so of a piece, so unbearably painful, that the lady in the hat was afraid to come face to face with the girls. She was afraid of seeing their faces, their terrible eyes. She hurried back to her bench, sat down and began looking down the lane. The lane was deserted. She turned back the glove on her left hand and glanced at her watch.

"He's late. That's all I need!"

She took a rusk from her handbag, broke off a piece and put it into her mouth. Then, turning to one side, she saw a lean man of medium height wearing a straw boater. He was coming unhurriedly down the lane towards her.

She quickly took a powder compact from her bag, turned away a little, but then crossly snapped the compact shut.

"To hell with him! I shan't!"

The lean gentleman stopped for a while beside the woman with the board, exchanged a few words with her and then, in a leisurely way, went over to the lady who had been waiting for him.

"You're at least half an hour late," she said abruptly.

"Only a quarter of an hour," he replied, a smile creasing his hollowed cheeks.

"And yet you found time to start a conversation with that peasant woman."

"She's not a peasant. She's a very cultured lady. She's working for the blind, transcribing *Anna Karenina* for them."

"I can just imagine how important *Anna Karenina* is for those fools. Ugh—it's the last thing they need!"

"What's the matter?" he asked in a tone of affectionate reproach. "Surely it can't be wrong to be caring for these unfortunates?"

"Thank you for the lecture," she said with trembling lips.

"Well, it's all been thought out very cleverly, you know. That board has grooves in it and she uses a little stick to press points into the paper and arrange them in a different way for each letter. On the other side of the paper the points come up as little bumps, so the blind can read by feeling these little bumps with their fingers. It's extraordinarily interesting."

"Well, I think it's uncivilized," she said, interrupting him.

"What?" he asked in surprise. "What's uncivilized about working for the blind?"

"It's uncivilized to keep me waiting. You could have amused yourself with Anna Karenina later, after I'd gone."

He shrugged and sat down.

"I can see you're not in a good mood today."

"Good heavens, how absurd! Obviously you've decided to compensate for your stupidity by being rude," she muttered, and turned away.

He leant forward and looked at her benignly.

"Hold on there," he said. "What's the matter? Is it your nerves? Or have I done something wrong? Hmm?"

His feigned affability utterly enraged her. Instead of answering him, she silently took the rusk from her handbag and began nibbling it.

"Why are women always munching on something?" he asked with a smile.

He had to respond somehow or other. And so he had. But even as the words were coming out of his mouth he realized he was saying the wrong thing.

Her nose turned white with fury.

"Women munch on something because they haven't even had time to drink a little tea... because they didn't want to keep someone else waiting... because of their delicate sensibilities... and now I'm starting to get a migraine. That's why women are always munching on something..."

She knew she was speaking stupidly, like the very worst of fools, and this only enraged her still more. Yet she could not bring herself to stop. It was as if she was racing headlong down an infernal railway track, drunk on her own despair, mindless and furious.

"Better to be late, I'd say, than to get yourself so worked up," he said. "And in half an hour we'll be able to have some breakfast."

She looked at his face; it was close to hers. She saw the deep folds around his mouth and on the left a porcelain tooth with a gold band. The tooth decided everything. She shouldn't have seen it. For the sake of beauty, this tooth had been inserted into that pale, elongated mouth, the corners of which had a lilac tinge. It had been put there to please, to captivate, to attract love, so that others would come running when he called and then wait for him. But he—he would be late, he would allow himself to make fun of her and her nerves. Oh! What a beast!

> Oh, open up! Oh, open up
> The joyous doors to our bright heaven!

The girls' voices, sad yet unaware of their sadness, were ringing out from the bank.

She looked at him again and saw that he had slipped a large ox-eye daisy into the buttonhole of his coat. This was the last straw.

"Well, aren't you the dandy!"

Overwhelmed by a surge of inexplicable loathing, she snatched the flower and flung it onto the bench.

"How vulgar!" she said with a gasp, almost a groan. "That is you through and through. Through and through! Go away! For heaven's sake, just go! Otherwise I—"

"All right, Vera Andreyevna. Calm down. If I annoy you as much as that, I'll go."

He had already taken several steps, but he paused in sad bewilderment.

"I am utterly at a loss… Perhaps you'll allow me to

accompany you, even so. Forgive me, I don't even know...
Well, then, God be with you."

Impatiently she turned away.

By the time she raised her head he was already in the
distance.

"Will he turn back or not? Will he or won't he? No, he
won't."

Something like a heavy wave seemed to roll down from
her head and shoulders. Her eyes darkened, her ears began
to ring, her heart thumped. So, now it was over. She felt
utterly drained. She was so tired, so deflated.

"What have I done? How crude! How stupid! The devil
knows why! What's wrong with me?"

Her entire body began to shake with a strange, mirthless
laughter.

"Heavens! I think I'm weeping..."

Probably it was because on her way here, to the sea,
to meet this sweet, wonderful man, she had been thinking
of another sea—a sunny, southerly sea. And of cheerful
friends, a chic restaurant on the waterside, and a young
Italian woman who had sung in a passionate voice to
the strumming of a guitar: "*L'amore è come lo zucchero!*"[1]
And of dear eyes that had gazed at her with adoration
and love.

> Oh, won't you shine! Oh, won't you shine
> Your friendly light on my dark land!

Beneath the wan sky the freaks were still singing; the sorrow of their voices was floating into the bitter fog.

Now another two girls emerged from a side path and walked towards the bench where she was sitting and weeping. One of them was thin and dark. Her eyes had sunk deep back into their sockets and her eyelids were firmly stuck together. Only a black strip of eyelash indicated where her eyes would have been. The other girl was tow-headed, with cloudy grey eyes both turned towards her nose. She was snub-nosed and a little plump. The girls were walking hand in hand. In a fluid voice the snub-nosed girl was saying, "It's just too beautiful to describe. The sea is brightest blue, and suddenly it becomes angry and dark. Then it's all a deep dark blue, with little white sea-sheep prancing and playing on it. And it's so pretty and gay that some sailors don't want to go home—not for anything. And how beautiful the shore is! There just aren't any words for it. The grass is a darling green and the little flowers in the grass are white and red and yellow and deep blue. And above each flower dances a butterfly. And whatever colour the flower, that's the colour of the butterfly."

"Why are they dancing?" asked the dark one sceptically. "Don't they need to eat?"

"It only takes them a minute to eat. They swallow the dewdrops from the flowers—that's all they need. And then they dance some more."

"But you've never seen them," said the dark one, suddenly irritable. "You haven't seen since you were born."

"It doesn't matter whether I've seen them. I know anyway."

"You think everything is beautiful. Probably you even think Darya Pavlovna is beautiful."

"Darya Pavlovna is like a flower of God."

"But what about her voice? 'Don't let go!' She screeches like an owl."

"Her voice is neither here nor there. Darya Pavlovna herself… Oh, what's this?"

They had reached Vera Andreyevna. The snub-nosed girl felt the bench with her hands.

"Sit down," she said. "My, what have we here? A little flower? You know what? A very handsome boy came and saw us and threw us this flower."

"What are you saying?" asked the dark one in astonishment. "Really?"

"Oh, what a sweet little flower! What a sweet little flower," the snub-nosed girl crooned tenderly, feeling the crumpled daisy with her fingers. "And each little petal is different. This one is a delicate blue, and this one is pink. Here, feel it—you can tell right away that it's pink. And this one is yellow. But this one—you may not believe it, but it's pure gold. Heavens, how much joy there is. And all of this joy is for us. All this joy has been given to us. In one little flower. Yet there are millions of little flowers just like it scattered all over the earth. With butterflies fluttering above them. And everything is so beautiful, it's so beautiful that some angel just won't be able to help itself, it will secretly wing its way down from heaven and give some little flower or butterfly a kiss, then go back up behind the clouds and smile at us from on high. Hush! Listen. Can you hear? The angel's laughing!"

"Girls!" called Darya Pavlovna from the water's edge. "It's time!"

The blind girls got to their feet and joined hands. The snub-nosed girl paused. "Can you hear it? Can you hear it?" she asked, turning her head towards the bench where the woman in the hat was quietly weeping. "Can you hear the angel?"

And both girls, smiling joyfully, began to amble along in an uneven, awkward gait towards the shore.

1948

THY WILL

1

The guests were being slow to arrive. It was already past ten o'clock and the hostess was getting cross.

"It's impossible, the way people behave now! Some guests won't turn up until after the theatre—and they'll just want to go straight in to dinner, while others have been sitting here and wearing one out since nine," she said, not thinking how discourteous this might be to the guests who had arrived at nine.

But these were old friends with whom she didn't need to stand on ceremony—three of her fellow bridge players, and then Doctor Pamuzov, two young actresses and an affected youth with slicked-back blond hair and a pointed little face. The youth so resembled an albino mouse that you half expected him to have red eyes.

The conversation was flagging; no one was coming up with any juicy new gossip.

"Will that Anna Brown be joining us this evening?" asked one of the ladies.

"I really don't know," replied the hostess. "She dropped by on Thursday and, if you ask me, she's got a screw loose up here."

She tapped her forehead.

"You can be absent-minded, but not *that* absent-minded. It was the stuff of farce. She had been sitting here for some time when suddenly she jumped up and started staring at the wall calendar. 'I must go,' she said, 'I really must go.' 'What's the hurry?' I asked. 'No,' she answered, 'I should have gone ages ago—look, it's already the sixth of Thursday.' 'Good heavens,' I thought. 'What *is* she on about?' But then she rubbed her temple, blinked a few times and said, 'Pardon me, I thought that was a clock.'"

"How ridiculous!" the women all exclaimed.

"Well, well," said Doctor Pamuzov, shaking his head. "That doesn't sound good."

"Well, if you ask me," barked one of the ladies, whose distinguishing feature was an enormous round brooch supporting her third chin, "your Miss Brown is simply a fool who's putting on airs."

"Yes, she's putting on airs," the others all chorused. "And why Anna 'Brown' when everyone knows she's a plain old Anna Brunova? Who does *she* think she is?"

"But that's a stage name," said the hostess, coming to Anna Brown's defence. "It's what people do."

"Stage names are neither here nor there. What matters is talent."

"Yes, talent. Which she hasn't got."

"Of course not. Gerbel *created* her."

"Pianists like her are ten a penny."

"If Gerbel hadn't given her such a brilliant review…"

"Well, if you ask me," boomed the lady with the brooch, drowning out all the other voices, "if you ask me, your Anna Brown is simply a fool who's putt—"

Suddenly she broke off mid-word. Eyes bulging, she was looking in horror somewhere above the hostess's head. Everyone turned. They saw a tall, dusky woman. Smiling graciously, this woman leant forward and held out her hand.

"Hello, my dear."

It was Anna Brown.

"Hello, darling!" trilled the hostess. "I'm absolutely delighted to see you! Isn't this just lovely?"

And everyone tried to look welcoming, while glancing furtively at one another as if to ask, "Do you think she heard?"

Doctor Pamuzov couldn't contain himself and started shaking with mirth.

"Forgive me. I've just remembered a joke. Oh, my! I'll tell you later. It really is very funny indeed!"

And once again he was shaking, snorting, coughing and wiping tears from his eyes.

Suddenly everyone began talking at once, not listening to one another.

"We thought you'd gone away!"

"There aren't any concerts now."

"Of course not. The season's over."

"But maybe your students are keeping you here?"

"Surely not? Haven't your students left, too?"

It was all quite absurd. Everyone seemed to be asking questions of Anna Brown and then immediately answering on her behalf. And there she was, listening calmly, as if none of this had anything to do with her.

"Darling!" exclaimed the hostess anxiously, while looking indignantly at the doctor, who was still shaking with mirth. "You look exhausted."

"I am. I keep getting headaches and I feel a bit cold."

"Cold? In this heat? The papers say there have been cases of sunstroke."

"Sunstroke?" said Anna Brown in sudden astonishment. "How strange! Sunstroke—in the middle of winter?"

"The middle of winter? I'm talking about now—June."

Anna Brown frowned.

"Yes, yes, of course. It's June. I've got everything back to front."

Some more guests arrived and the hostess rushed off to greet them.

The evening was getting lively. Card tables were being set up, and two long-nosed maids in white caps were serving tea and biscuits.

The young man who looked like an albino mouse went over to the piano with the two actresses. Softly touching the keys, he began languidly humming something.

Anna Brown whirled around. Pressing her hands to her temples, she exclaimed, "Dear God! Please—anything but music!"

But they didn't hear her and went on humming.

Anna began quietly making her way to the door.

Still more guests were arriving, but there didn't seem to be anyone she knew. Or maybe she just didn't recognize them. And then her attention was caught by some other woman. There was something terribly restless and unpleasant about her. First Anna noticed the woman's beautiful, elegant dress. It was skew-whiff across the breast—two loops had been pulled over one button. Then she took in the woman's unkempt hair. As for her face, it was as if she hardly even had a face—only the unbearably strained expression of her large, weary mouth and her unpleasant dark eyes.

"Dear God! What's wrong with her?"

Anna drew closer. This woman moved too, towards her. Yes, it was herself. It was her own reflection in the large mirror.

"Seems I really am in a bad way!"

The foyer was furnished like a small living room, and the door out onto the stairs was half open. There were several gentlemen smoking on the landing.

"Should I go home?" Anna said loudly. She shook her head and looked around. Next to the door stood an exotic plant. The plant looked stunted but it was in a very large tub, and tucked away behind it was a low armchair.

"Just what I need."

She sat and drew the thick, plush curtain hanging by the window towards herself.

"Perfect. Now I can do some thinking."

She couldn't go home. The previous evening she had felt such dread as she approached her house that she had to sit down on a bollard—she had no idea how long she had stayed there. Going home could be very frightening. The night before last her elder sister had come and sat on her bed and said tenderly, "Why make things so hard for yourself? You'll only wear yourself out." This sister, who had died four years ago, had never really loved her, and it was very strange suddenly to hear her speaking so affectionately. If she had still been alive, she would have done nothing but judge Anna. But Anna knew she had done nothing wrong. She was right. And everything that she had done had been carefully thought through. If she had not left him, he would have left her, and that would have hurt even more. She had merely precipitated the event; she herself had chosen where to draw the boundary. It was a real breakthrough—to draw a boundary oneself. But hardly anyone seemed to grasp this. She had heard, not long ago, about a prisoner whose cell was six steps in length. Every time he reached the wall he wanted to smash his head against it, so tormented was he by this limit imposed on his freedom. Six steps—that was all. Then he decided he would take only four steps. He drew a boundary, of his own free will, and he felt free. These four steps are my freedom. As for your six steps, you can keep them. What would her own life be like now if she had clung to the six steps of their relationship? She would be waiting, watching, checking. Would he ring or wouldn't he? Would he drop by or wouldn't he? Would he send a concert ticket or wouldn't he? Would he ask her over or wouldn't he? But it was even worse when he did give himself away. Like when he said something after being lost in thought. Four times now he had come to and at once said something about the singer Zarnitskaya. He was writing an article about her. It was true that she had a good voice, but why would he get so lost in thought about *that*? People said that he had *created* Anna Brown the pianist. His review had been stunning... Stunning... "But I know now," she said to herself, "that what inspired him to write that review was not just artistic rapture. So why should I believe in the purity of his rapture for this singer's talent? But be that as it may, it's not the heart of the matter. Every affair, like a stone thrown up into the sky, reaches its ordained height and then falls back down to earth. The more powerful the force that impelled it upwards, the harder it falls. Well, I wasn't going to wait for it to fall. I didn't want it to kill me on its way down, so I chose to set a limit to its ascent myself. I couldn't prove anything, but I had a presentiment and that was enough for me. The real problem is that we live on two planes of existence! One is straightforward reality. The other is made up entirely of presentiments, impressions, incomprehensible and insuperable sympathies and antipathies. Of dreams. This second life has laws and a logic all of its own, for which we cannot be held accountable. Brought out into the light of reason, they surprise and shock, but we cannot overcome them. Now and again a man who has led a decent, honest life will end up in court, and the court will never be able to get to the bottom of what motivated his crime. And the defence he trots out will be utter balderdash, because the terrible laws of the second plane of his life are incomprehensible, and therefore inadmissible on the plane of reality."

She suddenly had a vivid recollection of that last evening. He had asked her over and she had gone round, in a state of feigned excitement, full of lies, cheerful and bright. He was ambitious, so she filled his ears with flattery. She told him about all sorts of wonderful responses to his articles; she had embellished and embroidered the truth, mentioning envious people who didn't even exist and aiming clever jibes at them. She told him about letters and flowers being sent to her by the editor of the magazine he worked for. He felt flattered: it was because of *him* that she was turning down this fascinating and potentially useful admirer. He was smiling, stroking his head with roguish self-satisfaction. Then he got up, embraced Anna, seated her on the divan and knelt down before her. The usual ritual of their amorous evenings. And when the words "usual ritual" came into her mind, she knew this was the moment. "All right, that's enough. Now, while he's entirely mine, I'll draw a boundary of my own free will. I'll put an end to our intimacy…" He was embracing her legs and burying his face between her knees, and suddenly, in an abrupt movement, she pushed him away with both hands. Raising his head, he looked at her in confusion. And this face with its flared nostrils and a dark vein bulging across its brow—this face looked frightened and pitiful. And somewhat repulsive.

She got up, smoothed her hair and in a voice so plain and natural that she even deceived herself, she said, "That's enough of all this. Aren't you finding it all rather tiresome already? Really, I'm surprised at you!"

Nonchalantly she made her way out of the room. She stopped in the doorway and, without turning around, she said, "I may give you a ring in a day or two."

He didn't see her out and didn't reply. Since then they had not met.

She had brought it off perfectly. That she'd found his face repulsive was exactly what she had needed. It made her job easier. Only one thing was wrong: when she got home, triumphant and quietly laughing, she found herself listening involuntarily for the phone to ring. The next day was no better, and with each following day it was even worse. The trouble was that she was still hoping. She needed to do something that would make it impossible to keep hoping.

She lived on a quiet street, and every time a car went by it seemed to be Gerbel's. Every time the telephone rang she thought it was him. She stopped going to concerts. She was afraid to be around other people she knew in case she happened to hear his name.

Then came this obsession over the key. She still had the key to his apartment. She had used it so as not to disturb his manservant when she came over late at night.

What should she do with the key? Post it back to him? Leave it with the concierge? Somehow nothing seemed right. But why not? Evidently because this would put an absolutely indisputable full stop to everything. It would be the end. If she was shying away from this full stop, it must mean she was still hoping for something. But as long as she was still hoping, she would find no peace. She had to stop hoping. Even if she put the key in the post or left it with his concierge—even then she would have no peace. Even then she would be waiting for something, still pathetically hoping for something. If only he would go away forever—or better still, die—then she could rest easy.

She could slip out right now and go down the stairs. No one would notice; the door would remain just as it was, almost closed but not completely. She could cross the street. Yes. There was no one about. Although the yardman was sure to be in his usual place, by the gate. He wouldn't notice her. He'd be bundled up in a sheepskin coat with his collar pulled up around his ears. It was snowing—he wouldn't hear footsteps. He'd be asleep... Oh, someone had said it was summer now. Maybe it was, but yardmen wear sheepskin coats in summer, too—they always feel cold at night...

...How quickly I've got down the street and round the corner. On the left is the Neva; I'd better not look. In summer, during the white nights, the Neva looks so sad and still, so hopeless—it can sap all your strength of spirit. But I need strength of spirit—it's what I need more than anything. I should get the key out now or I'm sure to drop it and make a noise. But what if he's not at home? No, that's impossible. Since I've decided to come, he must be here. He's sleeping.

Here we are. The apartment is dark. The same familiar smell, as unsettling as ever. Cigarette smoke and eau de Cologne. Although in another apartment the same smoke and the same eau de Cologne would smell quite different. There it would be ordinary, but here it's always disturbing. Here's the bedroom. The curtains are drawn across the door, but there's light coming through the gaps. I could see whether my portrait's still there or whether he's taken it down. But why should I? It's all the same to me. I haven't come to check things like that, I've come to impose my will. Here on the bedside table should be the little blue saucer that goes with my teacup. He loved it for some reason and kept it after I broke the cup. And on the saucer a pair of cufflinks. No, don't think about the saucer. There's a certain repellent tenderness about it. And I mustn't look at the bed either. I should go over to the commode and feel around for a cold, long, flat object... And carefully pull out the blade. Now everything will be easy. People always do this in gloves, that's why I've got gloves on now. I go quickly up to the bed. I need to feel for his face. No, I can see—there's light falling right on the pillow. His head is thrown back. How easy it all is. One movement, one moment. And the key? I toss the key onto the table in the foyer. The yardman is asleep. Thick snow blankets his shoulders. He hasn't heard a thing. And the snow will cover my tracks. And now I'm back here again, back in my place behind the tub with the stunted plant. But how tired I am, and how I'm trembling!

There was an excited hubbub.

"Time for dinner!"

"Dinner is served!"

Someone was looking at her. They seemed pleased.

"So this is where you've been hiding!" said the hostess. "Let's go in for dinner."

Anna rose to her feet, swaying slightly to one side. Everyone was chattering cheerfully as they made their way into the dining room. In she went with the rest of them.

"Please have a seat! Allow me, hmm?"

It was the same as ever. Guests approaching a laden table always become strangely animated, like beasts, and everyone wants to say something—it doesn't matter what.

"Well, well, hmm. Yes, yes! Is anyone sitting here? Allow me! Hmm!"

In the midst of all this amiable silliness Anna was standing calmly at her seat, next to Doctor Pamuzov.

"How pale you are!" he said, and even frowned. "You really ought to take a little, you know, a little cure!"

The maid ran up to the doctor.

"A telephone call for you, sir."

The guests continued confusedly seating themselves. The doctor soon returned.

"Good heavens!" he exclaimed. "What sad news. Terribly, terribly sad. Our poor Gerbel has died under the knife. That was the hospital on the phone. He had appendicitis. He was operated on this morning by Professor Ivashov himself. The operation went well, but his heart couldn't take it. He died at five o'clock this afternoon."

Anna heard the words distinctly: "Gerbel has died under the knife." She was standing, holding on to the back of the chair with both hands. And then something strange happened. The table and overhead light suddenly shifted to the right. She gripped the chair tightly; then, without letting go, she fell to the floor.

2

The blinds had been lowered on the windows and on the balcony door, but it was still hot in the office.

The furnishings were exactly what one expects in the office of a serious doctor, the director of a sanatorium. There were enormous bookcases; in one of them, behind a pane of glass, were all kinds of nickel instruments. The writing desk was as big as a double bed and on it were thick notebooks with stiff green bindings.

The doctor had a big nose and hair so smoothly pomaded that it looked as if a tub of black varnish had been poured over his head. His eyes were small, sharp and unpleasant. He rose slightly and offered Anna his hand. On the desk before him was a letter from Doctor Pamuzov—Anna had given it to the nurse that morning, to pass on to him.

"Sit down," said the doctor; this was not an invitation but a command. "On this chair here, facing the light. Your name?"

"Anna Brunova."

"What?"

"Brunova. Brown. Whatever. You already know, so why are you asking?"

"I'm asking so that I can hear how you reply. Your age? How old are you?"

"Thirty-five."

"Does that mean forty?"

"No. It means thirty-eight."

"Put the pencil down and stop fidgeting. You're distracting me. Why did you say thirty-five?"

"Out of habit."

"I see! Excellent. This habit indicates a desire to appear younger—better, in other words. It indicates a desire to do well in life. A normal, healthy desire. Now do you see why we insist on our patients answering our questions? Keep your hands still. What is today's date?"

"It's the twenty-eighth... no, the twenty-ninth. I can't remember. Look, Doctor, I'm afraid this is all rather tedious. No normal person would answer you right away. Anyone who's the least bit normal would be surprised by the irrelevance of your questions. They won't be able to answer until they understand why you're asking."

"You don't need to concern yourself with that," said the doctor with an ironic little smile. "That's already been taken into consideration. How are you feeling now? Are you sleeping well? Of course, you've had a terrible nervous shock and you need to recover."

"A shock? Not at all. Obviously Doctor Pamuzov has

shared his own conjectures with you. I've just been a bit under the weather and I need to have a rest. That's why he sent me here."

"Why is your hair cut so short? Or do you always wear it that way?"

"I had a fever; my hair was getting all matted. Then it got hard to brush. I was shedding hair all over the place. Good heavens! What does it matter to you? I'm healthy, I want a rest, and that's all there is to it."

"I shall be the one to judge the state of your health, not you."

"I'm just so tired! So terribly, terribly tired!" Anna said. It took her a big effort to stop repeating these words. She wanted to go on and on repeating them, endlessly, for as long as she lived.

He looked at her carefully, then suddenly said, quite simply and softly, "Yes, I know, my dear. You're fatigued by the road and the heat. It's terribly close today. There's going to be a thunderstorm. All my patients are on edge today. Go and have a good rest. Keep out of the sun and stay away from the beach. There will be time enough for that. Go along and lie down, my dear. Have you got a nice room?"

"It's lovely."

"Excellent. If you need anything, don't be shy. Just let me know."

The room really was lovely. It was on the third floor. The window looked directly out onto a tree, almost onto its crown, which was dense with leaves and very dark.

"What kind of a tree is that?" she asked the chambermaid.

"I'm not sure. It looks like a local rowan tree. Or else an acacia. Here in the Caucasus everything is different. Mind you don't open the window—clouds of little bugs will come in off the tree."

"I'm like a dryad, living inside a tree," thought Anna. "But what's this tree called? I think Rosalinda sounds right. Sweet Rosalinda, my new friend. How will we get on together?"

The night air felt very close. She opened the window, and clouds of bugs did indeed come into the room. She had to close it again.

That night she slept better than at home, but she knew it was only a matter of time until she got used to her surroundings. Then her thoughts would catch up with her.

Early in the morning she opened the window. One of Rosalinda's boughs reached straight into the room. Anna took the bough in her hand like a rough and furry paw and squeezed it.

"Hello, Rosalinda. You have a warm paw. We're going to live together."

The day was unbearably close. It was impossible to stay indoors, so Anna went out to the market square.

The market was already over. In the empty stalls were the remains of spoilt plums and tangerines. The ground was littered with banana skins and there was a smell of hot dust. The dust got between your teeth and it felt gritty, like fine sugar. In the middle of the square was a group of people, standing in a circle and roaring with laughter. Anna went up to them. In the centre of the circle, swaying slowly from side to side as she walked, was a she-bear. She was a dirty, brownish black, as shabby as an old doormat on which many people had wiped their boots. In the bear's nose was a ring attached to a chain. Her handler was a huge, black-nosed man whose cheeks were covered with brownish-black fur like the bear's.

Jerking the chain a little, he was saying, "Well, now, Shura Ivanovna, show us how the ladies walk in the park."

The bear held one paw up behind her head and shimmied from side to side. The spectators guffawed, the little boys squealed. Shura Ivanovna opened wide her enormous lilac maw; it was evident that she enjoyed being liked.

"Shura Ivanovna," said Anna to the bear, "We're sisters, you and I! We're both *artistes*. Does the approval of your audience matter a great deal to you? My dear, my darling! Once it mattered to me, too."

"Now, Shura Ivanovna," said the handler, "ask the ladies and gentlemen to give us a few million so we can get ourselves some beer and some cake."

Once again Shura Ivanovna opened wide her lilac maw. Turning one paw over, she held out a narrow, bare Gypsy's palm. Enormous and clumsy, letting out little growls, or perhaps grunts, she made her way around the circle.

For some reason Anna was beginning to feel uneasy and sad. She turned round and headed back for the sanatorium.

She passed a boarded-up lemonade stand. A torn yellow poster pasted to its side was hanging down like the ear of an ancient elephant. Even a trifle like that could harbour such unexpected sadness. It must have reminded her of something. Of course, the smart thing to do would be to think of something else and not let herself remember.

And then something dreadful made her stop. At the entrance to the sanatorium stood the youth who looked like an albino mouse, the youth who had been at that dinner party. This was nothing so very dreadful in itself—but it was dreadful that this youth should have come *here*…

She turned away, drew her head down between her shoulders and slipped in through the door. How terribly her heart was pounding. There was no good reason for it. Only nerves. And even though nothing had happened, she knew she would find it difficult to calm down now.

It was quiet in her room, and after being outside it seemed rather dark.

On the table lay a large bouquet of roses, wrapped in silky paper, with a letter.

My beloved Anna Brown!

Press these roses to your face. Don't be afraid. You do not know me and you never will. Tonight I am leaving. I have not missed a single one of your concerts. I was more than listening; I was also watching you. I love you, Anna Brown.

N.

Anna read this strange letter and suddenly found herself weeping.

"Why am I weeping?"

Then she remembered reading about a zoo where the animals had hardly been given anything to eat. A commission was sent to investigate. When the vet entered one of the cages and began stroking a dying lioness, the beast became hysterical. *Those of us who have been tortured cannot be treated with kindness: scorn and the scourge are our oxygen. Tenderness we cannot bear.*

She didn't even unwrap the bouquet. She dropped it into one of the chest drawers, then lay down and began to think.

"I won't, of course, go down to dinner. The albino mouse is there. In fact I should probably leave. It's no good talking to the doctor. He'll keep saying it's nervous shock. Pamuzov has written to him about how I fainted when I heard a certain person had died. So I guess I'll go home. In the mornings the pigeons will be moaning up on the rooftops. The piano with its yellow teeth will be sitting and waiting. The phone there won't ring. And it's all for the best, of course, because everything's hopeless. What's stopping me? What's stopping me from living? I am not, after all, mad. I know full well that it's not my fault. That is, to *their* way of thinking, it's not my fault, because they don't know. And even if they did know, they wouldn't accept it. But I know that *I did it.* So what of it? Yes, I did it. Because I wanted to. I reduced six steps to four. And then I put an end to the whole wretched business…"

The room had become dark. Or had she fallen asleep without noticing? She did this sometimes. And on waking, she immediately entered the same train of thought, as if she'd had the same thoughts in her head even in her sleep.

It was dark. The air was black and dense. The day had been especially close. There was going to be a thunderstorm. Nights like this were called sparrow nights: if a sparrow flew up into the electricity-filled air, it would die and fall straight to the ground.

She had to keep on thinking. At least once she had to think everything through right to the end.

Why was I so sure that he was drifting away from me? Well, there were any number of signs. Why didn't he call after me as I was leaving? There are two possible answers. Either he was deeply hurt and he was waiting for me to make the first move—after all, I'd said I would phone in a few days. Or else he was glad to be rid of me so easily. I was gone, and good riddance! Without any scenes or drawn-out explanations. But no, that can't be right. He couldn't not have asked himself questions. He couldn't not have wondered why I was acting the way I did. Which means the first answer is the right answer. He was deeply hurt. He was waiting for me to make the first move. But it was impossible for me to make that move, because it would just have led to more of the same—suspicions and presentiments and despair. No, everything's fine as it is. There was only one way out, only one door. And I opened it.

Rosalinda's shaggy paw was brushing against the glass. A breeze?

Anna went to the window. In the blackness outside, the black boughs were motionless, scarcely discernible against the sky. The boughs were perfectly still. Just one leaf, right by the window, was pulsing strangely. It was quivering. Just one, like the vein in Anna's throat.

"Rosalinda! You're not in pain, too, are you?"

She ought to go downstairs, where there were people. Here it was rather frightening.

But downstairs was deserted. Evidently everyone had already gone to their rooms. There was only the sound of soft, ragged chords coming from the small drawing room. Anna pushed open the door and went in.

The room was almost dark, apart from a tiny lamp by the grand piano. The albino mouse was leaning an elbow on the keyboard and weeping. Then he wiped his eyes and his nose, and, picking out the chords, he began to sing softly:

> My bright little budgerigar was dying.
> He was not the cleverest of birds.
> I have heard of birds of many words,
> But your dear name was my bird's only word.
> And as he lay dying, he bequeathed to me
> His longing for a brighter, finer sun
> Than any in the world. He bequeathed to me
> Your name, his single word, his one and only one.

He reached the end and once again began to weep.

"Didn't he hear me coming in?" wondered Anna. "The poor, queer thing."

"Young man!" she called out. "What are you so upset about?"

He let out a loud shriek.

"Oh! You frightened me! It's not a good thing to frighten me."

"Forgive me. Why are you weeping?"

"I'm weeping because the bright little budgerigar has died."

"Did you really have a budgerigar, or did you invent it for the song?"

"No, it never even existed. And that's even more painful. If it had lived in the real world and then died, it would be different. But it was living only inside of me. Not even that. It wasn't even living, it only died inside of me, and that's almost more than I can bear."

He blew his nose miserably.

"You'd better go," he said with a sob. "You wouldn't understand anyway. And I want to go on suffering. I beg you, please go."

She turned round and went through the empty dining room and out onto the terrace. To the right, beside the kitchen door, something was clanking and seemed to be groaning. She went up closer. It was the she-bear, Shura Ivanovna. She had been chained to a tree and was walking round it in circles. She would take a few steps in one direction, the chain would grow taut and pull, and she would bellow and turn back. Then she would take a few steps in the opposite direction, the chain would grow taut again—and again it would pull at her and again she would bellow and turn back. She must have been going back and forth like that for some time, unable to believe what was happening and continuing to hope that maybe, this time, the chain wouldn't stop her.

"Shura Ivanovna! Shura Ivanovna!" Anna said. "Do you really still have hope? You have to choose where to draw the boundary—only then can one live. The only people in the world who are truly living are those who have managed to draw a boundary round evil. The strong in spirit used to withdraw from the world into the desert. Because earthly life can never grant a complete and elevated joy, they renounced it. They withdrew into caves and catacombs, accepting suffering and death—but what they did not accept was this loathsome world, with its niggardly joys. How full of anguish you are, Shura Ivanovna, you poor, unfortunate creature! It hurts me to look at you!"

She went back inside and wandered the dark rooms until she found the stairs and went up to her room.

How was she going to live through this sparrow night? She didn't have the strength. There was a little box full of morphine in case her neuralgia flared up. Nothing was hurting now. But she had a lot of morphine. Forty ampoules. Enough for a long rest. An eternal rest.

She went to the window.

There were Rosalinda's paws, still black as black—and, just as before, a single leaf was quivering and pulsating.

What does one need to overcome the despair that floods the world?

They say that a scorpion surrounded by a ring of fire will thrust its sting into its own breast. It kills itself. It chooses, of its own free will, to put a limit to its suffering.

What a dreadful black night! In the distance there was a flash of lightning. Like someone quickly opening and closing their eyes.

She reached out and pushed aside the sturdy, springy bough. Now the sky was visible. And the stars—large, small, near, far. There were even the kind that can be felt but not seen.

Yes, the scorpion imposes its will. But what if…

A terrible suspicion flashed through her mind, like the lightning that had only a moment ago lit up the black world.

What if it wasn't the will of the scorpion? What if it was the will of the one who had surrounded the scorpion with the ring of fire? "Not a hair from his head shall fall unless He wills it."[1]

She threw back her head and pushed the black branches even further away. Her eyes swept across the thousand-starred expanse of the incomprehensible and merciless heavens.

"So this is who has surrounded me with a ring of fire!"

She released the branches and turned round. Thoughtfully she lit the lamp and took the small box out of her suitcase.

"So be it. May the scorpion thrust its sting into its own breast."

She smiled bitterly, as if she were weeping, the corners of her mouth turned down.

"If that's the way it is, then may Thy will be done."

1952

AND TIME WAS NO MORE

"JUST ONE left till morning."

What does this mean? I keep repeating the words in my head. They've got stuck there. I'm fed up with them. But this often happens to me. A sentence or part of a tune will get stuck in my head and won't leave me alone.

I open my eyes.

An old woman is kneeling down on the floor, lighting the little stove. The kindling crackles.

> And my stove is crackling away.
> It lights up my bed in the corner
> Behind the bright-coloured curtain.

How often I'd sung those lines.

The bright-coloured bed curtain is gathered into pleats; light is shining through its scarlet roses.

The old woman, who is wearing a brown shawl and a dark headscarf, is hunched into a little ball. She's blowing onto the kindling, clanging the iron poker against the stove. I look at the little window. Sunlight is playing against the frost on the glass.

No sooner has the light of dawn
Begun to play with the clear frost
Than…

Just like in the song. How does it go on? Ah, that's right:

Than the samovar has begun to boil
On the oak table… [1]

Yes, there's the samovar, boiling on the table in the corner, a little steam escaping from under its lid. It's boiling and singing.

Along the bench outside struts the cockerel. He comes up to the window, tilts his little head to one side and looks in, his claws clicking against the wood. Then he moves on.

But where's the cat? I can't live without the cat. Oh, there he is, stout and gingery, purring as he warms himself on the table behind the samovar.

Someone has begun stamping inside the porch, shaking snow from their felt boots. The boots make a soft thudding sound. The old woman has got laboriously to her feet and waddled to the door. I can't see her face, but it doesn't matter. I know who she is…

I ask, "Who's that?"

She replies, "It's that fellow, what's his name…"

I can hear them talking together. The old woman, standing on the threshold, says, "Well, I suppose I could roast it."

There in her arms, upside down, is an enormous bird, black with thick red eyebrows. A wood grouse. It's been given to us by the huntsman.

I must get up.

Next to the bed are my felt boots—my beloved white *valenki*. Long ago in St Petersburg the Khanzhonkova film company organized a hunting trip for a group of actors and writers and their friends. We were meant to be hunting for elk. They drove us out over the firm white snow to Tosno, where we had a long, convivial lunch with champagne. Early the next morning we set out on low, wide sledges to the edge of the forest. How I loved my pointy-toed white-felt skiing *valenki*. I remember my white cap, too. Against the snow neither my head nor my feet would be visible. No beast would recognize me as a human being. It was a hunting ruse all of my own invention.

A steward of some sort showed us all to our correct spots. We were told not to smoke or talk, but we decided it couldn't do any harm if we only talked and smoked a little bit. I was standing with Fyodorov, the writer. We could hear the cry of the beaters. Later we found out that some elk had come, taken a look at us through the bushes and gone away. They hadn't liked what they'd seen. Instead of the elk, some hares leapt out—one of them right in front of me. Not moving at any great speed, it slipped slyly from bush to bush—neither quite running away nor quite taking cover. Fyodorov quickly raised his gun and took aim. "Don't you dare!" I yelled, jumping up and flinging my arms open right in front of him. He began yelling even louder—something like "You foo—", except that the word got stuck in his throat, and "That could have been the end of you!" I didn't mind him yelling at me. What mattered was that we'd saved the hare. My white, slim, nimble *valenki* did a little dance in the snow.

Later my *valenki* went missing. The maid's husband, a drunken layabout, had stolen them and sold them for drink. But now they'd come back again. Here they were by my bed, as if this were the most ordinary thing in the world. I slipped my feet into them and went into the little box room to get dressed.

There's a narrow window in the box room, and a small mirror on the wall. I look at my reflection. How strange I seem. My face could be from a childhood photograph. Anyone would take me for a four-year-old. I have a cheeky smile and dimples. As for my hair, it's short, with a fringe. It's fair and silky and it lies close to my head. It's just like it was when I used to walk down Novinsky Boulevard with my nanny. And I know exactly how I used to look then. When we were going down the front staircase, the big mirror on the landing would reflect a little girl in an astrakhan coat, white gaiters and a white *bashlyk* hood with gold braid. When she lifted her leg up high you could see her red flannel pantaloons. Back then all of us children wore red flannel pantaloons. And reflected in the mirror behind this little girl would be another figure just like her, only smaller and wider. Her little sister.

I remember how we used to play on the boulevard, my sister and I and other little girls like us. Once a lady and a gentleman stopped and watched us for a while, smiling.

"I like that little girl in the bonnet," said the lady, pointing at me.

The thought of her liking me was intriguing. I immediately opened my eyes wide and puckered my lips, as if to say, "Look at me! Aren't I wonderful?" And the gentleman and his lady smiled and smiled.

On this Novinsky Boulevard I so loved there was also a big, bad boy, about eight years old, who hung around being naughty and picking fights. His name was Arkasha. Once he climbed up on top of a bench, tried to look impressive and poked his tongue out at me. But I stood up for myself. Even if he *was* big, I wasn't afraid of him. I taunted him, saying, "Arkasha eats baby *kasha*! Arkasha eats baby *kasha*!"

And he said, "Yah, you're just a little squirt."

But I wasn't afraid of him and I knew I would always be able to make fun of spiteful fools, no matter how high they climbed.

Then there was that proud moment of my first bold triumph, my first triumph of ambition. There on that same boulevard. We were walking past our house when Nanny pointed to a short, stout figure standing on the balcony.

"Look, there's Elvira Karlovna. She's come out for some fresh air."

Elvira Karlovna was our nursery governess. We were

little and her name was so hard for us to say that we just called her "Baba". But suddenly I felt bold.

"Irvirkarna!" I called. Not "Baba" but "Irvirkarna"—like a big girl. I said it in a loud ringing voice so that everyone would hear that I could talk like a big girl. "Irvirkarna!"

Evidently I had once been bold and ambitious. Over the years I lost all this, more's the pity. Ambition can be a powerful force. If I had been able to hold onto it, I might have shouted out something for all the world to hear.

But how wonderful everything was on that boulevard. For some reason it's always early spring there. The runnels gurgle as they start to thaw; it's as if someone's pouring water out of a narrow little jug, and the smell of the water is so heady that you just want to laugh and kick up your heels; and the damp sand shimmers, it's like little crystals of sugar and you want to put some of it in your mouth and chew it; and a spring breeze is blowing into my woolly mittens. And off to one side, by a little path, has appeared a slender green stem. It stands there, quivering. And the lamb's-fleece clouds whirling about in the sky look like a picture from my book about Thumbelina. And the sparrows bustle about, the children shout, and you take all this in all at once, all in one go, and *all* of it can be expressed in a single whoop of "I don't want to go home!"

All this was in the days when my hair was fair and silky. And now, all of a sudden, my hair's like that again. How strange. But is it really so very strange? Here in this little house with the cockerel strutting along the bench, what could be more ordinary?

Now I'll put on my little cap, the one I wore on that hunting trip, and go out on my skis.

I walk out onto the porch. There, standing against the wall, are my skis. No sign of the old woman and the huntsman. Eagerly I slip my feet into the straps. I grab the poles, push off and glide down the slope.

Sun, the odd powdery snowflake. One snowflake falls onto my sleeve and doesn't melt; it's still crystalline when it blows away. I feel so light! I'm held by the air; happiness is carrying me along. I've always known and I've often said that happiness isn't a matter of success or achievement— happiness is a feeling. It's not founded on anything, it can't be explained by anything.

Yes, I remember one morning. It was very early. I'd been on my knees all night long, massaging the leg of a very sick patient. I was numb from cold and trembling from pity and fatigue as I made my way home. But as I was crossing the bridge, I stopped. The city was just beginning to wake up. The waterside was deserted apart from a longshorewoman the likes of whom you'll see only in Paris. Young and nimble, a red sash around her waist and pink stockings on her legs, she was using a long stick to fish for rags in the dustbins. The still sunless sky was just brightening in the east, and a faint haze, like pencil shading on pink blotting paper, showed where the sun's rays were about to burst through. The water below wasn't flowing as water is supposed to flow but whirling around in lots of flat little eddies, as if dancing on the spot. It was waltzing. And trembling gaily in the air was a faint ringing sound—perhaps the sound of my fatigue. I don't know. But suddenly I was pierced by a feeling of inexplicable happiness—a feeling so marvellous it made my breast ache and brought tears to my eyes. And reeling from fatigue, laughing and crying, I began to sing:

Wherever the scent of spring may lead me…

I hear a rustling behind me. The huntsman. Now he's standing beside me. I know his face, his outline, his movements. His earflaps are down; I can only see him in profile. But who is he?

"Wait," I say. "I think I know you."

"Of course you do," he says.

"Only I can't quite remember…"

"There's no need to remember. What use is remembering? Remembering is the last thing you need."

"But wait," I say. "What's that sentence that's been bothering me? Something like: 'Just one left till morning.' What on earth does it mean? Something nasty, I think."

"It's all right," he says. "It's all right."

I've been ill for so long, and my memory is poor. But I do remember—I made a note: I want to hear the *Lohengrin* overture one more time, and I want to talk once more to a certain wonderful person, and to see another sunrise. But *Lohengrin* and the sunrise would be too much for me now. Do you know what I mean? And that wonderful person has left. Ah, I remember that last sunrise, somewhere in France.

Dawn had just begun to glow, its wine-red hue beginning to spread. In a moment the sun would come up. The birds were getting agitated, twittering and squawking. One little bird was loudly and insistently repeating, "*Vite, vite, vite…*"[2] Tired of waiting, it was urging the sun on. I joined in this reproach to the sun, saying (in French, of course, since it was a French bird), "*Il n'est pas pressé.*"[3] And suddenly there was the sun, round and yellow, as if breathless and embarrassed about being late. And it wasn't even where I'd expected it to be, but somewhere far off to the left. Out came the midges, and the birds fell silent and got down to their hunting.

The poetic conceit that birds greet the rising of the sun god with a hymn of rapture is ever so droll. On the whole birds are a restless, garrulous tribe. They make just as much fuss when they're going to bed as when they wake up, but you can hardly claim that they're hymning the sun then, late in the evening. In Warsaw, I remember, in one of the squares, there was what you could call a sparrow tree. In the evening people would gather to watch the sparrows go to bed. The birds would flock around the tree and make a clamour you could hear all over the square. From the tone of their twittering you could tell that these were squabbles, disputes, brawls and just plain mindless chatter. Eventually everything would calm down and the sparrows would settle in for the night.

Although, I shouldn't reproach the birds for this garrulousness. Nature gives each bird a single motif:

"cock-a-doodle-doo" or "chink-chook" or just plain "cuckoo". Do you think *you* could get your message across with a sound as simple as that? How many times would *you* have to repeat yourself? Imagine that we human beings were given a single motif according to our breed. Some of us would say, "Isn't the Dnieper wonderful in fine weather?" Others would ask, "What time is it? What time is it?" Still others would go on and on repeating that "the angle of incidence is equal to the angle of reflection." Try using a single sentence like that to rhapsodize about the Sistine Madonna, to expound on the brotherhood of nations or to ask to borrow money. Although, maybe this is exactly what we *do* do and we just never realize it.

Sunrise! How varied it can be, and how I love it in all its guises. There's one sunrise I remember well. I waited for it a long time; for some reason I was really longing for it. And there in the east was a strip of grey cloud or light mist. I raised my arms like an ancient pagan worshipping the sun and beseeched the heavens:

> Sun, our god! Oh, where are you?
> We are arrayed in your flowers,
> Our arms upraised to the blue,
> We are calling, invoking your powers…

And then there it was, an orange coal ringing through the grey mist. Slowly before us rose a bronze sun, swelling, incandescent, malicious. Its face was blazing with rage; it was quivering and full of hate. Sometimes sunrise can be like that…

And I remember another very curious sunrise.

In a patch of grey there suddenly appeared a round hole, like the spyhole in a stage curtain that actors look through to check the size of the audience. Through this little hole in the sky peeped out a hot yellow eye; then this eye disappeared. A moment later, as if deciding—Now!—out jumped the sun. It was very droll.

Sunset, on the other hand, is always sad. It may be voluptuous, and opulent, and as richly sated with life as an Assyrian king, but it is always sad, always solemn. It is the death of the day.

They say there is a reason for everything in nature—the peacock's tail serves to perpetuate the species, the beauty of flowers attracts the bees that will pollinate them. But what purpose does the mournful beauty of sunset serve? Nature has expended herself in vain.

Here's the huntsman again, standing beside me.

"Where's your gun?" I ask.

"Here."

It's true, I can see his gun behind his back.

"And your dog?"

"There."

Up bounds his dog. Everything's as it should be.

I feel I ought to say something to the huntsman.

"How do you like my little house?" I ask. "When it gets dark, you know, we light a lamp."

"Does Nanny light it?"

"Nanny? Oh yes, yes, the old woman—that's Nanny," I say, remembering.

Nanny… She had died in an almshouse. She was very old. When I visited her, she would ask, "Just what are these granchilder? Some country folk keep coming round and saying, 'But Grandma, we're your granchilder.'"

"They're your daughter Malasha's children," I explained.

Malasha had been our housemaid when I was little.

I remember it all so vividly it's uncanny. Someone has spilt some needles on the window sill and I'm stroking them. I think they're absolutely wonderful. And someone is saying, "Lyulya has spilt the needles."

I hear but I don't realize that this Lyulya is me. Then someone picks me up; I'm touching a plump shoulder tightly encased in pink cotton. This, I know, is Malasha. And as for the needles—I've loved needles and everything sharp and glittery all my life. Maybe I began to love them back then, before I realized that Lyulya was me. We were talking about Nanny. She was very old. And now she's here in this little house. In the evening she lights the lamp; from outside the little window shines orange, and out from the forest comes a fox. It comes up to the window and sings. You've probably never heard the way a fox sings? It's just extraordinary. Not like Patti or Chaliapin, of course—but far more entertaining. It sings tenderly and off-key, in a way that's utterly bewitching: very soft, yet still audible. And the cockerel's outside, too, standing on the bench, its comb like raspberry gold with the light shining through it. It stands there in profile and pretends not to be listening.

And the fox sings:

> Cockerel, cockerel,
> With your comb of gold,
> Your combed little beard,
> And your shiny little head,
> Come look out the window.

But the cockerel clicks its claws on the bench and walks away. Yes, at least once in your life you should listen to a fox singing.

"It sings at night," says the huntsman, "but you don't like night, do you?"

"How do you know? Does that mean you've known me a long time? Why is it so hard for me to remember you when I'm quite certain that really I know you very well?"

"Does it matter?" he says. "Just think of me as a composite character from your previous life."

"If you're a composite character, then why are you a huntsman?"

"Because all the girls of your generation were in love with Hamsun's Lieutenant Glahn.[4] And then you spent your entire life seeking this Glahn in everyone you met. You were seeking for courage, honesty, pride, loyalty and a passion that ran deep but was held in check. You were, weren't you? You can't deny it."

"But wait… You said I don't like the night. That's true. Why? What does it matter? Tyutchev said, and he's probably right, that it's because night tears away the veil that prevents us from seeing the abyss.[5] And as for the anguish inspired by the stars—'The stars speak of eternity'—what could be more terrible? If a person in pain gazes up at the stars as they 'speak of eternity', he's supposed to sense his own insignificance and thus find relief. That's the part I really can't understand at all. Why would someone who's been wronged by life find comfort in his complete and utter humiliation—in the recognition of his own insignificance? On top of all your grief, sorrow and despair—here, have the contempt of eternity, too: *You're a louse. Take comfort and be glad that you have a place on earth—even if it's only the place of a louse.* We look up at the starry sky the way a little mouse looks through a chink in the wall at a magnificent ballroom. The music, the lights, the sparkling apparitions. Strange rhythmical movements, in circles that move together and then apart, propelled by an unknown cause towards an incomprehensible goal. It's beautiful and frightening—very, very frightening. We can, if we like, count the number of circles made by this or that sparkling apparition, but it's impossible to understand what the apparition means—and this is frightening. What we can't understand we always sense as a hostile force, as something cruel and meaningless. Little mouse, it's a good thing that *they* don't see us, that we play no role in *their* magnificent, terrible and majestic life. Have you ever noticed how people lower their voices when they're looking at the star-filled sky?"

"Nevertheless, the stars speak of eternity," said the huntsman.

"Eternity! Eternity! How terrifying! 'Forever' is a terrifying word. And the word 'never' is no different—it is eternal in the same way. But for some reason 'never' frightens us still more. Maybe this is because 'never' includes a negative element, almost a prohibition, which we find abhorrent. But enough of that or I'll start feeling wretched. A while ago, a group of us were talking for some reason about how impossible it is to grasp the concept of infinity. But there was a little boy with us who made perfect sense of it just like that. He said, 'It's easy. Imagine there's one room here, and then another, and then another five, ten or twenty rooms, another hundred or million rooms, and so on and so on… Well, after a while it gets boring, you just can't be bothered any more and you say, *To hell with it all!*' That's what it is—that's infinity for you."

"What a muddle you're in," said the huntsman, shaking his head. "Eternity and starry despair, a singing fox and a little boy's prattle."

"But to me everything seems quite clear. I just want to talk without any logic or order, just the way things come to me. Like after morphine."

"Precisely," said the huntsman. "After morphine. Because this little house of yours never really existed either. It's just something you used to like drawing."

"Look, I'm tired and ill. Does it really matter? When all is said and done, we invent our entire lives. After all, don't we invent other people? Are they really, truly the way they appear to us, the way we always see them? I can remember a dream I once had. I went to the home of a man I loved. And I was greeted there by his mother and sister. They greeted me very coldly and kept saying he was busy. They wouldn't let me see him. So I decided to leave. And as I was leaving, I caught sight of myself in the mirror and let out a groan. My face was fat and puffy and I had tiny squinting eyes. On my head was a hat with bugle beads, the kind that used to be worn by elderly shopkeepers' wives. On my shoulders was a brown cape, and on my short neck a filthy, coarsely knitted scarf.

"'Good God! What's wrong with me?'

"And then I understood. This was how those women saw me. And I know now that you will never find even two people on earth who see a third in the same way."

"You seem to have set great store by dreams," said the huntsman.

"Oh yes. Dreams, too, are life. I've seen and experienced much that is remarkable, beautiful, even wonderful—and yet I don't remember it all and not all of it has become an essential component of my soul in the way that two or three dreams have done. Without those dreams I wouldn't be the person I am. I had an astounding dream when I was eighteen—how could I ever forget it? It seems to have foretold my whole life. I dreamt a series of dark, empty rooms. I kept opening doors, making my way through one room after another, trying to find a way out. Somewhere in the distance a child began to cry and then fell silent. He had been taken away somewhere. But I walked on, full of anguish—until, finally, I reached the last door. It was massive. With a great effort, pushing against it with all my weight, I opened this door. At last I was free. Before me was an endless expanse, despondently lit by a lacklustre moon. It was the kind of pale moon we see only by day. But something was gleaming in the murky distance; I could see it was moving. I was glad. I wasn't alone. Someone was coming towards me. I heard a heavy thudding of horses' hooves. At last. The sound was getting closer. And an enormous, bony white nag was approaching, its bones clattering. It was pulling a white coffin sparkling with brocade. It pulled it up to me and stopped... And this dream is my entire life. It's possible to forget the most vivid incident, the most remarkable twist of fate, but a dream like this you'll never forget. And I never have done. If my soul were reduced into its chemical components, analysis would reveal the crystals of my dreams to be a part of its very essence. Dreams reveal so very, very much."

"Yours is a very nice little house," he says, interrupting me. "And it's a good thing you've finally reached it."

"You know," I say, "today my hair is just like it was when I was four. And so is the snow. I used to love resting my head on the window sill and looking up to watch the snow falling. Nothing on earth creates a sense of peace and calm like falling snow. Maybe because when something falls it's usually accompanied by some noise, by a knock or a crash.

285

But snow—this pure and almost unbroken white mass—is the only thing that falls without any sound. And this brings a sense of peace. Often now when my soul feels restless, I think of falling snow, of silently falling snow. And always there's one snowflake that seems to come to its senses and does its best, zigzagging its way through the crowd of obediently falling snowflakes, to fly back up into the sky."

The huntsman didn't speak for a long time. Then he said, "Once you made out that there are five doors through which one can escape the terror that is life: religion, science, art, love and death."

"Yes, I think I did. But do you realize that there is a dreadful force that only saints and crazed fanatics can defeat? This force closes all these doors; it makes man revolt against God, scorn science for its impotence, turn a cold shoulder to art and forget how to love… It makes death, that eternal bogeyman, come to seem welcome and blessed. This force is pain. Torturers the world over have always known this. The fear of death can be overcome by reason and by faith. But only saints and fanatics have been able to conquer the fear of pain."

"And how have *you* overcome your fear of death?" he asked with a strangely mocking smile. "By reason or faith?"

"Me? Through my theory of a world soul—a single soul, common to all people and animals, to every living creature. It is only the ability to be aware of this soul, and above all to give it expression, that varies according to the physical make-up of the creature in question. A dog can distinguish between good and evil every bit as well as a human being can, but a dog of course can't put any of this into words. Anyone who has carefully observed the life of animals knows that the moral law is inherent in them, just as it is in human beings. Which reminds me of a certain little hare, a silly little woodland creature. Someone caught this hare and it soon grew tame. It liked to stay close to its owners, and if they quarrelled it always got terribly upset. It would run back and forth between the two of them and it wouldn't calm down until they made up. The hare loved its friends and wished them to have a peaceful life. This was for their sake, not for the hare's, because their quarrels did not affect it directly. What upset the little wild beast was the suffering of others. It was a bearer of the world soul. This is how I feel about the world soul, and this, therefore, is how I feel about death. Death is a return to the whole, a return to the oneness. This is how I see things myself; this has been *my* important illumination. There's nothing mathematical about it, certainly nothing that can be proved. For some people the concept of the transmigration of souls has been an important illumination. For others, the illumination that matters has been that of life after death, and redemption through the eternal torment of remorse. For others still, like my old nanny, what mattered most was devils with pitchforks. But I'm telling you what has been important for me. And there's one more thing I can say. Yes, let me tell you a story. Listen. There once was a woman who had a vision in her sleep. She seemed to be kneeling and reaching out with both her hand

and her soul to someone whom she had loved and who was no longer among the living. She was staying in Florence at the time and the air in her dream—probably influenced by Simone Martini's *Annunciation*—was translucent gold, shimmering as though shot through with rays of gold. And within this extraordinary golden light and blessed intensity of love was that ecstasy no one can endure for more than a moment. But time did not exist, and this moment felt like eternity. And it was eternity, because time was no more. As it says in the Book of Revelation, 'And the Angel lifted up his hand to Heaven and swore by Him that liveth forever and ever that there should be time no more.' And then the woman realized that this was death, that this is all there is to death: it is something tiny, indivisible, a mere point, the moment when the heart stops beating and breathing ceases, and someone's voice says, 'He is dead now.' That's eternity for you. And all the elaborations of a life beyond the grave, with its agonies of conscience, repentance and other torments—all this is simply what we experience while we're alive. There is no place for such trivial nonsense in eternity. Listen, huntsman, when I'm dying, I'll say to God, 'Oh Lord! Send your finest angels for my soul that was born of Your Spirit, for my dark, sinful soul, which has rebelled against You, in its sorrow always seeking but never finding...'"

"Never till now," corrected the huntsman.

"Never till now," I repeated. "And bless my body, created by Your Will, bless my eyes that have looked without seeing, my lips that have grown pale from song and laughter, and bless my womb that has accepted the fruit of love, all according to Your Will, and my legs…"

"… that have been kissed so many, many times," interrupted the huntsman.

"No, I won't say that. I'll simply say, 'Oh Lord, bless this body and release me into the immortality of your world. Amen.' That's what I'll say."

"But you've said it!" exclaimed the huntsman. "You've said it now!"

"I may have said it, but I'm not dying yet."

My skis came to a stop. I looked down at my feet. The white-felt *valenki* were gone. In their place were tall, yellow-leather boots laced right up to the knee. I knew them well. I had worn them when I went to the front during the war. I began to feel strangely apprehensive.

"I don't understand," I said.

The huntsman was silent. Suddenly, with a slight bend of his knees and a single co-ordinated movement of his entire body, he pushed off and quickly glided ahead and down a slope. Then he flew up over a hillock and disappeared from view. Far ahead he appeared fleetingly at the top of another rise.

"Hello-o-o!" I cried out. "Come back! I don't want to be alone!"

What is his name? How can I call out to him? I don't know. But I can't bear to be left all alone.

"Hello-o-o-o! I'm frightened…"

But no, this isn't quite true: I'm not frightened. I'm just used to thinking that I'm frightened of being alone. I'll go back to my little house. Yes, I still have something on which I can build life. I've still got the little house I once drew… But I'm cold. So cold.

"Come back! Hello-o-o-o-o!"

"It's all right, I'm right here," says a voice beside me. "There's no need to shout. I'm here."

I turn this way and that way. No one is there. Just the whitest white all around. The snow lies heavy on the ground. It's no longer that light, happy snow. There is a soft tinkle, the tinkle of fine glass. Then the sharp pain of an injection into my hip. Right before my eyes are the folds of a thick apron with two pockets. My nurse.

"There," says the voice, "your last ampoule. That's it until morning."

Warm fingers take hold of my wrist and squeeze it. Far, far away someone's voice says, "Heavens. There's no pulse. She…"

She. Who is this "she"? I don't know. Maybe it's that little girl, the girl with the silky hair who didn't understand that she was Lyulya.

How very quiet it all is…

1949

ACKNOWLEDGEMENTS

In addition to Clare Kitson and Natalia Wase, who have both made many helpful suggestions, as well as contributing one translation each, we wish to thank all the following for their help: Michele Berdy, Kate Beswick, Maria Bloshteyn, Inna Chuyeva, Olive Classe, Mahaut de Cordon-Prache, Richard Davies, Lydia Dhoul, Boris Dralyuk, Morgan Giles, Roland Glasser, Edythe Haber, Katia Hyrahuruk, Alina Israeli, Sara Jolly, Simon Jones, Iulia Kristanciuk, Erik McDonald, Olessia Makarenia, Mark Miller, Elena Ostrovskaya, Natasha Perova, Diana Postica, Stella Postica, Irina Rodimtseva, William Ryan, Elena Trubilova, Tamara Turcan, Wendy Vaizey and Elizabeth Yellen. Anne Marie Jackson also thanks Robert and Elizabeth Chandler and Irina Steinberg. Robert Chandler also thanks many former students from translation classes and workshops who have inadvertently contributed to this collection.

An earlier version of 'Subtly Worded' was published in the journal *Index on Censorship* and 'The Dog' was first published in *Russian Magic Tales from Pushkin to Platonov* (Penguin Classics, 2012).

'The Lifeless Beast' was first published in *The New England Review*, Vol. 34, #3–4 (2014).

'Time No More' was first published in *The Stinging Fly*, Vol. 2, #27 (2014).

NOTES

INTRODUCTION

1 When a literary anthology was being prepared to com-
memorate the tercentenary of the Romanov dynasty, Tsar
Nicholas II was consulted as to which contemporary writers
should be included. His response was: "Teffi! Only Teffi!"
See O.N. Mikhailov, 'Nezhny talant', in O.N. Mikhailov,
D.D. Nikolayev and E.N. Trubilova (eds), *Tvorchestvo N.A.
Teffi i russky literaturny protsess pervoy poloviny XX veka* (Moscow:
Nasledie, 1999), p. 5.

2 M.M. Zoshchenko, 'N. Teffi', in *Ezhegodnik Rukopisnogo otdela
Pushkinskogo doma na 1972 god* (Leningrad: Nauka, 1974),
p. 141.

3 L.A. Spiridonova, 'Teffi', in *Russkaya satiricheskaya literatura
nachala XX veka* (Moscow: Nauka, 1977), p. 162.

4 Teffi worked for *The Russian Word* (*Russkoye Slovo*) until the
Bolsheviks closed it down in 1918. By 1917 it had achieved a
circulation in excess of 1 million, making it one of the world's
largest papers. See Louise McReynolds, 'Newspapers and
public opinion', in *Between Tsar and People* (Princeton: Princeton
University Press, 1991), p. 241.

5 Quoted in I.V. Odoyevtseva, *Na beregakh Seny* (Moscow: Khudozhestvennaya literatura, 1989), p. 73.

6 Marc Raeff, *Russia Abroad: A Cultural History of the Russian Emigration 1919–1939* (New York & Oxford: Oxford University Press, 1990), p. 4.

7 From a letter by Teffi dated 14 December 1943, quoted in E.M. Trubilova, 'V poiskakh strany nigde', in *A.T. Averchenko, N.A. Teffi: Rasskazy* (Moscow: Molodaya gvardiya, 1990), pp. 221–22.

8 Robert Chandler, *Russian Magic Tales* (London: Penguin, 2012), p. 166.

9 The Soviet experiment enjoyed widespread sympathy among leading literary critics in the West. See W. Bruce Lincoln, 'Émigrés against utopia', in *Between Heaven and Hell: The Story of a Thousand Years of Artistic Life in Russia* (New York: Viking, 1998).

10 N.A. Teffi, 'Tot svet', *Russkiye novosti*, 3 August 1945, p. 4.

11 From a letter by Teffi quoted in L.A. Spiridonova, 'Teffi', in *Russkaya satiricheskaya literatura nachala XX veka* (Moscow: Nauka, 1977), p. 169.

12 Stanislav Nikonenko, 'Nesravnennaya Teffi', in N.A. Teffi, *Moya letopis'* (Moscow: Vagrius, 2004), p. 14.

13 See E.M. Trubilova's essay 'Rozhdyennaya v voskresen'ye', in N.A. Teffi, *Sobraniye sochineny*, vol. 7 (Moscow: Lakom, 2001), p. 8.

14 Poet and critic Georgy Ivanov, quoted in V. Vereshchagin, 'Teffi', *Russkaya Mysl'*, 21 November 1968, p. 8.

A RADIANT EASTER

1   *paskha*: A sweet cream-cheese dish eaten at Easter (Russian).

THE CORSICAN

1   From the 'Warszawianka' or 'Warsaw song', the Russian lyrics
of which are traditionally attributed to Gleb Krzhizhanovsky
(1872–1959). During the early twentieth century this song was
one of the most popular revolutionary anthems in Russian-
held Poland.

2   A Maximalist was a member of the extreme-left faction of the
Social Revolutionary Party, known from 1906 as the Union
of Social Revolutionary Maximalists.

3   Vera Figner (1852–1942), a notorious revolutionary figure,
took part in an attempt to assassinate Alexander II.

THE HAT

1   Savva Mamontov's Private Opera was an important opera
house in late-1800s Moscow. It brought together many of
the finest voices and composers of the day.

PETROGRAD MONOLOGUE

1   *Mir iskusstva*, or World of Art, was an artistic movement
that flourished in Russia at the beginning of the twentieth
century.

2 Yeliseyev's Emporium in its Art Nouveau premises at 56 Nevsky Prospekt, St Petersburg, was the flagship shop of Russia's wealthy Yeliseyev merchant family. This landmark establishment, which sold fine food and wine, first opened its doors in 1903 and is still trading today under new ownership.

3 Lina Cavalieri (1874–1944) was a beautiful Italian opera soprano much loved in pre-revolutionary St Petersburg.

ONE DAY IN THE FUTURE

1 The quotation "Don't cry, my child. One day we shall see the heavens glittering like diamonds" comes from Chekhov's play *Uncle Vanya*.

ONE OF US

1 *C'est affreux*: That's terrible (French).

2 *sans façon*: familiar (French).

RASPUTIN

1 Vasily Rozanov (1856–1919) was a controversial and well-known writer. His best work, much of it an attempt to reconcile Christian teachings with an assertion of the importance of sexuality and family life, is deeply personal. A somewhat Dostoevskyan figure himself, he married Polina Suslova, a woman twice his age who had once been Dostoevsky's mistress.

Rozanov died of starvation in the aftermath of the Bolshevik Revolution.

2   Alexander Izmailov (1873–1921) was a prominent journalist and literary critic.

3   Alexander Kuprin (1870–1938) was a popular writer of short stories and novels. He emigrated to Paris in 1920. Impoverished and homesick, he returned to the Soviet Union in 1937 and died within the year.

4   Leonid Andreyev (1871–1919) was a prolific writer of short stories, plays and novels and one of the foremost representatives of Russia's Silver Age of literature. Andreyev emigrated to Finland shortly after the Revolution.

5   "Madame V——" may refer to Anna Vyrubova (see below), although elsewhere Teffi refers to her by name.

6   Grigory (or Grisha) Rasputin is sometimes referred to as a monk, but he never took holy orders and had no official connection to the Orthodox Church. Here Teffi uses the vaguer term "elder". Rasputin was often thought to have belonged to an extreme Christian sect known as the Khlysts, but these rumours have never been proven. There is no doubt, however, that he lived the life of a religious "wanderer" for several years and that he was widely believed to be endowed with healing abilities.

7   Anna Vyrubova was a close friend of the Tsaritsa and an intermediary between Rasputin and the royal family. She was also a childhood friend of Prince Felix Yusupov, the orchestrator of the plot to murder Rasputin.

8   The Khlysts were a mystical sect. Often the subject of lurid speculation, they observed ascetic practices and ecstatic rituals as a way of attaining grace.

9   This is how the Orthodox Church refers to the women who, early in the morning of the third day, came to Christ's tomb and found it empty.

10 Alexey Frolovich Filippov was a banker and the publisher of writings by Rasputin. Ivan Fyodorovich Manasevich-Manuilov was a police agent. He had "suggested that Filippov organize a literary soirée, and he himself had told Tsarskoye Selo about the soirée, attributing the initiative to Filippov. And he had passed on to the security branch [...] the list of literary invitees. All the people on it were well-known 'leftist writers'. Which was why there had been a call from Tsarkoe Selo interrupting the meeting." See Edward Radzinsky, *Rasputin: The Last Word* (London: Phoenix, 2000), p. 403. Manasevich-Manuilov had evidently wanted to compromise Filippov both in the eyes of the tsarist authorities and in the eyes of Rasputin himself. In the original, Teffi uses abbreviations to refer to Filippov and Manasevich-Manuilov, probably in order not to embarrass people still living.

QUE FAIRE?

1   Fyodor Tyutchev (1803–73) is commonly seen as the finest Russian lyric poet after Pushkin. Avril Pyman has translated the relevant lines of his as follows: "Russia is baffling to the mind, / not subject to the common measure; / her ways—of a peculiar kind... / One only can have faith in Russia." See

Robert Chandler (ed.), *Russian Poetry from Pushkin to Brodsky* (London: Penguin, 2014).

MARQUITA

1   It is clear from Raichka's surname, Blum, that she is Jewish. Her stage name, Tsvetkova, is a Russian translation of this name. Both names mean "flower".

2   Both "Sasha" and "Sashenka" are affectionate forms of the name Alexandra.

HEART OF A VALKYRIE

1   *Puisqu'on est toujours mécontent*: Because they're never happy (French).

2   *femmes de ménage*: household staff (French).

THE DOG (A STORY FROM A STRANGER)

1   Vanya is referring to an old Russian saying that a person in love will oversalt their dishes when cooking.

2   In the late nineteenth and early twentieth centuries Hermann Friedrich Eilers supplied flowers to the court and owned a large florist's shop opposite the Kazan Cathedral.

3   The Stray Dog was a café in St Petersburg, a famous meeting place for writers and poets. Between 1911 and 1915 nearly all the main poets of the time—regardless of their political or

artistic affiliations—gave readings there. In its critical portrayal of at least some aspects of this legendary institution, Teffi's story in many ways anticipates Anna Akhmatova's *Poem without a Hero*.

4   Mikhail Kuzmin (1872–1936), a homosexual, was known as "the Russian Wilde". A gifted composer as well as a major poet, he sang his own songs at The Stray Dog, accompanying himself on the piano. Both in a newspaper obituary and in a later memoir, Teffi writes of Kuzmin with considerable respect, but she is critical (at least in the obituary) of his followers, whom she saw as affected and talentless.

5   Oscar Wilde used to wear a green carnation in his buttonhole. Wilde owed his fame in early-twentieth-century Russia mainly to his trial and imprisonment, but many of the leading poets of the time—Konstantin Balmont, Valery Bryusov, Nikolai Gumilyov, Mikhail Kuzmin and Fyodor Sologub—translated his work.

6   'The Waves of the Danube' was a popular waltz composed in 1880 by Iosif Ivanovici, a Romanian. In the United States it has become known as 'The Anniversary Song'.

7   That is, officers of the Cheka—the first of the many titles given to the Soviet security service.

THE BLIND ONE

1   *L'amore è come lo zucchero*: Love is like sugar (Italian).

THY WILL

1   The quotation is a paraphrase from 1 Samuel 14:45.

AND TIME WAS NO MORE

1   From the poem 'The Bell' by Yakov Polonsky (1819–98).

2   *Vite, vite, vite*: Hurry, hurry, hurry (French).

3   *Il n'est pas pressé*: It's in no rush (French).

4   The huntsman Thomas Glahn is a central character in Norwegian novelist Knut Hamsun's work *Pan*, first published in 1894. Hamsun was a hugely influential figure from the 1890s until the Second World War. In 1920 he was awarded the Nobel Prize for Literature.

5   The narrator is referring to one of Tyutchev's best-known poems, 'Day and Night'.

PUSHKIN PRESS

Pushkin Press was founded in 1997, and publishes novels, essays, memoirs, children's books—everything from timeless classics to the urgent and contemporary.

This book is part of the Pushkin Collection of paperbacks, designed to be as satisfying as possible to hold and to enjoy. It is typeset in Monotype Baskerville, based on the transitional English serif typeface designed in the mid-eighteenth century by John Baskerville. It was litho-printed on Munken Premium White Paper and notch-bound by the independently owned printer TJ International in Padstow, Cornwall. The cover, with French flaps, was printed on Colorplan Pristine White paper. The paper and cover board are both acid-free and Forest Stewardship Council (FSC) certified.

Pushkin Press publishes the best writing from around the world—great stories, beautifully produced, to be read and read again.